The Awakening of
Sunshine Girl

Also by Paige McKenzie with Alyssa Sheinmel

The Haunting of Sunshine Girl

The Awakening of Sunshine Girl

BOOK TWO

The Haunting of Sunshine Girl series

PAIGE MCKENZIE

WITH ALYSSA SHEINMEL

Story by Nick Hagen & Alyssa Sheinmel

Based on the web series created by Nick Hagen

Illustrations by Paige McKenzie

WEINSTEIN
BOOKS

WITHDRAWN

Printed in the United States of America

Library of Congress Cataloging-in-Publication Data is available for this book.
ISBN 978-1-60286-274-6 (print)
ISBN 978-1-60286-275-3 (e-book)

Published by Weinstein Books
A member of the Perseus Books Group
www.weinsteinbooks.com

Weinstein Books are available at special discounts for bulk purchases in the U.S.
by corporations, institutions, and other organizations. For more information,
please contact the Special Markets Department at the Perseus Books Group,
2300 Chestnut Street, Suite 200, Philadelphia, PA 19103, call (800) 810-4145, ext. 5000,
or e-mail special.markets@perseusbooks.com.

Editorial production by *Marra*thon Production Services. www.marrathon.net

Book design by Jane Raese
Set in 11-point Baskerville

FIRST EDITION

1 3 5 7 9 10 8 6 4 2

For my family.
You know who you are
and you know what you did.

Someone Else
Is Watching

I sensed it the instant she passed her test.

The feeling began in my center: a small, tight twist, as though someone had taken hold of my guts and pulled tight. Unbidden, an image of what she might look like today blossomed behind my eyes: sixteen years old. Her father's eyes. Her mother's . . . I don't know. All I can remember now are her eyes.

I don't want to remember anything more. I don't want to think about whom she might look like, sound like, act like. I've been setting aside such curiosities for years now. They have no place in my life. They'll only interfere with what must be done. And it must be done. It should have been done sixteen years ago, but he took her before I could. I've had years now to gather my strength.

Sixteen years to plan it.

Sixteen years to envision it.

Sixteen years to steel myself for the task that's fallen at my feet.

I'm ready to eliminate her. I just have to find her first.

CHAPTER ONE
Haunted

Sixth-period biology isn't where most people expect to see a ghost, but I'm not like most people. After making a note about the genetic similarities of rhesus monkeys to humans, I look up to see an old lady standing in the corner of our classroom who clearly doesn't belong there. She's short and at least ninety years old. Or maybe, I should say, she *was* at least ninety. She's wearing a pink terrycloth robe with embroidered flowers along the neckline. Her eyes are intense, small and sunken into her skull. She doesn't blink as she stares at me, and it sends shivers along my spine. Quickly I glance around the room to reassure myself I'm the only one who sees this. No one is reacting like we have a sudden, oddly dressed guest lecturer, so I know she's a ghost. I'm the only one who can see her, and she needs my help.

I'm new to this luiseach thing, so I try not to be too hard on myself when my first instinct is to ask for a hall pass and run out of the room. Instead, I casually reach toward the woman, trying not to draw too much attention to myself. I need her to come closer if I'm going to help her move on.

Mr. Packer moves his lecture from monkey to pig genetics, and I know I should be taking another note, but I can't. I extend my arm a little further and focus on the woman. It works, and she begins to move toward me. She passes through three of my classmates, and they have no idea, although I do notice one of them shudders and looks around for the source of the cool breeze. He wouldn't believe me if I told him.

As the woman gets within a few feet of me, I stretch my arm out even farther, hoping I can touch her and help her move on without anyone noticing. The woman's jaw begins to chatter with excitement as she nears. Her mouth opens just enough to let out a sickening dark liquid that pours down her robe. Suddenly I know how she died: she was lying alone in her bed, too weak to sit up, when she began coughing. She coughed until she choked. Her name was Elizabeth, and it wasn't the most peaceful death in the world, but at least it wasn't the most violent either. Now I need to help her move on.

Her eyes remain locked with mine, and I wonder whether she sees me or is looking straight through me. I've never seen anything like this before, and suddenly I want to scream. I just want to make it all go away, for her and for me. I stand, and my chair lets out a groan as it slides against the floor. I reach out and touch her shoulder, closing my eyes as a sense of peace washes over me. Just as quickly as she appeared, Elizabeth dissolves into a bright ball of light. Within seconds the last particles of light fade into the air.

"Can I help you, Sunshine?" Mr. Packer asks, as if there wasn't just an oozing ghost in his classroom. I open my eyes and suddenly realize how ridiculous I looked standing in the middle of the room, my arm stretched out in front of me, my eyes closed.

"Um. No. I'm fine," I answer, quickly sitting down as half the class laughs out loud. Before Mr. Packer can resume his lecture—and before my face can reach peak redness—the bell rings. I grab my things and rush out of the classroom. Why do luiseach have to come into their powers at sixteen? It's hard enough being sixteen without having to deal with all of *this* at the same time. I run out into the parking lot and sigh with relief when I see Nolan's lanky body leaning against the car, waiting for me.

"How are you feeling?" he asks, unaware of what just happened in bio.

It's the first day back after winter break, and around us our classmates chatter about their Christmas presents and tropical vacations, about the trees they trimmed and the candles they lit, about the movies they saw and how late they slept. Their voices fill the air around us, and, still thinking about the woman I just helped move on, I can't decide whether or not I'm glad I'm so different from them.

"Nervous," I finally answer Nolan, brushing my long, curly brown hair away from my face with my fingers and securing it with an elastic band. I don't want anything obstructing the view for what I'm about to do.

"Don't be nervous," Nolan says as we walk across the parking lot. "You're a natural. You've done it once already, right?"

"Yeah, but that was just a practice run. And I wasn't alone then."

"Do you want me to come with you?" he offers.

"No," I say, digging in my bag for the car keys. "I have to do it by myself." Part of me does want Nolan to come with me, though. He could grab the steering wheel if I suddenly have to help a spirit move on. But I don't tell him that. I have to learn to be a luiseach *and* a functioning normal person at the same time. I unlock the door and toss my purple patch-covered backpack onto the backseat, then lean against our silver sedan beside Nolan. "I can do this. I can drive all the way to the hospital alone."

Mom cringed when she handed me the keys this morning. I've had my license for months; I passed the test before we moved here from Austin, Texas, in August. But I haven't been doing much driving. Before we moved, with my shiny new license burning a hole in my pocket, I thought I'd be begging Mom for time behind the wheel in our new hometown. But nothing's been anything like I thought it would be since we moved here.

Mom works long hours, and I'm kind of trapped in the house when she's not there. She finally offered to let me take the car to get myself to and from school—it's a long walk, and January in Ridgemont, Washington, is flippin' cold—but I had to promise to pick her up from the hospital whenever she needs a ride home. I'm happy to do it. I mean, it's only fair, right? But the ride to the hospital isn't exactly a nice straight line from point A to point B. I have to get on the freeway, and then I have to drive on the twisty road around the mountain that towers above our town. You'd think they'd have made the road to the hospital easier—I mean, ambulances have to get there at top speeds, right?

The truth is, it's not really the twisty roads that have me worried; it's the fact that my mentor/father, whose name I now know is Aidan, keeps sending lost spirits my way to remind me he's waiting to talk to me. I wrap my arms around myself.

"Another spirit?" Nolan asks, lowering his voice to a whisper.

I nod, unable to speak because my teeth are chattering. I can't see the spirit yet, but I know it's near. Luckily, with Nolan standing close, I'm not *too* cold because being near him keeps me a little bit warmer. Still, I pull the too-long sleeves of my navy blue cardigan over my wrists because apparently when spirits touch me, my temperature plummets and my heart races. Which has happened *way* too many times in the forty-eight hours since I met Aidan. Well, *met* might be a bit of an overstatement. *Met* implies we shook hands, exchanged pleasantries, that kind of thing.

"You can't avoid him forever, Sunshine," Nolan says, leaning on the car beside me. He's wearing a bluish-gray hooded sweatshirt with a scarf, gloves, and a rather silly-looking bright yellow snowcap with a red ball on the top. I'm still not entirely used to seeing him without his grandfather's leather jacket. I'm not sure he even owns another coat. But on New Year's Eve he gave me the jacket he loves so much and insisted I keep it even after all the craziness happened. It's hanging in my closet at home now, still not entirely dry. "You should talk to him."

"That would be a lot easier if I had the slightest idea of what I wanted to say to him."

Okay, maybe that's not entirely true. There are about a million things I want to say to him. Well, a million things I want to *ask* him: Why did you abandon me? How could you endanger my mother? Who is my birth mother? Where have you been all these years? Why haven't you come forward until now? What made you think this was the right way to introduce yourself: *Hi, I stood by silently while your mother almost died so I could test you while you figured out you weren't the person you thought you'd been your entire life—that, in fact, you weren't technically a* person *at all?*

But when he showed up in my driveway on New Year's Day, I found myself completely tongue-tied. When he held out his hand and told me his name, explained who he was—my birth father, as if his milky-green cat eyes identical to mine didn't do the talking for him—I could barely even control my muscles enough to make my own hand shake his. I opened my mouth, but the only sounds I could manage were pathetic little mumbles of *Whydidyou howcouldyou whendidyou* before I finally realized it was all too much. I shook my head and ran inside, leaving Nolan all alone on the porch with him.

The guy may have been my birth father, but he was also the person who put my mom—my adopted mom, but my *real* mom nonetheless—in danger so he could test my newly activated supernatural skills. I'd believed that when I finally saw him I'd give him—as Mom would say—a piece of my mind. But instead, my mind went totally, miserably, shockingly blank.

"He told me he needed to talk to you," Nolan says for what's probably the twelfth time.

"I know," I answer. "But I'm not ready to talk to him yet."

"I understand that." Nolan nods slowly. "And I get where you're coming from. But you're going to have to talk to him eventually, so why not get it over with?"

Finally I spot the spirit that's been making my teeth chatter. It's a man in his midtwenties. Immediately I know his name was Ryan Palmer. His face is pale blue, his lips purple, and his eyes are blood shot. He drowned, and it looks like a terrible way to go. I step to the side of Nolan to reach the man and touch him on the shoulder. I close my eyes and help him move on. It feels as natural as breathing. I can't tell if helping this amount of spirits is normal or if Aidan really is sending every single local spirit in my direction. It feels like he thinks I need a reminder that he's waiting. Like there's even the slimmest, smallest chance I might forget he's here.

That he's my mentor.

That he's my father.

That I'm a member of a race of magical-mystical-guardian-angel-types for the entire human species.

Those aren't exactly the kind of details a girl could just forget willy-nilly. However much she might want to.

"Can we please, please change the subject?" I beg, squeezing the car keys in my hand so hard it hurts. Part of me just wants to go. To hop in the car and drive off before the next spirit is drawn to me. I mean, it may feel good to help the dead find peace, but it can also be quite frightening when someone didn't die so peacefully and they suddenly appear. Luckily I haven't had to help any murder victims yet.

"All right," Nolan acquiesces, leaning against the car beside me. "What do you think of our new visual arts teacher?"

If I could playfully shove him like half the girls across the parking lot are doing with their boyfriends, I would. Not that Nolan is my boyfriend. He's not exactly *not* my boyfriend either. I mean, he's my boy and he's my friend and he's really cute (even with that ridiculous hat) and I'd love it if he *could* be my boyfriend, but we can't touch each other because every time he gets too close, I get queasy and not in the weak-in-the-knees, good kind of way. Feeling ill every time the boy you like touches you has never been the opening setup to a great romance.

"That's not really changing the subject," I joke, smiling just a little bit. Our new visual arts teacher, Mrs. Johnson, is nothing at all like our old one. Victoria Wilde wasn't even a teacher at all, it turned out. Aidan planted her at Ridgemont High just so she and I could find each other. But now she's gone, and I don't know where.

"I should get going," I say finally, pushing myself off of the car. "I can't put this off much longer."

"My thoughts exactly," Nolan answers, but we both know he's not talking about driving.

"Plus, if I have to look at that silly hat any longer, I might have a seizure or something." I grin, glad that I managed to make a joke. Nolan smiles, impervious to my teasing.

I settle into the driver's seat, checking my mirrors and adjusting my seat even though I already did all of that before I drove to school this morning. I push my sleeves back up over my wrists so my hands are free to grip the steering wheel. The door still open, Nolan leans down to say good-bye.

Looking through my windshield, I see other girls kissing their boyfriends before they drive away. Maybe I'll have to add that to my list of questions for Aidan, if I can just get my vocal chords to work in his presence next time I see him: Why can't I kiss the boy I like so much?

No. I will not ask him that. That's way too personal for a person I barely know, even if he is my birth father. Anyway, I don't even know whether Nolan *wants* me to kiss him. He's never tried to kiss me. But, then again, the past few months since we met haven't exactly been romantic; in fact, they've been terrifying. A high creepiness factor doesn't really lend itself to lingering stares and heaving bosoms and long walks in the rain across the moors.

Get a grip, Sunshine. You're a luiseach, not the main character in a Brontë novel.

"Good luck!" Nolan shouts, shutting the door for me.

Right, it's time to drive. As I shift the car into drive and pull out of the parking lot, Nolan's tousled sandy hair is visible in my rearview mirror. He must have taken off his hat, and I can't help but smile. It doesn't occur to me that this might be the last time I smile for a very long time.

CHAPTER TWO
Emergency

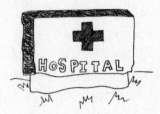

These aren't nice, pretty, baby flurries. They're big, fat, wet snowflakes, so heavy that the windshield wipers can barely move across the glass in front of me. The already intimidating drive from Ridgemont High to Mom's hospital has turned downright treacherous. I inch along at a snail's pace, which gives me plenty of time to think about the fact that the drive isn't the only reason I'm not looking forward to picking Mom up. I mean, I'm definitely looking forward to the picking-her-up part; it's the *hospital* part I'm not so crazy about.

I never used to be queasy about hospitals. Mom was—is—a neonatal nurse, and when I was a baby, I was a regular at the hospital's day care back in Austin. Later, when Mom's schedule was crazy and she couldn't find a sitter for me after school, sometimes I'd hang out at the nurse's station, quietly doing my homework. I got used to the sound of sirens and crying babies and even doctors and nurses shouting for aid.

But everything's different now. The last time I was at this hospital I helped a spirit move on. In fact, it was my very first time helping a spirit move on. But that's not what's making me drive even slower than the slowest of cars on the road in front of me; it's the fact that the last time I was at this hospital was also the day they told me Victoria was dead. Hearing those words was like a punch to the gut, like I'd never catch my breath again.

My thoughts are drowned out by the sound of sirens screaming. Ambulance after ambulance comes careening out of the hospital parking lot, and I'm barely able to pull into a spot before it starts.

It's just one spirit at first. A young man who died seconds ago, a victim of a multiple-car pile-up on the freeway I just left behind. His name is Matt, and he's sitting in the passenger seat beside me, his piercing blue eyes unwavering as he stares at me. He died from some sort of major trauma to his torso. I try not to let my gaze drift down to his midsection. I know seeing his wounds will be terrifying, so instead, I stare back into his eyes, which are filled with sadness. His was the car that started it. His bald tires skidded over a slick patch, drifting across the median and into oncoming traffic. I can feel the tremendous guilt saturating his spirit; he won't know peace until he moves on.

But before I can help him, I feel something else. Another spirit. A woman this time, Kimberly, who's only a few years older than I am. She's standing beside the driver's side door waiting for me. Her injuries don't look as traumatic as Matt's, but blood is dripping from her ear. A head injury killed her, mostly hidden by her hair.

Two spirits this close to me, this quickly, is overwhelming. Even though heat is blasting from the vents behind the steering wheel, it's suddenly so cold in here that I can see my own breath coming out in hyper little pants because my heart is pounding, beating faster than it ever has before.

Another spirit is near. I gasp at what I see and look away as quickly as I can. His wounds are horrific. No one told me I'd see spirits in such graphic detail. But then again, I've been avoiding my mentor, the one person who can tell me things like that. Before I have time to process what's happening, another spirit is here, waiting for my help. I can't see Matt anymore, the man whose bald tires caused this tragedy. I want desperately to help him move on, but I can't find him. I can only feel the overwhelming cold from all of them at once. I sink into the gray upholstery of my seat as though someone has placed an enormous weight around my neck, pressing me down, down, down.

I've never known cold like this before. I should have zipped my jacket before I got in the car, should have put on the multicolored crocheted hat and gloves that are sitting uselessly in my backpack in the backseat. I should have put on boots with thick socks instead of my sneakers when I got dressed this morning. I should have borrowed Nolan's ridiculous hat.

I manage to focus on my fingers, still gripping the wheel, and I'm not surprised when I see they're turning blue at the knuckles. I try to catch my breath, but it's run away without me. I can't keep my eyes open; I've been deprived of oxygen for too long, and I'm about to pass out. Mustering whatever strength I have left, I press down on the horn as hard as I can, like I think I can scare the spirits away.

Mom opens the door on the passenger side, and my overworked heart leaps. "Didn't want to run out in the snow to pick up your poor old mom so you just honked the horn?" she says with a smile that fades away the instant she sees the state I'm in.

"Sunshine!" she shouts, reaching across the car and putting her warm fingers on my neck. When she feels my pulse, she pulls back for a second in shock. But then she goes right into nurse-mode. She unclicks my seatbelt and pulls me across the car and onto my back on the snowy ground. She starts performing CPR and somehow manages to get the attention of the EMTs across the lot at the same time. The next thing I know, I'm on a gurney being wheeled into the hospital, my mother squeezing one of those airbags I've only ever seen on television, trying to breathe air back into my lungs.

If I could talk, I'd tell her it's no use. The doctors can't help me; they're not qualified to treat this kind of thing. Thanks to Nolan's research, I know that a luiseach like me can't be killed by a dark spirit, but I find myself wondering whether an onslaught of light spirits can kill me. I'm panting so hard that my lungs ache. The doctors and nurses are shouting around me as I'm wheeled into the ER and hooked up to their tubes and machines.

"We need to stabilize her heart!"

"We need to raise her body temperature!"

"We need to figure out why the heck an otherwise healthy sixteen-year-old girl just got wheeled into the ER with hypothermia and cardiac arrhythmia."

Okay, maybe they didn't shout that last one. But it's not difficult to guess it's what they're all thinking.

In all the chaos, as I drift in and out of consciousness, I can feel the warmth coming from my mother's touch. Her hand on my arm is a tiny source of heat keeping me connected to the world of the living, a small flame in the darkness. Suddenly I have a better understanding of what it must be like for the spirits who find me after they pass.

And then, it all stops. Not the flurry of physicians around me but the pounding in my chest, the freezing of my extremities. The sound of the heart monitor they'd hooked me up to shifts from a screeching wail into a steady beep. The warming blankets they'd packed around me feel too hot; in a snap I go from shivering to sweating.

The weight on my shoulders lifts. The spirits have vanished. My tunnel vision fades, and everything is bright again. Mom slips out of nurse-mode and back into mom-mode. She shoves the machines aside and leans down over me, wrapping me up in a tight hug.

"Mom," I gasp. "I just started breathing again. I don't think smothering me is the best idea." I expect her to laugh at my joke, but instead she goes on hugging me, her cheek pressed against mine. I can feel that her face is wet with tears.

"I'm okay," I say, and she finally releases me. She turns to face the doctors surrounding my bed, each of them looking more baffled than the last.

"What happened to my daughter?"

"We don't know, Kat," someone answers. I look at his ID tag and see his name is Dr. Steele. The same last name as Lucy from *Sense and Sensibility* by Jane Austen. Apparently with my vital signs back to normal—I think—I'm back to relating my life to the stories of my favorite writer. At least some things never change.

"What do you mean, you don't know?" Mom stands, looking confused. "There has to be an explanation for an episode of this magnitude."

I close my eyes. There's an explanation all right, just not one my mother—or pretty much anyone—would believe. Like most people—like me, before the past four months—Mom believes in science and reason, not magic and mystery. I couldn't convince her our house was haunted even after a demon had taken possession of her body. Especially after the demon possessed her.

"We'd like to admit her for observation," Dr. Steele offers finally. "You can stay with her overnight."

"Of course I'm going to stay with her," Mom snaps, and I actually feel kind of sorry for Dr. Steele. It's not his fault he doesn't know what's wrong with me. Not his fault he'll never be able to answer my mother's questions to her satisfaction. Not his fault that from now on she's probably going to be haunted by the idea that he's a terrible doctor.

"I'm okay, Mom," I say again, and she turns from the doctor to face me, fresh tears brimming in her eyes.

It's clear she doesn't believe me. I'm not sure I do either.

CHAPTER THREE

The Truth

They put me in a private room in the pediatric wing. One of the perks of being a nurse's daughter, I guess. The bed is right next to the window, and I gaze outside, looking at the snow coming down. Like the rest of our little town, Ridgemont Hospital is surrounded by towering Douglas firs, and the snow clings to their branches, making the evergreens look ever-white instead. Even though my temperature has rebounded, a chill runs down my spine.

Why did whatever was happening to me stop all at once like that? Why did my heartbeat go back to normal and my fingers turn from blue to pink? Did I help those spirits move on without realizing it? Or did they just float away when they discovered how useless I was, in search of a better, more competent luiseach to help them? Of course, deep down inside I already know the answer. When I turn from the window to the door, I see him standing right in front of me.

He was the better, more competent luiseach. He helped all those spirits move on, drawing them away from me like a magnet. And he's been waiting patiently ever since for the right moment to talk to us.

The last time I saw Aidan it had been only twelve hours since my mother was released from a demon's possession. It had been just a few minutes since I learned Nolan was my protector, since I learned that although Victoria was declared dead right here in this very hospital, she stood up and walked away—very much alive, still enough of a luiseach that a demon couldn't kill her.

Once again it feels like there are about a million questions bubbling up in my throat, like the words are literally fighting among my vocal chords, arguing over which one of them gets to be spoken first. But before I can say a thing, Mom looks up from her chair beside my bed and says in her calm, collected, professional nurse voice, "Can I help you?" She probably thinks he's lost, that he's here at the hospital to visit someone else.

She has no idea that he's here to see me.

Aidan steps inside the room, his right arm extended formally in front of him. He's wearing a perfectly tailored black suit and black wing-tip shoes; a gunmetal-gray tie is tied tightly around his collar. His hair is several shades darker than mine, almost black, and his skin is paler. His nose is straight as an arrow, and I bet he never wrinkles it like Mom and I wrinkle ours.

He looks nothing like my mother, in her pastel-colored scrubs and black clogs, and nothing like me, in my hospital gown and socks. Most everyone else in this hospital is probably dressed more like Mom and me than they are like him. Still, somehow he makes me feel like we're the ones who are inappropriately dressed.

"My name is Aidan," he begins. "It's nice to meet you, Katherine."

"Kat," Mom corrects automatically, the way she always does whenever anyone calls her by her full name. She stands up, no doubt wondering how he knew her name.

"I just wanted to see how Sunshine was doing," Aidan continues, and I bite my lip so hard it hurts. Because now Mom is about to ask how he knows *both* of our names.

I shake my head. I don't want him here, filling Mom's head with questions.

All those words that had been battling it out in my throat calm down long enough for me to say, "I think you should probably leave."

It's the first real sentence I've ever managed to say to him, and I can't help feeling a little bit proud of myself. If I can manage one sentence, soon I'll be able to manage another, which means I'll be able to ask him all of my questions eventually. But I don't want to ask them now. Not here. Not in front of Mom. Not yet.

"I think I should probably stay," Aidan counters calmly, settling into a chair across from Mom's on the other side of my bed. He gestures for her to sit and she does, perhaps off-put by how at ease he seems in here with us. His pants don't even wrinkle when he sits. Before I can protest, Aidan continues, "She's not going to believe you if I'm not here to prove it."

"To prove what?" Mom stands again, her arms folded across her chest. She takes a deep breath, still anxious about what happened to me, still waiting for the doctors to show up with an explanation for why her daughter nearly had a heart attack. "Are you some sort of specialist?" she asks, still searching for a reasonable explanation for this poised man's presence. Her voice is more high pitched than normal, so I can tell she's anxious. "Did they call you in for a consult? Do you have new information on my daughter's condition?"

Mom must think Aidan's here to deliver some kind of hopeless diagnosis. And in a way I guess he kind of is. It probably doesn't help matters that he's dressed like he runs a funeral home or something. I reach out and take her hand in mine. Her skin is clammy and cold.

I close my eyes, like I believe that maybe when I open them, Aidan won't be here and maybe Mom and I won't be here either. Maybe we'll be magically transported back home. And not home to our house here in Ridgemont. Home to our old house in Austin, with its sun-dappled backyard and the windows flung open wide to let the warm air in. The house where we lived for the sixteen years before I discovered I wasn't even human. Before I knew ghosts and demons really existed. The house where I lived when I was still normal.

Well, as normal as I ever was.

But when I open my eyes, of course we're still here. Aidan is still here. And worst of all, Mom is staring at him. She pulls her hand from mine and covers her mouth instead. Because she's just noticed Aidan's eyes. The eyes that look exactly like mine.

"Someone please tell me what's going on here," she whispers breathlessly, her eyes darting back and forth between us.

I've never wanted to tell anyone anything less. I mean I've never kept a secret from Mom. (Not unless you count the past few months, when she wasn't really Mom at all, but a shell of herself while the demon took up residence, and I definitely don't count that.) This whole not-telling-Mom-about-everything-that-I've-discovered-about-myself-and-about-everything-that-happened-to-her feels really, really unnatural. I've spent sixteen years telling her *everything.*

But once I tell her, *everything* will change. Will she still look at me the same way when she knows what I am? Will she still laugh at my jokes, make fun of my clumsiness? Will we still argue over who gets the last slice of pizza and cook together using recipes we printed off the Internet? Will she still tell me she loves me more than anything else?

A lump rises in my throat. Part of me thinks she'd rather hear Aidan offer up some diagnosis than the truth. At least she'd know what to do with a diagnosis. But there's no cure for being born a luiseach.

I sit up, blinking away my tears. "How are you going to prove it?" I ask slowly. My second full sentence aimed in his direction.

"Trust me." He looks directly into my eyes. Trust him? He's the one who put my mother's life in danger. Who turned my entire life upside down, turned me into Alice falling down the rabbit hole. Does he even care that he's about to change everything again?

"Sunshine," she begs with a gasp. I wish I could hug her, but I'm attached to so many wires and tubes that I can't figure out how to put my arms around her. "Please explain this to me." The sound of her voice makes me realize I have no choice but to do what Aidan says. Because I can't go on keeping the truth from my mother. Gently I pull her down to sit on the edge of the bed beside me. I square my shoulders and swallow the lump in my throat and start talking.

I start with the fact that Aidan is my birth father. Before she can launch into her own tirade of questions—*How did you find my daughter? How could you abandon her as a baby?*—I rush ahead, explaining I've inherited certain special traits from my birth parents.

"What kind of traits?" Mom asks sharply. "Recessive genes carry all kinds of traits." She's speaking so quickly that all of her words run together. "Look at your eyes. And I suppose you might have inherited certain medical conditions—but I can't think of any genetic explanation for what happened to you this afternoon—"

"It's not that kind of condition," I break in. "I mean, it does explain what happened to me this afternoon, but not for any *medical* reason."

"Don't be ridiculous." Mom shakes her head, standing up once again. She walks around the bed and stands over Aidan, still seated calmly in his chair. Mom is tall, taller than I am, but Aidan is taller. (Clearly I didn't get my vertical-challenged-ness from him.)

"Allow me to explain, Katherine—"

"Kat," she interrupts, her arms still hugging her own chest.

"Kat," he echoes. "When your daughter arrived at the hospital today—" I exhale, grateful he referred to me as *your daughter*. "She was met by an onslaught of spirits that had recently been released from their mortal coils, victims of the accident on the freeway."

Mom's mouth drops open. I think she wants to protest, but something in Aidan's voice keeps her quiet. Even when he's talking about spirits, he sounds every bit as calm and rational as a college professor talking about facts and figures.

"The presence of so many spirits at once overwhelmed her." He continues, "It takes a great deal of training to handle multiple spirits, and even among the well trained, few of us are prepared when taken unaware like that."

"Few of us?" Mom echoes. "Few of who?"

"Luiseach," I say quietly. "Luiseach." I repeat the word, louder this time. "It's an ancient species of guardians who've been around as long as humans have been living and dying. It's their job to help spirits move on after people die. And to exorcise spirits who've gone dark."

Mom looks at me like I'm speaking Chinese. I'm tempted to tell her the word *luiseach* is actually Celtic in origin, that it means light-bringer, although Nolan thinks the word might be so old that it predates the Celtic language altogether. He was going to look into it, and if anyone can find out, it's Nolan.

"This is absurd," Mom declares. "You don't even have proof that you really are my daughter's birth father, and you certainly can't just show up sixteen years after abandoning her in a hospital and lay claim to her with these outrageous stories." Unlike me, clearly Mom isn't tongue-tied around Aidan. "I don't know what you're trying to achieve here, but you can't just brainwash my daughter into believing fairy tales. I'd like you to leave right now, and if you don't, I'm calling security." She reaches for the phone at the side of my bed, but I can see that her hands are shaking. Still, she tries to sound as calm and authoritative as Aidan as she says, "My daughter is recovering from a serious cardiac episode, and I don't think this kind of stress—"

Before she can finish, Aidan takes hold of her arm, shocking her into silence. She drops the phone.

Mom's face goes slack, her eyes closing heavily. "What are you doing?" I ask frantically, sitting up and reaching for her. Immediately I get tangled up in the myriad wires and tubes I'm connected to.

"Don't worry," Aidan says.

"Don't worry?" I shout. "The last time you did something to her she was possessed by a homicidal demon!"

It's the most I've ever said to him, and much to my surprise, the words slipped out easily. My worry for Mom's safety is so much bigger than my fear of and anger at Aidan.

"I'm showing her what happened on New Year's Eve," he explains calmly.

I'm overwhelmed by the idea of Mom seeing what we went through on New Year's. I wasn't sure whether I was ever going to tell her about the danger we were all in that night. I knew she'd blame herself, even though it wasn't her fault. My eyes well up with tears as I watch her face, knowing she's experiencing those horrifying moments for the first time.

"I don't know if . . ." my voice fades away, unsure how to express my thoughts.

"It's all right. I'll show her something more positive now," Aidan says, as if he's reading my mind. "I'll show her a little of what you and I can feel. The spirits that float through this hospital, coming loose from their bodies as death grows near. The spirits that have left this place behind, leaving nothing more than a shadow in their wake."

Even though Mom is here in the room with us, it feels like she's somehow absent.

"I'm not sure I can feel that," I protest, but Aidan nods slowly. "You can." His voice is soft but insistent. "Close your eyes. Concentrate."

I don't want to take my eyes off Mom, but I also want to know exactly what she's feeling right now, so I let my eyelids drop. "Concentrate," Aidan whispers.

"On what?" I squeeze my eyes tight.

"Relax. Let it flow over you. Open yourself up to receive it."

I take a deep breath and try to relax all of my muscles, rolling my shoulders down my back, slouching so my stomach curls into a C. Almost like I'm trying to fall asleep.

And then I feel it. It's nothing like the cold shiver that a spirit's actual presence or touch brings; it's more like a hum, a heartbeat, a sense that the very air is alive, a sort of electric charge in the air.

"Wow," I say, opening my eyes. For just a second I swear Aidan smiles at me.

"Consider that your first lesson," he says. He doesn't add: *Just imagine what you might learn if you come with me and begin your training.* He doesn't have to. I can't help but raise one eyebrow as a response.

Quick as a snake, he lets go of Mom and she drops onto my bed, sitting up straight as a ruler. When she opens her eyes, I see a look of absolute wonder coming over her freckled face as she realizes that the world is much more mysterious than she ever believed it could be. She blinks, her gaze landing on Aidan as though she's seeing him for the first time. I reach out and take her hands in mine.

"Katherine," Aidan begins. "Kat," he corrects himself. "There's a reason you named your daughter Sunshine."

CHAPTER FOUR

Tears

Aidan excuses himself politely, leaving me alone with Mom. She's wearing a cream-colored cardigan over her pastel scrubs, and she's pulled the sleeves down over her wrists, just like I do. I wonder whether she got cold when she felt the spirits too. She looks more than a little dazed, and when I squeeze her hands, I'm surprised to discover that my own are trembling.

I'm seriously frightened. More frightened than I was in the parking lot hours earlier. Maybe even more frightened than I was when we moved into a haunted house.

What if my mother never looks at me the same way again?

Even though I sometimes think of Nolan as one of my best friends—and even though I've been calling Ashley, my best friend in Austin for just about as long as I can remember—the truth of the matter is I've always only had *one* best friend. And even though it might sound super-dorky-cheesy, I don't care: my mom is my best friend.

The idea that anything could change terrifies me.

"I'm sorry I didn't tell you sooner," I begin. "I've only known about Aidan since New Year's Day."

"You don't have to apologize." Mom stares into my eyes. The look of wonder is stripped from her face. Her always-pale skin looks a few shades whiter than usual. She turns to face the door like she's wondering who might show up next. Nurses rush back and forth in the hallway; doctors stand around examining charts. A bouquet of balloons floats by on its way to the maternity ward to congratulate a new parent. I can see Mom's hands shaking, and I reach out to hold them.

"Mom?" I prompt. "I know this is a lot to take in—"

"Understatement of the century," she says softly.

I nod. "I know."

"Has he introduced you to your mother?" Her voice cracks on the last two syllables, and I put my arms around her.

"*You're* my mother," I insist fiercely, hugging her so tight it must hurt, but she doesn't complain. Finally, when it feels like she's stopped shaking, I say, "And no. He hasn't told me anything about the woman who gave birth to me." I choose my words carefully. "It's just one of a long list of questions I have for him."

Mom nods. "I think I've started a list of my own," she says, then sighs. "I always knew this day would come."

"You did?" I ask incredulously, smiling awkwardly, again raising my eyebrow without meaning to. Mom knows what I'm thinking.

"I didn't mean the whole magical powers part of it," Mom answers. She manages a small smile as she brushes tears from her eyes. We're both crying now, but eventually Mom catches her breath and continues, "I meant that . . . I guess all adoptive parents wonder about the day their children's birth parents might show up on their doorsteps, right? Though to be honest, I thought the odds in your case were pretty slim, given how we found each other."

I nod. Someone—Aidan, perhaps?—left me at my mother's hospital as an infant. There were no official papers for my birth parents to sign before they gave me away, no records hidden in some bureaucratic vault somewhere revealing who they had been.

"But," Mom continues, now serious and dry-eyed. "I always knew it was a possibility. And I wanted that for you," she adds quickly. "If you wanted to know, then I wanted you to have every detail about where you'd come from and why your parents gave you up. So I guess . . ." She pauses. "I guess part of me is relieved Aidan showed up."

"Relieved?" I echo. That's just about the last word I'd have expected her to use right now.

Mom nods slowly. "I was scared sometimes, worried that you'd want to know where you came from and we'd never be able to find out and you'd never have the closure you needed."

"I still don't have closure," I protest. "This feels like the opposite of closure actually. It feels like the beginning of something that's going to change everything. I'm not even technically human anymore." I bite my lip. Technically I never *was* human—I was born a luiseach.

Mom shifts on the bed, lying down beside me and putting her arms around me. I rest my face against her shoulder just like I did when I was a little kid. "There's one thing it hasn't changed, Sunshine. One thing it never, ever could."

I swallow. "What's that?"

"It hasn't changed how much I love you. You could tell me you were descended from a family of wolves or rabbits or aliens, and I would still love you all the same."

I start crying all over again, but I'm smiling too, breathing in the scent of Mom's mango-scented shampoo.

"As a matter of fact," Mom continues, "this actually explains a lot."

"It does?" I ask, my teary eyes wide.

Mom reaches out and tucks one of my curls behind my right ear. "I knew you were special," she concedes, shaking her head. "I just didn't know there was a name for it."

By the time I wake up in the morning and the doctors have checked up on me, it's clear there's no reason for us to stay here any longer; they could run a million tests and never find out what's wrong with me. Anyway, it's not wrong with me anymore. For now at least.

Mom's sitting in the chair beside the bed, exactly where she sat when Aidan showed up last night. It looks like she hasn't slept a wink.

"'Morning, Sunshine," she says groggily.

"There's something else I have to tell you."

"Okay." Mom takes a deep breath. She sits up straight, like she's bracing herself for something big. Guess I can't blame her after last night.

"Aidan isn't just my birth father. He's also my mentor." Ever since he showed up, in fact, I've been calling him my *mentor/father* in my head. I can't think of him without imagining a slash cutting its way between the two words. Neither word feels natural.

"What does that mean?" Mom asks.

I recite the facts I know by heart. "Every luiseach has a mentor. When they turn sixteen, they're supposed to begin working with them. Training, I guess."

"What kind of training?"

I shrug. "I don't really know. Nolan's been trying to research it—"

"Nolan was there on New Year's!" Mom interrupts, remembering some of what Aidan helped her see just hours ago. Sometimes I forget she wasn't exactly all there over the past few months when Nolan and I became close. She probably doesn't even remember the times he came over, helping me figure out what the heck was happening to her.

"Nolan is my protector," I explain. "A luiseach has both a mentor and a protector. We didn't know he was mine until New Year's Day either."

"As though you didn't have enough going on that day." Mom grimaces, and I know she's thinking about Victoria. I bite my lip and wrinkle my nose, a habit I got from her. I sit up, my paper-thin hospital gown wrinkling beneath me. Instantly I decide *not* to tell Mom that Victoria isn't actually dead anymore. Her entire belief system has already been monumentally shaken; I don't want to completely shatter her understanding of the way the world works. She doesn't need to know that sometime after the doctors and nurses declared her dead, Victoria stood up and walked out of the hospital, every bit as alive as she'd been before the water demon attacked her.

"Umm . . . right. It was a big day. But anyway, the point is that ever since New Year's, Aidan's been trying to get me to start working with him."

"And you don't want to?" Mom asks gently, leaning forward. She swallows. I'm sure the idea of me doing much of anything with this near-stranger is scary for her. I know it is for me.

"I don't know what I want," I answer honestly. "Actually I want to go back to six months ago when you and I still lived in Austin and I didn't know anything about ghosts or ancient Celtic words or mentors or demons or any of it. I want to un-become a luiseach."

"Honey, it sounds to me like this isn't something you can un-become. You didn't even *become* it to begin with. You were born this way." Before I can explain you can (sort of) un-become a luiseach, Mom continues. "But maybe . . ." She takes a deep breath, hesitating, like whatever she's about to say next is going to be difficult. "Maybe you should start working with Aidan."

"Really?"

"I've been thinking about this all night." She nods solemnly. "I know Aidan helped me see what you two are, but I still don't fully understand what happened to you yesterday, and I know it wasn't safe. Your heart was beating so fast, I thought that you couldn't possibly survive it. So . . . if there's some sort of luise-ach training that can get your body under control so whatever happened to you in the parking lot never happens again, then I don't think you should risk going another second without learn-ing everything you can."

I close my eyes, remembering how it felt yesterday. I thought I'd never catch my breath; I thought my heart would explode from the effort of beating so quickly. What will I do if there's another accident nearby, maybe a bigger one? What if next time Aidan doesn't show up in time to help all those spirits move on before they become too overwhelming?

"I'm new to all this, but I know I want my daughter safe. And," Mom adds shyly, dropping her gaze, "it will give you a chance to get to know Aidan, to find out all the bits and pieces of your history that I can't tell you. To ask all of those questions you haven't had a chance to ask yet."

I reach out and take her hand in mine. She's right, of course. Training with Aidan would be the perfect chance to start going through my list of questions one by one.

As long as I *am* a luiseach, I need to get these spirit-sensations under control. Seriously, that should be lesson number one on the very first day of luiseach training, right?

"How do we get in touch with him to let him know what you've decided? Do you have his cell phone number?"

The idea of Aidan with a cell phone at his ear is so absurd that I almost burst out laughing. Instead I just shake my head and blink, looking around the empty hospital room. A lost spirit hasn't visited me since yesterday, which can only mean one thing: Aidan is close. I'm pretty sure he already knows.

That Woman

That woman approached me today, the one who worked alongside Aidan for all those years, nearly as close to him as I used to be.

She claims she was married. She claims she had a child of her own, one whose life was taken by a demon. And she claims that after years of standing by Aidan's side, he forced her to give up her powers in exchange for helping her poor daughter's beleaguered spirit move on.

She says Aidan never made good on his promise. She says her daughter's spirit still lingers here on Earth. Yet that woman can't find it, so even I can't help the poor child move on.

That woman won't stop crying.

I want to turn her away, but I know how it feels to be betrayed by Aidan, just as I know how it feels to trust him with the most sacred parts of yourself. After the things we exposed to that child while she was in the womb . . . just thinking about it makes me tremble. That baby, and the things we did to her—all of it was a mistake.

As became crystal clear the very instant she was born.

I trusted Aidan to do what had to be done. I trusted that woman too. I thought they understood the girl had to be destroyed, no matter how tiny her pink hands and feet, how piercing her cries, how round her little mouth, or how green her enormous eyes.

It was months before I realized he didn't do what we'd discussed. That he'd allowed the child to thrive. I must admit it: for one selfish instant I was relieved. More than relieved—I was overjoyed. But I shoved my joy aside. Such feelings didn't matter: the child must be eliminated, no matter my personal feelings on the matter. There was the greater good to bear in mind.

Aidan refused to see reason. He wouldn't reveal the child's location. I did everything in my power to find her. Most of our people rallied to my side, but even our collective powers weren't enough to locate her. The child was only an infant when Aidan took her, and by the time I discovered what he had done, it was impossible to distinguish her from the other lost and abandoned children. We checked every foster home, every adoption record, but there was no sign of her. Aidan erased all traces of the girl.

So I waited. It was only a matter of time. Now that she has come into her powers, I can sense her. After all, my blood pumps through her veins as well.

And now, here is that woman telling me that Aidan used her offspring for the girl's test. Telling me she knows where the girl is now. Weeping as she admits that for all these years her loyalties were misplaced. She offers to lead me to her.

I won't think about what that baby might have grown up to look like, sound like, act like all these years later. I won't hope she was raised with love and support, that she had a good life up until now. I won't be proud of her for passing her test.

I will only find the girl—and eliminate her.

CHAPTER FIVE
Danger

Aidan is waiting at the house when Mom and I get home from the hospital, wearing yet another perfectly pressed suit. This one is slate gray, with a pale blue tie secured tightly around his neck. I wonder if he even owns a pair of jeans, like the ones I'm wearing as I close the car door behind me. I wonder if he thinks that my mother is a slob because she's still wearing the scrubs she wore when he met her, the same ones she slept in, sitting beside my hospital bed all night long.

"You should get packed," Aidan instructs as we step inside the house. I notice he doesn't wait for Mom to invite him in.

"Packed?" I echo.

"Wait a minute," Mom interjects. "I said my daughter could begin her training with you. I had no idea that meant you'd be taking her away."

Aidan nods solemnly. "I understand your hesitation. But I'm afraid we cannot afford to waste any more time."

"You mean that what happened last night might happen again?" Mom blinks and I shudder, remembering how cold I was in the car.

"No," Aidan answers. "Although, I suppose it might. But that is not the danger I'm concerned about at the moment."

"My daughter is in danger?"

"She's been in danger almost from the moment she was born."

I reach out and take Mom's hand. "What do you mean?"

"All I can tell you is you're not safe here anymore and I'm taking you someplace where you will be."

"Safe from what?"

He doesn't answer.

"I'm not letting you take my daughter away from me without a good reason."

"There are about a dozen reasons, all of them very good," Aidan looks directly into Mom's eyes. "But I can't explain now." He glances at his watch. "Time is of the essence." Despite the cool January air, I think I see a hint of sweat on his upper lip. Wherever he's taking me, he wants to get on the road right away.

"Will my birth mother be there?"

"No," Aidan sets his lips into a line so straight and firmly shut that I can tell he's not going to elaborate.

"What about school? It literally just started again."

"Believe me, school isn't important right now. The lessons you have to learn—"

"I know you're new to this whole parenting thing," Mom interrupts, "but I don't go around telling my daughter school isn't important."

"Apologies." Aidan glances at his watch once more, even though there's no way more than a minute or two has passed since the last time he looked. "Sunshine's teachers won't even notice she's gone," he promises. "They'll send you a report card at the end of the school year just as though she never left."

Mom opens her mouth to protest—I know what she's going to say, something about learning being more important than grades—but this time I'm the one who interrupts. "What do you mean at the end of the year? Just how long am I going to be gone?"

"As long as it takes."

Another nonanswer answer. I'm about to ask *As long as what takes,* but I have a hunch he's not going to answer—again!—so instead I pull my phone out of my pocket and dial Nolan's number. I've already talked to him once this morning to tell him exactly what happened last night.

Before I can hit the call button, I shiver as a wave of cold air crashes into me. It's the unmistakable coldness of a nearby spirit, but this time it's different. The sensation hits me like someone throwing a bucket of ice water over my head. Then I notice Aidan's slightly outstretched hand, summoning the nearby spirit. He's pulling it toward us with such strength and focus that my jaw drops in wonderment. In the blink of an eye the dead man's spirit is upon us. He's in his midsixties, half of his face is limp, sagging toward the ground, and the other half is filled with fear. He died from a severe and sudden stroke.

Quickly Aidan touches the man's shoulder, and the spirit dissolves into a ball of light. Aidan's face doesn't register a single emotion. At once I'm in awe of his ability and disturbed by his lack of emotion. Is that my future?

Suddenly I remember what I was doing, and I hit the call button and press the phone to my ear as I wait for Nolan to pick up.

"What about Nolan's teachers?" I ask. Report card or no report card, Nolan's going to be pretty upset about potentially missing a semester or more of school.

"Nolan isn't coming," Aidan answers.

"What do you mean he isn't coming?" I echo, ignoring Nolan's voice saying *Hello* on the other end of the phone line. "He's my protector! How safe can wherever you're bringing me be without him?"

"Our work doesn't require him. And you know by now a protector's role isn't to protect you physically. He protects you by gathering the information you need to complete your tasks."

But . . . I only know that because *Nolan* helped me figure it out. I don't think it ever occurred to me that, whatever I was agreeing to when I said I'd start working with Aidan, Nolan wasn't going to be a part of it.

"Where am I going to get the information I need if Nolan isn't there to help me?"

Aidan looks surprised by my question. "From me, of course," he replies simply.

On the other end of the phone I hear Nolan hanging up. I don't have to call back and ask him what he's doing. I already know.

He's on his way here.

Later, after Mom has served Aidan tea at our kitchen table and he's more or less convinced Mom that I should go with him, and after I've packed my clothes into an enormous duffle bag and stuff my backpack with every Jane Austen book I own (all six of them, obviously), Nolan is waiting for me on our front steps.

He's still wearing that silly hat, so I playfully pull it off his head and hand it to him.

"I can't take you seriously when you're wearing that hat," I joke. Nolan doesn't even crack a smile.

"This is ridiculous," he says.

"I know. It's an awful color combination." I hold up the hat. Nolan remains stone-faced. *Okay, Sunshine, stop trying to make the hat joke work.*

"No. *This* is ridiculous." He waves his hands as if he's trying to encompass our whole lives. "How am I supposed to protect you if I'm not with you?"

"Aidan said I don't need you." I bite my lip. I didn't mean to say it quite like that. I mean, that *is* what Aidan said, but I didn't mean to make it sound like I agreed.

"Here." I hold out his grandfather's butter-soft brown leather jacket between us. This jacket was the first thing I ever noticed about Nolan. When he gave it to me for good luck, I thought I'd never want to take it off. "Aidan says it's warmer where we're going. I won't . . ." I bite my lip again, stopping myself before I can say I won't need the jacket. Bad enough I already said I wouldn't need *him*.

Nolan shakes his head. "I want you to have it."

I hug the jacket to my chest and breathe it in. Just the scent of it brings me back to when Nolan and I first met. He didn't seem bothered by my embarrassing klutziness. He didn't think I was weird because I carried an old-fashioned camera around wherever I went and preferred vintage clothes to the brand-new ones most of the girls at Ridgemont High wear. Finally I say, "I want me to have it too. But can you . . . can you take care of it for me while I'm gone?"

Nolan nods, but he doesn't reach out to take the jacket, so I place it carefully on the steps beside him.

"And this," I add, taking my beloved Nikon F5 from around my neck. "Can you hang on to this for me?"

"Don't you want to take it with you?"

"I thought I did, but . . ." I trail off. Nolan gave me his jacket when I needed it. Now I want to give him something that's important to me too. I hold the camera out in front of me, and Nolan finally takes it, lifting the thick strap around his own neck.

"I've read Victoria's letter over and over." His voice is heavy with frustration. "I still don't understand what my role is in all of this." Nolan is amazing at research, the kind of person who's used to getting answers from books, articles, letters. I'm pretty sure this is the first time the written word has ever let him down.

I sit down beside him. "I'll make sure Aidan explains it to me. I'll ask him over and over and over again, and I won't stop until it's absolutely *crystal* clear. I'll be the most annoying mentee he's ever had."

Nolan looks up at me and smiles, though he looks tired. I don't think he slept much last night. Around dinnertime he called to find out how my drive to and from the hospital went, and I had to tell him what happened in the parking lot, how Aidan showed up, how we told Kat everything. I think he felt guilty he wasn't there every step of the way.

And now he's not going to be there for whatever my next steps will be either.

The front door opens behind us. Mom steps out onto the porch to let our little white dog, Oscar, out. Aidan is still waiting inside.

"I think it's time, Sunshine." Mom says.

"Okay. Just a sec," I answer, and she turns to go back inside.

Nolan waits for Mom to close the door. "Come here," he says softly, walking toward the side of the house.

Slowly I follow him. I start to ask why we're walking away—what does he want to do or say that he can't do or say in front of my mother?—but then I realize. I don't know how I know—it's not like this has ever happened to me before—but I just *know*. He wants to kiss me good-bye. Just like those couples I was so jealous of in the school parking lot yesterday. Just like the characters in my favorite Jane Austen books. (Okay, I know there's not much actual *kissing* in Jane Austen novels, but sometimes my imagination takes liberties.)

The twelve steps it takes to get around to the side of the house feel like twelve hundred. My heart is pounding—not a million beats a minute like it did last night, but just really *hard*, like I can actually feel the blood pumping through my veins one beat at a time.

CHAPTER SIX

Confessions

I want to kiss Nolan. Of *course* I want to kiss him. But I'm not sure I want our first kiss—my first kiss *ever*, by the way—to be a kiss good-bye.

Does Nolan think I'm going to be gone a very, very long time and this is his last chance to show how he feels about me? I mean, I want him to show me how he feels—if this really *is* how he feels—but not right now. Not like this. And not just because it's a kiss good-bye.

Ever since I met Nolan, his touch has had a . . . *strange* sort of effect on me. I don't mean in a romantic, makes-my-knees-weak sort of way, though I really wish I did. Being near him may make me warm, but only up to a point. If he gets *too* close, I don't feel good. I mean, I feel literally *sick* when he touches me, like I'm going to throw up or like I have a fever and need to lie down and get under the covers for a very long time. Which isn't exactly conducive to romance. Sure, there have been times when I've ignored the feeling—when he was bleeding or when he grabbed my hand to run through the torrential rain. But those were emergency situations. They were nothing like *this*.

Still, here I am, around the corner from our front porch, my back leaning against the outside of our house. The kitchen is on the other side of this wall. The same wall that actually disappeared a few days ago as I battled the demon that threatened to kill my mother and Nolan and to destroy Anna's spirit altogether. But right now this wall feels completely solid, like not even an earthquake could make it falter.

And that's a good thing, because right now I'm shaking so hard I need something solid to lean on.

I can feel Nolan's breath on my face. As he leans down, his tawny hair falls across his amber eyes. I inhale. The camera bumps up against my chest between us. But when his thumb traces my jaw, every muscle in my body stiffens as I try to control my gag reflex. Nolan drops his hand and steps back.

"Why don't you want me to touch you?"

I shake my head. There's no way to tell him that being this close to him makes me feel sick without sending the wrong message.

As if reading my thoughts, he prompts, "You can tell me the truth."

I nod. When I told Mom everything, she said that she'd love me the same no matter what, and I felt about a zillion times better than I had before. Plus, from the look on Nolan's face, it's clear that the truth he's expecting is for me to tell him that I don't like him *that way*, that I want to be just friends.

I'd rather he know the truth than believe I don't want him.

So I tell him. But Nolan doesn't look relieved. He backs away, one foot behind the other, like he can't get away from me fast enough.

"I'm sorry—" I begin, but Nolan shakes his head.

"I understand," he cuts me off.

"Maybe it's a luiseach thing," I suggest desperately. "Maybe Aidan can help me learn how to overcome it," I add, but it's the wrong thing to say. No guy wants to hear that the girl he wants to kiss has to *overcome* disgusting feelings in order to kiss him back.

I look down at my bright blue sneakers. I've hurt him. I've *really* hurt him. This doesn't feel better than keeping the truth to myself. This feels much, much worse.

"I better go," he says finally. Before I can call out *Wait* or *I'm sorry* or *Good-bye*—before I can say anything at all—Nolan stuffs his hat in his back pocket and heads around the corner, down our driveway, and into his grandfather's car parked just across the street. I wait for him to drive away, and then I go back to the front porch, where Mom is standing with her arms folded across her chest, holding herself to keep warm.

"He forgot his jacket," I say softly as Mom puts her arms around me. "Promise me you'll get it to him when I'm gone, okay?"

"I promise," Mom replies. I tucked Victoria's letter into one of the pockets so Nolan can take care of it while I'm gone.

Mom strokes my hair, frizzed from the Ridgemont moisture. Maybe wherever Aidan is taking me will be dry enough that my hair will actually behave. Not that I know where he's taking me. He just said that it was warm and that I needed to bring my passport.

I lean down and kiss Oscar on top of his soft little head, sending his tail-wagging speed into overdrive. Upstairs I kissed my taxidermied owl, Dr. Hoo, in exactly the same spot.

Aidan steps onto the front porch. "Take care of my baby," Mom's voice shakes as she faces him. She turns back to me, twisting my curls around her fingers. We've never been apart for so much as summer camp. "And call every day."

Her voice breaks on the last word and then she swallows. I know she's trying so hard to be strong for me, not to let on that she's scared—both to let me go and of what might happen to me if I stay behind. I know because I'm scared of the exact same things.

I have no idea how to say good-bye to her. She pulls me into her arms again and whispers, "You can come home anytime you want to. Just say the word, and I'll come rescue you." I nod into her hair. I know that if open my mouth to speak, I'll start to cry.

I lean down and lift my backpack off the ground, acutely aware of the weight of what's inside of it. Not just my books and some of the clothes I couldn't fit into my duffle bag: nestled between the Mustang T-shirt I stole from Mom and my tattered copy of *Pride and Prejudice* is something else. I decided to pack it at the very last minute: the rusty old knife that transformed into a torch on New Year's Eve when I faced the water demon.

I want to be prepared, no matter that Aidan said we were going someplace safe. Victoria said this weapon would manifest as whatever I needed it to be at the moment I needed it. I don't know what I'm going to need next.

I settle into the passenger seat of Aidan's long black sedan. He backs out of our driveway, and Mom gets smaller and smaller until Aidan turns the car and I can't see her anymore.

Once we get to wherever we're going, I'm going to move the knife from my bag to my back pocket. I'd rather have it within arm's reach. Just in case.

CHAPTER SEVEN

In Flight

Aidan's car has tinted windows and soft leather seats, and the controls on the dashboard look more like the ones on the Starship *Enterprise* than like the ones on Mom's old sedan. As we drive to the Seattle airport, Aidan tells me we're flying to Mazatlan in central Mexico. There's no direct flight from SeaTac to the Mazatlan airport, so we're changing planes in LA, and the whole thing will take more than ten hours.

"I've never even been out of the country," I say.

"I know," Aidan answers, pressing down on the gas pedal because we have a flight to catch. I wonder what else he knows about my life. Does he know Mom and I have pizza and movie night once a week? That I've never kissed a boy? That I prefer vintage clothes to new ones?

"When did you buy these tickets?" I ask suddenly. Aidan doesn't answer. "I only agreed to come with you a few hours ago, but you already had us on the next flight out of town."

"I booked tickets on every flight since New Year's Day,"

Aidan finally responds, as though that isn't a strange—and extravagant—way to make travel plans. "I wanted to be ready to go as soon as you agreed."

"Oh." I don't ask what he would have done if I kept *not* agreeing to go with him for much longer.

As we stand in line to board, I notice something, *someone*, strange in the terminal. There is a man looking at me, even as he walks right past us to an adjacent gate where another flight is boarding. Not just looking—he's staring. Almost like he knows me. But his face isn't friendly, like maybe he's trying to figure out why I look so familiar. He's wearing a long black coat and a wide-brimmed black hat, like someone out of a movie set in the 1940s. But that's not the weirdest thing about him; there seems to be a sort of . . . *darkness* attached to him, like a faint shadow is emanating from his body, surrounding him completely, unlike the rest of us, whose shadows are stuck to the floor beneath our feet.

"Did you see that man?" I ask Aidan, but he's already walking down the ramp to board the plane. I turn back toward the mysterious man, but before I can make eye contact, he walks past a pillar and out of sight.

We're sitting in first class. Enormous pillows and soft blankets wait on our seats, and as soon as we sit down, a flight attendant is asking for our drink order. I ask for a Diet Coke, unlike Aidan, who says, "Nothing, thank you."

"Isn't that the whole point of sitting in first class? You can have whatever you want, whenever you want it?"

"I just like to be near the front of the plane so I'm the first to get on and the first to disembark."

If you ask me, that's a total waste, but it doesn't look like Aidan's about to ask me.

I settle into my window seat, shove my backpack beneath the seat in front of me, and watch the rest of the passengers board the plane. I can't help noticing that they all look a lot more festive than we do. They're headed down south for fun, to catch some rays and warmth, a respite from the winter chill. I'm pretty sure we're the only two people here who aren't about to go on vacation.

Surely we won't be working twenty-four hours a day, right? Maybe I'll have time to work on my tan and get back some of the color that faded when we moved from Austin to Ridgemont. Mom would already be slathering sunscreen on her pale skin, even though we're still hours from landing south of the border.

"Where exactly are we going?" I ask Aidan as the plane ascends.

"I've been working at a facility a couple of hours north of Mazatlan for many years now."

"A facility?" I echo. Aidan nods.

"It's called Llevar la Luz." When he sees the blank look on my face—I don't know much Spanish—he translates: "Bring the light."

"Why Mexico?" Maybe he hates the rain and the cold as much as I do. Maybe I get that from him. Can preferences be hereditary?

"The warmth helps keep spirits under control," he answers softly. "It's easier to keep dark spirits at bay. There are a few spirits who are drawn to the warmth—fire demons, for example—but even they prefer the cold. They can hide more effectively in the cold."

"Why's that?" My ears pop as the plane climbs higher and higher.

"Think about it."

Is this what every conversation with Aidan is going to be like? Every time I have a question, he'll get all teachery and try to make me figure it out myself? I'm more interested in answers than in lessons, but I guess I don't have much choice.

Finally I respond, "Because our temperatures drop when a spirit is near, so if we're already cold it's harder to notice the difference?"

"Exactly," Aidan nods. I guess that's what he meant when he said he was bringing me someplace safe. Because I'm not exactly an expert at exorcising demons yet, I'll be safer where there's fewer of them and I can detect them more easily.

"Additionally a warm environment is easier on luiseach than the cold. Makes it easier for us to recover after a spirit touches us." I guess that means our preferences are kind of hereditary.

"So there are other luiseach there? Other mentees like me?" The captain announces that he's turned off the fasten-seatbelt sign.

"No. Not like you." Before I can ask what he means by *that,* he adds, "Llevar la Luz is where I've been conducting my research."

"What research?"

Aidan pauses before answering. Maybe he's worried the people on the plane around us might overhear and think he's nuts. Maybe they'll call Child Protective Services and send me back to Mom and Ridgemont before we've even begun, but then I remember what happened in the hospital parking lot and the look on Nolan's face when I didn't kiss him. I'm not entirely sure I want to go back. Not yet anyway.

"The mission of luiseach is to maintain a balance between humans and spirits, between the light spirits and the dark. It has been our sacred duty for hundreds, thousands of years, since the very dawn of humanity." He speaks as though he's reciting words he's said many times before.

"Is this your tried-and-true mentoring speech?" I attempt a joke, but Aidan doesn't seem to get it. Or, at least, he doesn't crack a smile. "I mean, every time you have a new luiseach to train, do you say the same thing?" I try to laugh, but it's no use. Jokes aren't funny when you have to explain them.

I'm not sure Aidan even knows what a joke is.

We may have the same eyes, but that's where our physical similarities end. He's tall, so tall that his knees touch the seat in front of them, even in first class. I've got plenty of leg room; if only he could borrow some of mine. His hair is so dark it's almost black, and his skin is paler than mine, without a single freckle marring it. He's kind of perfect looking, like a statue or Clark Kent or something. I bet he's never tripped. I bet he ties his shoelaces so tight that they never come undone.

Solemnly he explains, "As long as there have been humans living and dying on the Earth, there have been luiseach, guarding humanity and keeping the dark spirits from possessing them, forcing spirits to move on or destroying them altogether."

Thanks to Nolan's research, I already know this. Grr . . . just thinking about Nolan makes my stomach hurt. But it's impossible *not* to think of him because almost everything I understand about being a luiseach is thanks to him. "But because no luiseach has been born since me, the balance has been disrupted, right?"

He nods. "This is an unprecedented time in luiseach history."

Score one for Sunshine. I go through my mental list and land on another question.

"Your work—the work you and Victoria were doing—it was to restore the balance?"

Again Aidan nods. "In a way, yes. Part of my research is to find a solution to the growing darkness. The imbalance." Another question, another answer, even if he's not exactly chatty about it.

"Nolan said luiseach birth rates were dropping even before I was born. Do you know why?"

"It takes two luiseach parents to make a luiseach child."

"I know," I respond, and Aidan looks surprised.

"Nolan," I explain with a shrug, raising my eyebrow, even though saying his name out loud makes my stomach hurt even worse than *thinking* it.

"Our gene pool was shrinking. There are only so many luiseach, and the human race grows more numerous every year."

I remember something Victoria said. She and Aidan had a falling out after she married a human and had a child. Was Aidan angry because she'd given up the chance to have a luiseach baby and instead had a human child, Anna—a child who could be killed by a demon? Maybe there were more luiseach like her, ones who couldn't help falling in love with a human, luiseach who cared more about having a family than about producing children with powers.

The question I want to ask next—the question I've wanted to ask since Aidan first showed up on my doorstep—sits like a stone in the back of my throat: *Why did you abandon me?* It's like the words are trapped in there, stuck between my vocal chords, unable to get out.

So I ask something else instead. "Why do I feel so warm around Nolan?"

"He's your protector," Aidan explains. "When he's near, the spirits that might touch you settle down a bit so your temperature doesn't dip so low."

Before I can stop myself, I ask, "But then why can't I touch him? I mean, I *can* touch him, but it makes me feel . . ." I bite my lip. I *specifically* didn't want to ask Aidan this particular question. It's way too private, but it's also too late, because the words just flew out of my mouth before I could stop them.

Aidan doesn't answer right away, and I'm surprised to see that he looks flustered. He's actually tugging at his collar, and for a second I think he's going to loosen his tie. Maybe Aidan isn't so different from normal fathers, uncomfortable with the idea of his teenage daughter dating someone. Ashley told me her dad could barely look at her for days after he came home early from work one night and saw her making out with her boyfriend Cory Cooper in their driveway.

Not that Aidan is my father the way Ashley's father is hers. He's my mentor/father, and I've only known him for a few days. He's not even human.

Then again, neither am I.

Finally Aidan responds. "Nolan is human and you're luiseach."

"Victoria was married to a human."

"It's complicated," he says, then looks away, distracted. It takes me a second, but soon I feel it too. A man who passed away seconds ago.

"Where did he come from?"

"We're over Northern California right now. Even though we're airborne, for some of the spirits being set free from their bodies, we're the closest luiseach. They can't help being drawn to us."

I feel it when the spirit disappears. Aidan helped him move on without blinking an eye, too quickly for me to focus and see him. He looks like he barely felt anything at all, not the chill when the spirit arrived nor the peace when he left.

Aidan folds his arms across his chest and closes his eyes. "I'm going to get some sleep before we land."

I watch him for a moment, expecting him to shift in his seat, settle into his sleep, but he doesn't move. No one falls asleep that fast, right? But I know that it's even harder to rouse a fake sleeper than a real sleeper if the faker is determined to keep his eyes closed. From the way Aidan is squeezing his shut, I can tell he's more than a little determined.

I turn from my mentor/father to stare out the window at the clouds floating beneath us, trying to ignore the nagging thought that's running on a constant loop in my brain: if Aidan won't even give me a straight answer about Nolan, then what's he going to say when I finally do start asking some of the bigger questions?

Why did you abandon me?

Who is my birth mother?

Where is my birth mother?

Why isn't she here with you—with me?

I lean my forehead against the window and squeeze my eyes shut, pretending to sleep, determined not to open them until we get to Mexico.

Another thing that Aidan and I have in common.

CHAPTER EIGHT

Llevar la Luz

We land in Mazatlan and follow—or actually lead, given our place in first class—the plane's other passengers to the customs line. This is my first time getting my passport stamped, and I can't help feeling a little bit excited when the official-looking stamp presses down on the otherwise blank paper. I steal a glance at Aidan's passport on the counter beside my own. It's so covered in stamps that the customs officer has trouble finding a blank space to mark it. He finally smacks the stamp down directly on top of another one that looks like it's in French. Aidan speaks to the official in perfect Spanish.

At least I think it's perfect. I don't know enough Spanish to tell the difference.

The airport is crowded and hot. I mean, it's air conditioned, but no amount of artificial air can mask the heat that's beating down on this building from all sides.

We have to go through security again before they'll let us outside. Our bags go through an X-ray conveyer belt just like they did at the airport in the states. I wonder whether they'll notice the knife tucked away in my backpack. Maybe it will manifest as something else when the X-ray passes over it, disguising itself as a T-shirt or a book so security won't notice it.

An enormous black SUV with tinted windows is waiting for us in the parking lot. But unlike the car we left behind in Washington, this one is caked with dried mud in the wheel wells and along the bottom of the doors. I climb inside, trying to keep the bottom of my pants from rubbing against the dirt. We drive north along the coast for more than two hours. At first it looks like Mexico is the opposite of Ridgemont. Instead of gray, the world here is a collage of yellows and tans—sand and sun and not much in between. There are no towering Douglas firs to provide relief from the heat, no damp chill in the air to make me shiver.

But then the landscape shifts, going from arid desert to dense jungle. Definitely nowhere near those resorts you see in tourism commercials.

And it's still damp. As in *humid*. As in I think the frizzball on top of my head might actually grow bigger here than it was in Washington.

By the time Aidan stops the car, I have no idea where we are. Not that I've known where we've been from the moment we landed in Mazatlan, but now it feels like I know even *less*.

About thirty minutes ago we steered away from the ocean and began to climb the hillside. The farther we drove, the more uneven the ground beneath the car became until we were bouncing up and down so hard that I thought my head would smack against the roof, even with my seatbelt supposedly strapping me in. The road looked like little more than a path some-

one had carved out of the rainforest. Suddenly Aidan makes a
sharp left turn, and the trees all disappear as he pulls the car
into a clearing at the center of a circle of huge buildings, every
bit as tan as the dirt at our feet. The jungle around the buildings
feels like it's closing in, like whoever was in charge of holding it
back has long since left his post.

"Welcome to Llevar la Luz," Aidan says as he hefts my duffle
bag from the trunk of the car.

"So this place is kind of like a university?" I look around.
Each building is more ruined than the last: glass is missing from
half the windows, stucco crumbling down their walls. It looks
like something out of a movie about being trapped in an ancient
fortress in the middle of nowhere.

A horror movie. The kind you're not supposed to watch before you go to sleep at night.

Despite the heat, a chill in the air raises goosebumps on my
arms and legs. Aidan was right about one thing: the drop in
temperature is even more noticeable in the heat. Spirits are near.
I look around like I think I'll be able to see them. All that time
I spent in Washington, longing for my old life in Texas, and
now here I am closer to Texas than I've been in months—sure,
a totally different part of Texas, but still Texas—and my life is
even more different from what it was in Austin. Maybe it always
will be.

I hold my breath, waiting for another onslaught like the one I
felt in the hospital parking lot, hoping Aidan will step in before
I start having another spirit seizure. But the sensation doesn't
get stronger than the slight chill in the air, and my heart doesn't
start pounding like crazy.

It's as if something is holding these spirits back.

I glance at Aidan, trying to decipher whether he's doing something to keep the spirits from touching me, but if he is, it doesn't show.

"It was sort of like a university." It feels like I asked that question hours ago. "My wife and I ran it."

"Your wife?" The hairs on the back of my neck prickle, and the stone full of unanswered questions lodged in my throat loosens. "You mean my mom, right?"

Just saying the words *my mom* and meaning anyone other than Kat feels wrong, creepier than the creepiest of spirits. From now on I'm going to refer to her as my *birth mother* or *Aidan's wife*.

"Yes," Aidan replies shortly, like the answer is so obvious that the question wasn't really necessary. He drops his gaze and plays with his watch and then adjusts the cuffs of his shirt. Looks like his wife isn't his favorite topic of conversation. "There are places like this across the globe," he continues, waving his arm at the ruined buildings around us. I wonder whether those other places across the globe are in better condition than this one. "Most of them are just education centers, but this one became more of a lab over the years. It used to be populous with luiseach and mentor pairs, with a few protectors here to aid our work."

The fact that everyone must have left doesn't need to be said aloud. The emptiness is clear in the dilapidated buildings, in the fact that Aidan's is the only car in sight, in the way no one emerged to welcome us, in the sound of his voice echoing against the buildings across the courtyard.

"Why did they all leave?"

"As my experiments stalled, more and more of the luiseach who'd stood by my side left me."

"Including my birth mother?" I kind of regret asking this because when Aidan nods *yes*, it looks like his head weighs a million pounds.

Wow. She broke his heart.

He looks so sad that for a second I want to put my arms around him. Then I remember I've only known him a few days, and mentor/father or not, he's still more or less a stranger.

So I turn away, trying to look anywhere but at him. It must have been beautiful here once. Directly in front of us is what must have been a glamorous mansion. An enormous wooden porch wraps around it, like the kind you see in movies about the Antebellum South. But the pillars on either side of the front door are covered in vines so thick that the cement is crumbling beneath the weight of the leaves. There are so many holes in the wood of the front stairs that someone propped a giant plank across them like a ramp. Is this where Aidan and his wife lived? Is this where I was born?

The jungle is dense behind the house, growing up around it like it's just biding its time before it takes over completely. We're standing in what must have been a sort of courtyard, and across from the house in the other direction are three buildings, arranged in a half-moon, rounding out the yard's almost-perfect circle.

Nolan would love this place. He's probably been thinking about going to college since before he started kindergarten. I'll call him later and tell him every detail. He'll start researching luiseach training facilities, trying to discover where on Earth the rest of them are. Maybe they're in places as far-flung as Taiwan, Jerusalem, Buenos Aires, and Sydney. Maybe Nolan and I will start saving up so someday we can travel the world, seeing

each and every one of them, the way other teenagers backpack
from one famous landmark to another.

That is, if Nolan will even take my call tonight. I take a deep
breath and close my eyes, but all I can see is the look on his face
as I told him how it felt when he touched me.

I open my eyes. Beyond the three buildings across from the
mansion, I can make out the shadows of even more structures
between the trees. Maybe luiseach had to *apply* to come here just
like normal people have to apply to college. Maybe applicants
had to write essays about why *this* was the luiseach training facility that best matched the kind of luiseach they wanted to be
when they grew up.

Aidan lifts my bag over his shoulder and heads toward the
dark mansion in front of us. I follow, adjusting the straps on my
backpack. The house's door is enormous, big enough for four
people to walk through side by side, made of nearly black wood
and covered in intricate carvings. As we get closer I can make
out that almost all the carvings are different depictions of the
sun. *Bring the light* indeed. There isn't even a keyhole; whoever
put this door in place wasn't worried about normal things like
locks and keys.

"Where did everyone go when they left?"

Opening the door, Aidan solemnly answers, "They joined
the other side of the rift."

His words echo through the empty house. Or maybe it just
feels that way and they're actually echoing through my head.

CHAPTER NINE

Home Sweet Home

I didn't think any house could be creepier than our house in Ridgemont back when Anna and the demon took up residence there, but this place takes the cake. And I know *takes the cake* sounds like something someone about three times my age would say, but if the expression fits, wear it, right?

Unlike most of the other buildings in Llevar la Luz I've seen so far, the house is mostly made of wood rather than stucco. (I don't know what to call this place—a campus? A compound? A complex?) The wood creaks as I step over the threshold, a haunting sort of *hello*. Directly across from the front door is an enormous staircase, so wide that a dozen people could walk up or down side by side. It's so damp in here that the wood used to build this house still smells alive—it's like stepping into a forest instead of out of one. Maybe there's something to that. I can't imagine just how many spirits have passed through these walls over the years, seeking out the nearest, strongest luiseach. Maybe all that activity has kept the wood in the walls vibrant, alive in a way.

I run my hands along the wall in search of a light switch, hit some peeling wallpaper, and get a paper cut on my fingertip.

"Ouch!" I cry and suck on the cut.

"Careful," Aidan warns. "This place isn't exactly in the best condition."

That's an understatement. I finally find a light switch and flip it, but nothing happens. Keeping close to the wall, I look for another switch, heading deeper into the house, and flip it too. Nothing.

Finally I crash into what sounds like a ball of glass shards. I look down and see the remains of an enormous crystal chandelier. Where it must've once hung from the ceiling there are now wires hanging down, like another set of vines to match the ones outside.

This must have been the living room. Do mansions have living rooms? Maybe they called it something else. I wrack my brain for the right words from all the old novels I love reading over and over again. The sitting room. The drawing room. Even in the darkness I can see the furniture has been covered in white sheets, like someone dressed it up as ghosts for Halloween and then never undressed it.

A setting perfectly fit for the ghost I see next. At first I think it's a demon, covered in red and black peeling skin. I duck behind one of the sheet-covered couches. But then I realize it's a woman, her skin badly burned. *Way to be a good luiseach, Sunshine.* Her name was Marcy, and she was killed in an industrial accident only a few hours ago. She was working at a chemical plant, fell into a concentrated vat of paint remover, and passed away before they were able to pull her out. Even after her death, her skin continued to bubble and sizzle.

It's simultaneously terrifying and sad to see her badly burned and peeling skin. I want Aidan to notice her and help her, but he doesn't. Instead I get colder as she gets nearer. I close my eyes, knowing she'll appear behind the couch beside me at any moment. I'm being a wimp. This woman may look terrifying, but she needs my help.

I open my eyes, and there she is standing before me, her former appearance almost entirely dissolved in harsh chemical burns. I can't make out her eyes as I reach out and touch her to help her move on. An amazing ball of light appears, and an overwhelming sense of peace washes over me, so much stronger than anything I've experienced before. I stand in silence for a moment as this woman's spirit dissolves into the air.

I jump at the sound of Aidan dropping my duffle bag at the foot of the stairs. I turn around and make my way back toward the front door.

"I never go in there." Aidan nods in the direction of the room I just left. Yeah, I noticed, I think to myself. If Aidan saw the spirit, he's not letting on.

"Looks like no one ever does. Not that I could see much," I add quickly. "Do any of the lights work?" I'm starting to understand that this is how luiseach lives are. One moment you're helping a spirit, the next you're talking about what's for dinner. Or, in this case, what lights work.

"There's a generator out back. But it's not big enough to supply the whole house with power." That's not surprising—this house is enormous. "Most of the rooms on the second floor have electricity." He nods at the stairs.

I guess if you can only have power in part of the house, you'd want it to be upstairs. That's where the bedrooms usually are, where you go when it's dark.

Or, apparently, just where *I'll* be going when it's dark, as Aidan adds, "The second floor is all yours."

"I have the whole floor to myself?" That kind of sounds like a line out of one of those old books. The poor orphan girl taken to the mysterious mansion that she explores until she uncovers all of its secrets. Like Mary in *The Secret Garden* or Catherine in *Northanger Abbey*. Except I'm not an orphan. Right now I'm actually less of an orphan than I've ever been. And I have ghosts.

"My room is here on the first floor, off the kitchen." Aidan nods toward the darkness behind the stairs. "Technically speaking, that's the servants' quarters, but I find that it's the most efficient place to sleep. We haven't had servants here for nearly a century. It went out of fashion, you know."

I certainly don't know anything about the fashion of having servants. Besides, I'm too distracted by the fact that Aidan just said nearly a *century,* like it wasn't even all that long of a time. Just how old is he exactly? Victoria was sixty-seven years old and looked at least half that age—and she'd been Aidan's student.

"There are another couple of bedrooms right beside my own, but I thought you'd want more privacy than that." He sounds almost shy, like the needs of a teenage girl are a total mystery to him. He doesn't offer to carry my bag upstairs. Maybe he wants me to know the second floor is mine and mine alone, a totally private sanctuary. Maybe he got the generator for me too.

For the second time today I'm tempted to hug him, but I stop myself, rubbing sweaty palms together instead. The constant chill that permeated the space just outside the house—the presence of spirits—doesn't seem to reach the air inside the mansion. But I actually miss the chill. We've only been inside a few minutes, and I'm already sweating (not that I want to be visited by another spirit to cool down). My clothes are sticking to my skin, and I yank at the collar of my T-shirt, feeling wrinkled and wrung out. The exhaustion from all the hours we spent traveling is finally kicking in.

Aidan removes his suit jacket and folds it over one arm. His collar is still sharply folded around his neck, but even his perfect and straight dark hair looks a little bit wilted. Maybe he's tired too. "I'm sure you'd like to go upstairs and get settled. Get some rest after our travels."

Gingerly I step onto the first stair. This definitely qualifies as a *grand* staircase, like maybe once upon a time Aidan and his wife gave grand parties here and used the stairs to make a magnificent entrance. Each step is covered in what at one time must have been colorful Mexican tile, but the paint has long since faded, and half of them are cracked.

"Aidan?" I say softly, but when I turn around, he's already gone. I can hear his footsteps as he walks away to someplace behind the stairs in the opposite direction of the room with the furniture covered in sheets.

I grab my duffle bag, swing my backpack onto my shoulders, and start climbing. At the top of the stairs I drop my bags with a dull *thud*. The house groans in response, as though I hurt it somehow. It's nearly pitch dark up here, and I run my hands along the wall until I hit a light switch.

Thankfully this one turns on, though the tiny, dirty bulbs screwed into the chandelier above my head don't exactly give off what you could call *bright* light. Now I can see there's a long hall in front of me, dotted with big doors directly across from one another, three on each side, with an enormous bay window at the end. There's so much space between each door I can tell the rooms behind them must be huge. I take the knife out of my bag and slip it in my back pocket.

When I open the door closest to me, on the right, I'm hit by a hot, stale breeze, like the house is letting out a breath it had been holding in as long as the door was shut. I cough as dust collides with my face, and I run my fingers along the wall until I find another light switch. Some weak yellow light blinks down from the candle-shaped fixtures screwed into the walls, and I notice a few cockroaches scrambling for cover. *Yuck.* (At least they're not spiders, though.)

There are two enormous chairs framing a fireplace—who was the architect who thought a fireplace was necessary *here*? Wood-paneled walls are lined with packed bookshelves, lilac-colored velvet drapes cover the large windows, and the floor is covered in a matted cream-colored carpet. It looks more like a room you'd find in an English country manor rather than a house in the middle of a jungle. It would be the perfect Jane Austen fantasy if it weren't for the bugs crawling about, vines growing over the windows, and the humidity so powerful that the peeling lavender wallpaper looks like it's sweating.

When I close the door, the house inhales again. I spin around like I expect to find a giant standing behind me, taking enormous labored breaths, but there's no one there.

I open the next right-hand door, and inside is a bedroom. A big wooden bed covered in a peach blanket sits smack in the center of the room. I step inside and bounce onto the bed, giving it a try, feeling a little bit like Goldilocks testing out the three bears' beds. It's so covered in dust, it makes me sneeze.

Back to the hallway, and on to the next door: another exhalation, another bedroom. And another bed so covered in a dusty blanket—bright blue and silky this time—that I sneeze when I sit on it. But the lamp on the nightstand works and there are no visible bugs. Score one for the second bedroom.

I cross to the other side of the hall, opening the door closest to the bay window. The light switch in this room not only works; it reveals an elaborate crystal chandelier hanging down from the center of the ceiling that actually floods the room with bright white light.

The four-poster bed in the center of the room is so big that it could easily accommodate a family of five.

My breaths come quickly as I realize that this must have been my birth parents' room. I run my fingers along the back of a silky green chair at the foot of the bed. There is a fancy desk with a mirror behind it on the wall across from the door. No, not a desk—a vanity. Where women sit and put on their makeup. Where Aidan's wife sat to put on her makeup.

The wooden surface of the vanity is so smooth that it shines even beneath a layer of dust. There is a heavy brush she must have left behind; I bend down and see a few strands of brown hair still tangled in its thick bristles. I open the top drawer, and the strong scent of perfume fills the moist air. I sniff, trying to identify it—lavender, I think. With something else mixed in, something spicy to keep it from smelling too delicate. The drawer creaks when I push it closed, the scent fading until it's all but vanished.

Slowly and carefully I back out into the hallway, eager to leave this room exactly how I found it. Exactly how Aidan must have left it.

The next room, I'm relieved to discover, is a bathroom, complete with working lights and running hot and cold water.

The carpet behind the last door—first on the left at the top of the stairs—is so plush that I have to push extra hard to get the door to open. The curtains in this room are pulled firmly shut so the room is even darker than the rest of the house. I finger the wall just beside the door until I find the light switch, but the light won't turn on. I reach into my pocket. My fingers brush against the knife as I pull my phone out to use as a flashlight. For a split second I wonder which of the items in my pocket would be most useful.

Don't be ridiculous, Sunshine. You'd feel *it if there were spirits close by. Your heart rate would accelerate; your temperature would plummet.*

Wait. It's cool in here. Not, like, spirit-touching-me ice-cold, but a pleasant cool breeze circles the room, like this one part of the house has AC.

I choose my phone and flash a tiny beam of light around the room.

It takes my eyes a few seconds to adjust.

And then I gasp.

It's a *nursery.* Everything in here is white. I mean, it's grayish now, thanks to the dust, but it was all white once, so bright that it must have been cheerful. There's a crib in one corner and a dresser across from it. I open the dresser drawers, and inside are tiny little clothes, so small they look like they were made for a doll instead of a person. There's a white stuffed animal on the changing table, an owl that looks almost exactly like Dr. Hoo, identical to the toy I saw at Victoria's house, the one she said was Anna's favorite.

The stuffed bird's lifeless plastic eyes stare at me, practically glowing in the light. I take a step back, like I think this bird might take flight just like Dr. Hoo did one terrifying night. But the owl stays lifelessly still, and after a few moments I point the flashlight in another direction.

Every detail in this room was attended to: there are soft patches over the furniture's corners to keep a toddling baby from getting hurt. There are scented sachets in the drawers beneath the changing table to keep the air smelling fresh. There are tiny pink rosebuds on the otherwise white sheets on the crib, as though whoever decorated the room knew the baby was going to be a girl.

Which I was.

The breeze lifts my long hair off my shoulders. I point the light up, looking for the AC vents, for a ceiling fan, for any logical explanation. But there is nothing. No thermostat on the wall, no intricately carved vents by the ceiling. Even the windows aren't open, and when I try to open them, I discover that vines have pretty much sealed them shut.

This room has a breeze all its own. Like whoever filled it with all of this furniture wanted it to be as comfortable as possible.

I back out of the room. When I turn around, the door slams shut behind me all on its own with a bang so loud that I jump in surprise.

I regain my footing and stand in the hallway, panting as though I'd been running, staring at the door that just slammed shut behind me. I feel the need to put more distance between myself and the nursery.

I drag my bags into the second bedroom, across and down the hall. I manage to open one of the windows just a crack. I lean against the window frame and breathe in the outside air deeply. Not that it offers any respite from the heat. Not like the air in the nursery.

I shake my head. Someone made up that room carefully, attentively, *lovingly*. Someone—Aidan? his wife? both of them together?—was *excited* to have me, wanted everything to be absolutely perfect for the little girl about to be born.

How did they go from preparing that perfect room to abandoning me at a Texas hospital?

Aidan must have known I'd see the nursery when he sent me up here. Was he trying to tell me something? Did he want me to know there was a time when he'd had every intention of raising me, caring for me, *loving* me?

I shake my head and back away from the window. The bedroom I've chosen is decorated in bright colors. Instead of a plush carpet at my feet, there is the same blue, yellow, and white tile from the hall, though the colors are faded with age just like they are everywhere else. It's nothing like my room in Ridgemont, with its thick carpet and floral wallpaper, the pink so bright that it seems like decades wouldn't be enough to make the color fade.

I grab my phone and dial Nolan's number, anxious to tell him every last detail of this place. But I freeze before I hit send.

The expression on his face when I told him what I told him before I left Ridgemont blossoms in my mind's eye. Maybe if I just apologized—*No.* I bite my lip. Any apology I could offer would be hollow, pointless, *empty*. I can't take back what I said. Because it was the truth.

I glance at the phone. Looks like there isn't any service in here anyhow. I fall back on the bed, grabbing one of the pillows to press into my face, smothering a miserable groan. The pillow's so covered in dust that it makes me sneeze.

I roll over, and the knife beneath me slides from one side of my pocket to the other, like it wants to remind me that it's in there. I can't help but wonder: When will I need it next?

A Dead End?

That woman brought me to a rain-saturated town in the northwestern corner of the United States. She claimed this is where the girl lived. She told me her name: Sunshine Griffith, and I struggled to hide my smile. The girl's light was so bright that even the human who named her could sense it.

But we were too late. Aidan had already come and gone, taking the girl with him. Of course, I know exactly where he was headed when he left, but I can't go there. Not anymore. None of my people can get there. When we left, we also gave up the ability to step over its borders, wide as they stretch. Even that woman says she can't go there now.

Which means I have no more use for her. Although her birthright as a luiseach protected her from being permanently killed at the hands of a demon, she no longer has the power to see spirits and help them move on. Perhaps she'll try to live out her days as a human, though even she must sense the darkness gathering in the corners of the world. Sometimes I envy humans and their ignorance. They'll never have to do what I have to.

Even Aidan wasn't selfless enough to go through with it.

But the woman begs me not to leave her behind. She pleads for a place at my side. I tell her I have no reason to keep her—after all, the only information she offered me was a dead end.

I say perhaps she knew that it would be.

I suggest she may have been working for Aidan all along.

I'll make my way south and wait as close to the campus as possible. They can't stay hidden inside forever.

But before I leave that woman behind, she tells me that although the girl may be gone, her protector is still close by. And she offers to take me to him.

So I choose to keep that woman close. And I choose to stay.

For now.

CHAPTER TEN
Someplace Safe?

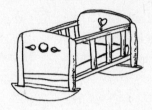

I'm still not asleep when I hear a voice. "Not again," I whisper to myself. The last time I heard a strange voice on my first night in a new place, it was the beginning of the test that turned my entire life upside down.

I get out of bed. My every step results in creaks and groans, as though my small-person footfalls are shaking the house to its foundation. I tiptoe across the room and open the door the tiniest crack.

I breathe a sigh of relief because the voice is one I recognize. It's not a spirit or a demon; it's just the sound of Aidan's deep baritone.

What has my life been reduced to that hearing my supernaturally empowered, long-lost birth father's voice has become the most *normal* explanation available to me?

But then another voice enters the conversation—duh, Sunshine, obviously Aidan was talking to *someone*—a voice I don't recognize, though it's almost as deep as Aidan's, so I can tell it belongs to a male. At first the words sound like nothing but gibberish. The last time I heard a strange voice speaking words I couldn't understand it was coming from my mother's mouth when the demon possessed her. What kind of creature is downstairs with Aidan now?

As the voices grow louder, I realize the second voice isn't speaking some mystical dead language but rather Spanish. I'm able to pick up a very few random words I've heard before: *dos, mañana, nunca.*

Nice one, Sunshine, you're mistaking Spanish for mystical dead languages. Such a worldly girl you are. I sigh at just how much my life has changed since turning sixteen.

I guess someone else is sleeping in one of the bedrooms downstairs. Someone who didn't abandon Aidan when the others left, someone he hasn't told me about yet. And apparently this someone is very upset about something because his voice is growing louder with each syllable.

"Keep your voice down," Aidan growls in English. "The girl is asleep upstairs."

I'm not asleep. Be as loud as you like.

"I'm sorry," the other voice answers, "but it's hard to keep quiet when one of our spirits escaped days ago and I still can't find it."

One of *our* spirits?

"You'll find it."

"And if I don't in time?"

"We'll cross that bridge when we come to it." Unlike whoever he's talking to, Aidan doesn't raise his voice. Which makes me want to run downstairs and shout, *How can you be calm at a time like this?* Because I know what happens to spirits who don't move on *in time*. They turn dark, like the demon who nearly killed my mother.

"A spirit shouldn't be behaving like this," the other voice argues. Aidan and his companion lapse back into Spanish, more words I don't understand until finally I hear one of them say *buenas noches,* which even I know means *good night.*

I listen to their footsteps creak across the hardwood on the first floor as they move across the room. Two doors click softly shut. Aidan and his friend, whoever he is, have gone to bed.

I close my door. It's so humid and hot in this room that I've long since flung the covers back. This old mattress isn't nearly as soft as my mattress back in Ridgemont. I swear I could literally feel each individual spring digging into my back. The idea of lying back down isn't exactly appealing.

But I know I should at least *try* to get some sleep. I don't know what Aidan has planned for me tomorrow, but I don't think he's the kind of teacher who'll excuse you from class just for being tired. Especially on the first day.

But first I drop to the ground and feel around in the dark until my hands hit the jeans I'd been wearing earlier. I dig the knife out of my back pocket and slide it beneath my pillow.

Suddenly this supposed "someplace safe" doesn't feel so safe after all.

The sheets twist around my sweaty legs, the lingering dust now wet and sticking to my skin. I squeeze my eyes shut. *Pretending* to sleep is almost as good as the real thing, right? Much to my surprise, within a few minutes my eyelids grow heavy and my breaths grow deeper. Within seconds I'm asleep. I'm dreaming.

The nightmare starts out innocently enough. There's a beautiful woman standing over me, curly brown hair framing her lovely face, her tanned skin the color of honey. She smiles at me, and I smile back automatically. She coos in response, reaching her arms out to hold me.

But then something in her face shifts. There's something desperate in her eyes. She looks like the evil queen from a fairy tale, beautiful but dangerous. Her hands turn into fists, her eyes narrow, and it looks like she's biting her tongue to keep from screaming out loud.

I understand that whoever she is, this woman wants to hurt me.

I open my mouth to scream, but the only sounds that escape are pitiful cries. I try to stand and run, but my muscles are too weak. My limbs won't cooperate with the messages my brain is trying to send them. I look down, trying to figure out what's wrong with my legs: Am I tied up? Are they broken and beaten?

What I see is even more horrifying.

They aren't *my* legs at all. Or anyway they're not the legs that I have *now,* the legs that trudged up the stairs of this strange and sad house a few hours ago. Instead, they're the helpless, kicking legs of an infant who should be sleeping in a crib like the one across the hall instead of in this enormous old bed.

I'm trapped in this small, vulnerable body. I wave my helpless baby arms around my head and try to speak, but my muscles and my brain aren't developed enough to make words. I'm not strong enough to do anything but cry and moan and kick pathetically against the blanket the woman wraps tightly around me, covering my face as I try to breathe.

When I finally wake up, my real-life teenage arms and legs are sore.

So much for getting plenty of rest before the first day of training.

CHAPTER ELEVEN

Lucio

The boy extends his hand in my direction. "Lucio," he says. I find myself staring at the tattoos running down the sides of his right pointer finger, bright white against his caramel skin. From here they look like words written in a flowing, loopy script, but I can't quite make out what they say.

When I came downstairs in search of coffee, the last thing I expected to be confronted with was a strikingly handsome boy, a wide smile on his face, perched on top of the kitchen counter with his legs swinging back and forth over the edge. I wasn't even expecting to be able to find the kitchen, but I did—after walking around in circles a few times.

"Huh?" I answer dumbly. I may have slept some last night, but I don't exactly feel rejuvenated this morning.

"Lucio," he repeats, hopping down from the counter, his tattooed hand still floating in the space between us. Still bleary eyed, I realize *his* must have been the voice I heard speaking with Aidan in the middle of the night. The voice was so deep that it never occurred to me he'd be so young—he looks only a few years older than I am. (Though if he's a luiseach, who knows, right? He could be eighty for all I know.) His skin is the exact color of the milky cup of coffee I'd been hoping to find down here. He's wearing a T-shirt and shorts—though his T-shirt is red, while mine is bright blue with a flock of birds flying across it—but unlike me, his hair is wet from a recent shower and his breath smells like toothpaste. I cover my mouth to keep my morning breath from escaping.

"I'm sorry, I don't speak Spanish."

"No, silly," he laughs, then explains in the same perfect, barely accented English I heard him speak last night, "That's my name. *Lucio*."

"Oh." I blush and reach out to shake his hand. He's only a few inches taller than I am. Nothing like Aidan, who towers above me. "I'm Sunshine."

"I know."

"Do you also know where a girl can get a cup of coffee around here?" There might not be electricity on the first floor, but there is an enormous old gas stove in the corner with a kettle of water steaming on top. Lucio hands me a mug and pours in some hot water.

"No coffee. Have some tea," he says like it's the same thing. He plops a tea bag into the mug and returns the kettle to the stove.

"Not quite what I was looking for," I answer, but I take a sip, suddenly very aware of the fact that I'm still dressed in the super-short shorts I slept in and that my hair is pulled into the messiest, frizziest bun in the history of hairstyles. I try to inconspicuously pull down on the legs of my shorts, making them a fraction of an inch longer, which I realize is pointless.

"There's milk in the icebox," Lucio offers, gesturing to a cooler set in front of an enormous—but powerless—stainless-steel refrigerator. "I think it's still good."

"You *think?*"

He shrugs, hopping back up onto the counter. He's wearing shorts, and I can't help but notice his muscular legs. I look away, feeling shy.

I blink and squeeze my mug, even though the water inside is so hot that it nearly burns me.

The kitchen is enormous, covered in the same ceramic tile as the room I slept in last night. It's not nearly as dark as the rest of the house; the window at the end of the room isn't covered in curtains, so some light actually gets in from between the vines growing over it. Lucio sits on the marble counter in the center of the room, right next to a sink with a dripping faucet. A long, scratched wooden table sits beneath the window beyond the counter. This must have been where the servants sat, back when having servants was in fashion. I peer through a doorway at the other end of the room and see a richly carpeted dining room, complete with a gleaming mahogany table surrounded by at least a dozen chairs. But I quickly turn away and sit on one of the wobbly wooden chairs in the kitchen instead, blowing on my tea to cool it.

"Good morning," Aidan says formally as he walks into the room. I stand up quickly, like I think I'm supposed to come to attention in his presence, like he's my drill sergeant and I'm his new recruit—in embarrassingly short shorts. For the first time since I met him (which isn't that long, I know) he's not wearing a suit. Instead, his khaki pants are perfectly pressed and his white button down is buttoned nearly to the top, and its sleeves are rolled up neatly above his elbows. I guess that's his idea of casual wear. "I see you've met Lucio. He works with me, one of the few who didn't leave our side." Aidan confirms that Lucio is a luiseach like me. Well, not exactly like *me*. Lucio's probably known he was a luiseach for a whole lot longer than a few months. "He'll help us out a bit this morning, but he was up late last night."

So was I. So were *you*.

"He'll be going back to bed to get some rest soon." The last part of the sentence is addressed to the other luiseach, not me. Like it's part of a conversation they've had before. Like Aidan is worried Lucio isn't getting enough rest.

Lucio jumps back down from the counter and grabs a cup of tea. He adds milk and honey and hands it to Aidan like he's done it a million times before. He clearly knows exactly what Aidan wants.

"What's he helping us out with exactly?" I don't add that I heard them arguing last night. That I already have an idea of what kind of work keeps Lucio up late.

"We have to start your training."

"Victoria's note said I'd be resuming the work that you and she had been working on together?" Victoria's note is the only explanation I have for what I'm doing here. I read it so many times that I practically memorized it before I left it with Nolan.

Aidan shakes his head. "We have a lot of ground to cover first."

"But then . . ." I wrinkle my nose, just like Mom would, if she were here—*boy, do I wish she were*—"what am I doing here if I'm not helping with your work?"

"Let's not get ahead of ourselves." Aidan turns from me to Lucio. "I'm just going to check in at the lab before we get started.

Can you take her to the playground?" Lucio nods. I get the idea that Aidan isn't talking about an actual playground. Wherever he's asking Lucio to take me probably won't include swings and a slide and seesaws.

Aidan turns back to me. "Get dressed. I'll meet you there soon." He turns on his heel. I get up and follow him.

"Meet me where?" I don't know if it's the bad dreams or the conversation I overheard last night or the fact that Aidan is leaving me with this boy I don't even know, but I suddenly feel completely helpless. Even if I wanted to leave, I couldn't. We're in the middle of the jungle. My cell phone doesn't work in this house. If Aidan left me alone, I'd be completely trapped.

I follow him out of the kitchen and around the stairs. "Promise you won't abandon me in the middle of Mexico!" I joke, but not really. The house takes a deep breath as Aidan opens the enormous front door. Before I can stop myself, the next eight words just come flying out of my mouth, "*Just like you abandoned me sixteen years ago?*" If I were in a cartoon, I'd slap my hand over my mouth like I had no idea where that sentence came from.

Aidan closes the door gently and turns around, furrowing his brow like I've just spoken Greek or something. Then again, maybe Aidan speaks Greek. He probably speaks everything.

"I never abandoned you. I thought you understood that now. Go have some breakfast. We have a lot of work to do today."

The door slams shut behind him. We've gone from hardly knowing each other to father–teen daughter cliché pretty quickly.

"Come on," Lucio says. "Get dressed. It's hard work, but Aidan's a good teacher."

"How do you know?"

"He's my mentor too."

"He is?"

Lucio laughs. "You see anyone else around here?" He raises his arms, indicating the otherwise empty house, empty buildings, empty campus. Aidan had no choice but to mentor Lucio. There was no one else left to teach him.

I head for the stairs, "You're the only other luiseach here, right?"

Leaning against the curved metal banister at the foot of the stairs, Lucio nods. "I grew up here. My parents were on Aidan's side until the day they died." With his left hand he toys with the tattoo on his right hand, like he's spinning an invisible ring on his finger.

"I'm sorry," I say quickly. My birth father may be cold and scientific and my birth mother may be a complete mystery, but at least I've always had Kat. When I came close to losing her, it made me sadder and more scared than I'd ever been in my whole life. I can't imagine how alone Lucio must feel.

"It was nine years ago. I was eight." He shrugs, but his shoulders look heavy. I do the math in my head: Lucio is seventeen years old. Which means he's been an active luiseach for at least a year.

"How did it happen?"

Lucio doesn't answer right away, and I open my mouth to apologize for asking—*that's none of your business, Sunshine!*—but before I can speak, he says, "A demon took them."

I gasp. That means that their spirits were destroyed. That Lucio is destined to forget them. "I'm sorry," I repeat softly.

"Thanks." Lucio runs his fingers over his scalp; his black hair is cropped very short. No chance of it falling across his eyes like Nolan's does. "Now, get dressed. We should get to work."

"Right." I take a few steps up the stairs and then freeze in my tracks. If Lucio is a luiseach, that means his parents were luiseach too. I turn around. "I thought luiseach couldn't be killed by dark spirits."

Lucio bites his thick—Ashley would call it *luscious*, but just the thought makes me blush—lower lip. He squeezes his hands into fists at his sides, and I can see the muscles working up and down his arms. "I didn't know you knew that."

"Why did you lie to me?" I'm annoyed this boy I hardly know thinks it's okay to lie to me.

"I didn't mean to lie. I just . . . it's easier to believe they were killed by a dark spirit."

"Easier than what?"

He takes a deep breath. "Easier than the fact that they were killed for what they believed in. The luiseach on the other side of the rift were interrogating my parents in search of"—he pauses—"of some precious information. When my parents didn't crack under pressure, they were killed for keeping their secret."

I cover my mouth with my hand. "I'm sorry," I say once more. I've known this guy for less than an hour, and I can't seem to stop apologizing to him.

"It's okay," Lucio says solemnly. "After my parents died, Aidan took me in. Over the years, when the others left, I stayed." From the tone of his voice it's obvious this boy really looks up to Aidan. "Go on." He mercifully changes the subject. "Get dressed. Believe me, you want to get out there before it gets too hot, even if you're planning on wearing those short shorts."

Instantly my face turns red and I turn away. Is he flirting with me? It's not a practice I have much experience with. I decide not to overanalyze it and skip up the stairs, taking them two at a time, even though my legs are still tired from kicking and squirming all night long.

I shudder as I remember my nightmare. I still have a lot to learn about the rift between the luiseach, but whoever's on the other side, they must be truly evil if they killed that nice boy's parents.

CHAPTER TWELVE
Lesson One

Lucio leads me into the jungle behind the house and up a muddy path on an even muddier hill. Enormous trees tower around us. I wonder how old they are.

"Don't worry," he says, without turning around. "This is all still part of Llevar la Luz."

"I wasn't worried," I pant at his back. It must be a million degrees out here, but Lucio has barely broken a sweat.

The top of the hill is flat and dry and open, like an enormous stage. It's gotta be the size of a football field. Or at least a baseball diamond. Whatever trees grew up here have long since been cut down. Which means no respite from the sun beating down overhead.

"Welcome to the playground." Lucio holds his arms out at the emptiness around us. He hops up onto a boulder and perches on it like an agile cat, running his fingers over his closely cropped black hair. "I know it doesn't look like much, but back in the day this was the coolest place on Earth."

"Why's that?"

"Used to be covered with luiseach pulling spirits to them from all across the world. Not just young luiseach in training with their mentors, but experienced luiseach honing their skills, practicing exorcisms, gathering strength. I'd sneak up here and watch, just itching for my sixteenth birthday so I could feel all the action myself."

"Sounds exciting."

"It was. 'Course, by the time I took my test, things around here were a whole lot quieter," Lucio gestures to the empty space around us. I close my eyes and try to imagine what it must have looked like when this enormous plateau was covered end to end with luiseach in training. But I can only picture it as empty as it looks now. I guess I haven't been a luiseach long enough to know what it's really like on an average day.

Lucio hops down from his boulder, nodding at the space behind me. Aidan's walking across the playground to meet us.

"I just took an inventory," Aidan says once he's close enough for us to hear. "But do another head count before you turn in."

"A head count?" I ask. "I thought we were the only people here."

"We are," Aidan answers.

"Got it, boss." Lucio starts jogging down the mountain, his steps as easy and assured as a cat's.

"And Lucio!" Aidan calls after him. "Get some rest. I need you strong."

"Strong for what?" I ask.

"Let's not lose our focus," Aidan says. "We've got a lot of work of our own to do."

"My mom really wants me to get better at handling multiple

spirits," I begin. "She's worried that what happened in the parking lot might happen again."

"It *will* happen again. But we'll get you stronger before it does. Before someone uses that particular weakness against you."

"What do you mean?"

"A luiseach can draw spirits toward him or herself. Which means a crafty luiseach could draw spirits toward a weaker luiseach nearby as well."

"Why would someone—"

"Let's not get ahead of ourselves," Aidan interrupts. "I'd like to start small. Close your eyes."

The look on Aidan's face tells me he's not the type of teacher who tolerates students who talk back too much, so I let my eyelids fall shut. The sun is so bright that even with my eyes closed, I see brightness; a collage of reds and oranges play against my eyelids.

"Concentrate," Aidan commands, like he knows I'm already distracted, paying attention to what I see instead of what I feel.

It's there, that feeling I first felt in the hospital, the electric hum of spirits in the air around me, spirits who may have departed from this very spot, spirits who may have come into being close by. I can feel what's left of them, like shadows falling over my skin. I'm filled with an odd sense of calmness, a connection to the past, to that moment of peace so many spirits have felt in this place.

"As you know," Aidan begins, sounding like Mr. Packer at the start of one of his lectures. *Should I be taking notes?* I can hear his footsteps as he paces slowly around me on the smooth stone surface. "Spirits are drawn toward the nearest luiseach, like moths to the flame. However, we can help them find us sooner.

We can pull spirits toward us from miles away, from across the country, from across the continent. If you concentrate, you can feel the instant a spirit is released from its body. Do you feel it?"

I take a deep breath, pressing my eyes shut tight. Somewhere, right at this moment, a spirit is being set loose. At first there's only the hint of its presence, barely enough to raise goosebumps on my skin. Last night Lucio said he was looking for a spirit and couldn't find it. Is this how he searches? By closing his eyes and waiting for the chill to set in? As suddenly as I begin to feel the spirit's presence arrive, it vanishes.

I open my eyes. Much to my surprise, Aidan's face is close to mine, our noses almost touching. "Don't let yourself get distracted," he says. I press my lips together. How did he know my mind was wandering? "Focus only on the task at hand. Seek it out. Concentrate."

I tense all of my muscles until I feel the chill again; my heart begins beating fast.

"Now draw him close. Trust your instincts."

Aidan must feel the spirit too, an eighty-year-old man named Miguel from San Antonio who smoked his first cigarette at thirteen and whose lungs slowly turned black and finally gave out.

"Don't lose your focus!" Aidan shouts, but his voice sounds terribly far away. "Draw him closer. Give him the peace he deserves."

I can taste smoke in my mouth as if I'm a smoker. As if I'm feeling what it was like to be this man. It's overwhelming.

"Concentrate. Remember what happens to spirits who don't move on in time."

"What's happening to me?" I manage to say right before I see him there, in front of us. He's so close that I'm shivering. I

stretch my arms out in front of me, drawing him close enough
to touch. His face, leathery and dried from years in the sun, has
an expression of wonderment and fear all at once, as if he's unsure of what's happening. The taste of smoke is overwhelming,
and I can hardly breathe as I touch his shoulder and send him
on his way.

And then, suddenly, peace. I'm so surprised that I fall to the
ground, gasping for air like a fish out of water.

Aidan stands over me. I expect him to bend down and offer
me some water or a hand, but instead he says, "Interesting."

"What?" My voice is hoarse.

"That man died from emphysema."

"I know." I also know that he left behind a son who begged
his father to stop smoking every year on his birthday. I know
that every year Miguel tried. And every year he failed.

I press my hand to my chest. I'm happy to breathe clearly
again and relieved I never let Vincent Warner talk me into trying cigarettes in eighth grade.

I wince at the fading taste of nicotine on my tongue. This
has never happened before. Am I getting stronger? Is it the playground? But before I have time to ask, Aidan says, "Let's try
again."

By the end of the day I've helped four more spirits move on and,
in addition to knowing what it feels like to die from emphysema,
I know what it feels like to die from sugar (a diabetic woman
in Arizona who went into insulin shock), lack of water (a man
who got lost in the desert and ran out of supplies), and too much
water (a surfer who drowned on the Cortes bank just south of

San Diego), and my chest aches like a rock is beating where my heart should be (an elderly woman in Costa Rica whose heart gave out).

"You did well," Aidan says. "Five spirits on your first try, some of them from great distances."

I know he's trying to be reassuring, but it doesn't *feel* like I did well. I'm exhausted from experiencing, even for the briefest moment, what it was like to be all those people when they died.

"Does this always happen?" I ask Aidan breathlessly when we finally leave the playground behind.

"No."

"You mean, over time, as I get stronger, I won't be so"—I search for the right word—"sensitive?"

Aidan shakes his head. "I mean I've never seen a luiseach *feel* the lives of the spirits she helps move on. It's as though you're experiencing their lives—and their deaths—yourself."

My breath quickens. "This doesn't happen to anyone else?"

"Not to my knowledge."

There may not be any spirits close by anymore, but now my heart is pounding for a different reason entirely. "What's wrong with me?"

"You appear to be particularly sensitive."

Mom used to say that too. I mean, not about spirits, obviously, but just about life in general. When I was five, I developed a whole plan to help save a homeless man we passed every day on the way to day care. When I was seven, my mom caught me stuffing an envelope full of pocket change. When she asked me what I was doing, I told her I planned to send it to the nice lady on the commercials with all the sad animals. Mom never seemed to think it was a problem, but it looks like Aidan would disagree. "Can you fix it?" I ask finally.

"I can certainly try," Aidan answers, as he writes a note in a small notepad he's pulled from his back pocket.

Worn out from my first full day of luiseach work, I shake my head. That doesn't sound as reassuring as I'd hoped.

CHAPTER THIRTEEN

Playtime Is Over

Another day, another lesson on the playground. This time Lucio's with us. As Aidan outlines today's goals, Lucio plays with his tattoo, runs his hands over his closely cropped hair, and bounces from one foot to the other like he's preparing to run away. More than once he cocks his head to the side like he's listening for something.

Maybe for the missing spirit?

"Are you ready to get started, Sunshine?" Aidan asks finally, tucking his notepad and pen in his back pocket.

"Sure," I answer, not wanting him to know I haven't actually been paying attention to him so much as I've been watching Lucio.

"Lucio is going to demonstrate first."

It feels like I've been in training forever. I'm now an expert at drawing willing spirits close: Aidan taught me to be perfectly still, to sense the nearest spirit—even if it's miles away. He taught me to control my breathing, flex my muscles, and draw that spirit close so I could help it move on. I've sought out spirits from clear across the country, spirits from as far away as El Salvador and Guatemala and even once a strange hermit-like man from all the way up in Vancouver who no one even knew was alive for the past fifty years. His strange, lonely aura made my skin feel icy cold as I helped him. Despite that, each time I helped a spirit move on I felt that same otherworldly sense of peace, as though I was exactly where I was meant to be, even if where I am is on an abandoned campus in the Mexican wilderness, thousands of miles away from the people I love.

If only that were all I felt.

"Do you see the way he's focused?" Aidan asks, forcing me to pay attention. I nod. Lucio closes his eyes and holds his hands out as though he thinks he can physically pull the spirit toward him.

Light spirits come to us easily like we're magnets, just like Victoria said. But today Lucio is dragging a more resistant spirit to him. He closes his eyes, and his chest and forearms clench.

It's not long before she appears in front of us, a frail-looking young woman, not much older than me. Her skin is a sickly yellow, and she's bald. It looks like she's been fighting an illness for some time.

I see the expression on Lucio's face change as the spirit moves on: his grimace becomes the slightest hint of a smile as the peace washes over him. Then he opens his eyes and shakes himself like a puppy after a bath.

"Why didn't she want to move on?" I ask.

Lucio shrugs. "Eighteen. Leukemia. Wasn't ready to stop fighting, but her body was."

How can he just rattle it off like that? I mean, he says it perfectly nicely—solemnly even—but he doesn't look *sad*. "Didn't you feel her sadness when she passed through you? You didn't feel the cancer destroying her blood?"

Lucio looks from me to Aidan. Finally Aidan explains, "Sunshine seems to be more sensitive than most."

Talk about an understatement.

Each time I've helped a spirit move on, I sort of *absorbed* some part of them; I felt what they felt at the instant they died—grief, relief, surprise. And the feelings stayed with me for hours after they'd vanished. Sometimes it's no more than a shadow: memories of the people they loved, the feeling of sunlight against their faces. But sometimes it's the ache of their deaths, the pain they suffered, the fear they faced.

Aidan thinks I just need to practice. A few dozen more spirits and I'll grow a thicker skin. I'm not so sure. It feels to me like the absorption is just getting *stronger* with each spirit who passes through me. Like with every spirit I help move on, I hang on to a little bit more of them, and I see them a little bit clearer.

"Now," Aidan says. "You try."

He takes my hands and I close my eyes. I concentrate on feeling that electric hum he showed to Mom in the hospital that day, the echo of spirits that have moved on, the pulse of those who haven't yet. I'm getting better at feeling connected to this energy.

"No," Aidan says as my focus lands on a ninety-eight-year-old grandmother named Marie. "Not her."

I open my eyes. "How did you know what I was about to do?" He squeezes my hands in his, like his touch explains the connection. "Luiseach can work together. For particularly tricky spirits, sometimes we have to join forces."

"So you're going to help me?"

"No." He shakes his head. "You're not reaching for anyone *that* tricky today. I'm going to *watch* you."

I get the feeling Aidan is the kind of dad who'd have thrown me into the deep end of the pool to teach me to swim. I'm supposed to be looking for resistant spirits, the kind that, left to their own devices, might turn dark. I know what's at stake when that happens.

So I close my eyes again and concentrate.

Then I find him. Sixteen years old, just like me. Lived in a suburb outside Tucson, Arizona. Riding his bike home from school—his parents promised him a car by graduation—when some car missed a stop sign and hit him. He was wearing his helmet, but the impact of the fall knocked it right off of his head. He lay on the ground, blood dripping from his skull, waiting for the ambulance to come. As he waited, he ticked off a list of the things he had yet to do: See the pyramids in Egypt. Drive his own car to and from school. Go to college. Pitch a perfect game, or even just a no-hitter or a one-hitter would do. Ask Meghan Waters out on a real date. Hold Meghan Waters's hand. Kiss Meghan Waters good night. Tell Meghan Waters how he felt about her.

Talk to Meghan Waters at all.

He didn't want to die without talking to Meghan Waters. And yet, as his eyes filled with blood and his brain swelled until it was simply too big for the skull around it, he knew that was his fate.

And now he's angry. Not at the tree that obscured the stop sign and not at the driver who hadn't slowed down when driving through a residential neighborhood. No, this boy—Eddie Denfield was his name—is mad at *himself* for all the chances he'd had that he hadn't taken.

So instead of being drawn to the nearest luiseach, he's been lingering by Meghan Waters's locker. Now I have to make him move on in spite of himself.

Even with Aidan's hands on mine, I reach my arms out just like I saw Lucio do. This must be why Lucio's muscles are so big: pulling spirits from across the continent takes strength. I'm flexing muscles I didn't even know existed. Tonight when I climb into bed, my entire body will ache from the effort of the day. My abdominals will be so sore that it hurts to take a deep breath, my legs so tired that it will feel like they weigh a million pounds.

Eddie Denfield wants nothing to do with me. At first loose papers in the hall begin to swirl about, and Eddie's former classmates take notice. They begin looking around for the source of the mysterious wind, but they won't find it. As I pull harder, Eddie gets angrier, holding on for dear life, *literally*. Lockers begin slamming shut one right after another all throughout the hallway. The girls are screaming and the boys are shouting. And then it happens. Meghan runs out of a classroom, trying to see what all the commotion is about, and Eddie spots her one last time. "You have to let her go," I say, unsure whether he can hear me. I can feel his resistance as I pull him farther and farther from the girl he's had a crush on since sixth grade. The sweat on my face turns cool as he comes close.

For a brief moment he's there right before me, his eyes filled with anger and blood and regret, his head smashed in and bleeding from the accident. He's been so focused on Meghan that he never noticed his leg was badly broken too, part of the bone sticking out of his flesh. As I quickly reach out to touch him he screams furiously at me in anger, feeling betrayed, even though I never knew this boy. Then he's gone, moving on with only the slightest sense of peace at the very last moment, but mostly with just one thing. Anger.

When I open my eyes, I'm angry too.

"Why did you make me do that?" I shout, pulling my hands from Aidan's grip. "He just wanted a chance to say good-bye!"

"Sunshine, do you hear yourself?" Aidan doesn't raise his voice. "It's your job to help spirits move on even when they don't want to."

"But he just needed a little more time—"

"I know," Aidan says softly. "We all struggle with that sometimes. But you know what happens if too much time passes."

He's right. A demon nearly killed my mother. Why did I want to let Eddie stay? Why am I so angry when I should feel peace?

Lucio whistles. "She really does take on what they're feeling, huh? *Freaky.*"

What he really means is *freak. I'm* a freak. A luiseach with a sensitivity problem no luiseach has had before.

"Maybe a protector could figure out why I'm so different?" I try. "That's what they do, right? Find information that might help us?" I bite my lip, hoping Aidan is about to launch into a lengthy explanation of protectors' duties.

Aidan shakes his head. "We'll keep working on it."

Something tells me we're not making as much progress as he'd like. He pulls out his notepad and writes something down as he walks away. I begin to follow, but Lucio grabs my hand and holds me back.

"Hang on. I want to show you something," Lucio says.

"What is it?" I ask.

"You'll see," he says as he leads me down another path.

CHAPTER FOURTEEN
Clementine

We walk down a path that's clearly used less often than the one we use to get to the playground. Overgrown with vines and loose rocks, I struggle to keep my balance.

"Where are we going?" I ask.

"You're not good with surprises, are you?" Lucio quips back, clearly amused by the situation. It's true, I'm not, but I'm not going to give him the satisfaction of knowing that, so I keep my mouth closed.

"I'm disappointing him," I say as I almost roll my ankle. The sun's getting low, and it's hard to see the ground through the thick shade of the jungle.

"Nah," Lucio says, trudging down the path with little trouble. He plays with the tattoo on his right pointer finger. He's the kind of person who's always moving.

"It'll get easier. Don't forget, you're descended from—"

"Two of the most powerful luiseach families in history, blah, blah blah." I cut him off before he can finish. Lucio grins as he glances back, and I smile back. "I'm still waiting for my genetics to kick in. It's a pretty good argument for nurture versus nature."

"What do you mean?"

"You know, because I was raised by a regular human instead of those two powerful luiseach, maybe I didn't inherit their powers after all."

"I don't think that's how it works." Lucio suddenly stops at the bottom of the trail. He motions with his hands to something green in front of him.

"An old tarp," I say as I realize what it is.

"It's not the tarp, it's what's underneath," he says and then just stands there, admiring the *idea* of whatever is covered by the tarp.

"Soooo . . . are you going to show me what's under the tarp?"

"Oh yeah!" He jumps forward and yanks it off.

"It's an old motorcycle," I respond, in a tone Lucio is clearly disappointed by.

"It's a 1967 Triumph Bonneville TT Special! She's my pride and joy." His grin is so wide that I can tell this is important for him, but I can't really wrap my brain around why he's showing me . . . *her*?

"She?" I ask.

"Clementine."

"Clementine?"

"She's a classic, so she needs a classic name." Lucio beams. "What do you think?"

His enthusiasm is infectious. "She's great," I grin.

"Shall we take her for a spin?"

"Really?"

"You can't come all the way to Mexico and not see some real Mexican culture. Plus, you deserve a break." Lucio jumps on the motorcycle and kicks some part of it to start it. I'm not entirely sure what's going on. I've never been this close to a motorcycle before, let alone to a boy asking me to ride one with him. Lucio motions for me to get on behind him, and to my surprise, I do. *Mom is going to kill me.*

I wrap my arms around him, and we lurch forward as he navigates the rocky path, but soon we're on a dirt road and moving quickly. It's a different road from where I came into Llevar la Luz with Aidan. We must be on the backside of the property.

The sun sinks below the horizon as Lucio deftly maneuvers the pothole-filled road. It doesn't take me long to feel completely safe as I hold onto him and watch the jungle pass by and finally fade into the distance behind us. Suddenly the Pacific Ocean comes into view in front of us, glowing as the sun sets above it. A tropical ocean breeze hits my face as we descend a hill toward what looks like a small coastal village twinkling in the distance.

For the briefest moment I close my eyes and pretend I'm not a luiseach. I pretend I'm not a sixteen-year-old girl whose whole life seems to be predestined for her. I pretend I don't have a responsibility to help lost spirits every day for the rest of my life. I pretend I'm on a journey to explore the far reaches of the Earth, and Lucio is my guide. I pretend I've been whisked away to a world that could only ever exist in my imagination. And for just a second I pretend Lucio is actually Nolan.

He hits the brakes and we slide to a stop across the dirt road. I open my eyes and look around.

"We're here!" Lucio proclaims as I climb off the bike and he sets the kickstand. True to Lucio form, he doesn't stop moving, and we're already walking into town.

"What's this place called?" I ask.

"I just call it the fishing village." Lucio shrugs like he's never given it much thought. We walk a couple of blocks into the town square, which seems to be bustling with energy as the locals go about their business. Small carts are set up throughout the square, selling a variety of things. Kids play in the fountain at the center.

"I didn't know places like this existed in real life."

"They do! Or at least this place does," Lucio responds. "I come here sometimes when Aidan gets to be a little too serious for me. He doesn't like it, but I think he knows I'd go stir-crazy if I never left Llevar la Luz. Not that this is technically leaving Llevar la Luz."

"What do you mean?

"Llevar la Luz stretches way beyond the campus."

"You're telling me Aidan *owns* this town?"

"Not exactly. But let's just say that a lot of this region is more or less *attached* to Llevar la Luz." Lucio holds out his arms, then adds, "Have a seat. I'll be right back." He motions to one of the many picnic tables set up throughout the square, and I sit as he runs off.

I notice the sound of music playing in the distance. It doesn't take long for him to return with four small tacos and two bottles of orange soda.

"You're gonna love these." He says as he hands me two fish tacos and takes the first bite of his. For a moment we sit in silence as we eat. The evening breeze blowing through town feels like heaven.

"Amazing, right?" Lucio grins, and I nod in agreement. "Hey, let me ask you something. That girl I helped move on earlier. How'd you know it was a girl? *I* was the one who pulled her in. We weren't working together, so how'd you know?"

"Well . . ." I pause. "She just looked like a girl."

"What do you mean?" Lucio asks.

"You don't need me to explain what a girl looks like, do you Lucio?" I tease, flashing him my best eyebrow raise.

"Are you telling me you can *see* the spirits when they're close?"

"Yes. Can't you?"

"No." Lucio shakes his head. "I just see a ball of light."

"Really?"

"I don't think anyone's ever *seen* them before."

I bite my lip. Why does it feel like my powers are different from everyone else's?

"That must be terrifying sometimes," Lucio offers gently, seeing my discomfort.

"I've had a couple of really gruesome ones," I confess.

"Can you see the darkness too?" Lucio asks, wide eyed.

"What darkness?" For the first time since I arrived here I remember the shadowy man I saw at the Seattle airport. He was surrounded by darkness. Is that what Lucio means?

"Aidan hasn't told you about that yet?"

"No."

Lucio presses his lips together, like he's worried he's said too much. "I'm sure it's coming up in a future lesson." He takes a drink of his orange soda, probably trying to buy himself a second to think of how to change the subject, but I'm not going to let him.

CHAPTER FIFTEEN

The Darkness

I wait patiently for Lucio to finish his drink. "Come on," I say, mock-whining, like we're five years old. "Give me a sneak peek of the lessons I've got coming to me."

Lucio shakes his head, but he's grinning, so I know he's about to give in.

"Okay. But if Aidan asks how you know, don't tell him it was me."

"No problem," I promise. "I'll just say it was one of the dozens of other luiseach here at Llevar la Luz."

Lucio laughs. "Excellent." His voice turns serious as he continues. "Aidan's been teaching you to pull spirits toward you from miles away, helping them move on one at a time."

"Yes."

"Most spirits want to be found. It's like they set off flare guns all across the world when they leave their bodies, just begging us to track them down and help them move on. But some spirits . . ." He trails off.

What was it that Professor Jones said about spirits who lingered on Earth too long? Nolan would remember immediately, but I have to search my memory. Eventually I hear the professor's scratchy old voice in my head: *Even the friendliest of spirits is dangerous. Because it simply should not be here. It is a fish out of water. A hawk with broken wings. A horse with a broken leg.*

Do you know what they do to horses with broken legs, child?

I didn't actually know until Nolan told me sometime later. Horses with broken legs are killed because it's the merciful thing to do.

I don't think dark spirits know about mercy.

"Some spirits don't want to move on," I supply. "The ones who feel their lives were snuffed out too soon. Who think they have unfinished business."

"Exactly," Lucio nods. "Earlier you got to that spirit before he could run and hide—"

"Eddie Denfield," I remember.

"Right. But sometimes we don't catch them in time. Spirits can hide from us."

"The opposite of spirits who do want to move on."

"Exactly. And when you're tracking a particular spirit, you can *feel* when it starts hovering on the edge of going dark. You can *feel* the darkness closing in."

"What does it feel like?" My voice comes out like a whisper.

"You know the peace you feel when you help a spirit move on? Imagine the exact opposite of that."

"No thank you," I say, and Lucio laughs out loud. "So that's what you've been doing since I got here? Tracking a spirit on the verge of going dark?"

He nods. "It's unusual, this close to the equator."

"Why?"

"Something about the warm air kind of . . . I don't know, makes them weaker, almost sluggish."

"So are all luiseach training facilities close to the equator?"

Lucio grins wryly. "Not the ones that are dedicated to studying dark spirits."

"But this spirit, the one you're tracking, it's behaving strangely—stronger than it should be?"

"I don't know why." Lucio runs his fingers over his closely cropped hair. "Maybe it's the . . ."

He doesn't seem to know how to finish his sentence, so I decide to try another question: "What did you mean when you said it was *one of our spirits*?"

"When did you hear that?" Lucio narrows his almost-black eyes.

"My first night here. I haven't exactly been sleeping soundly since I arrived."

"It's just . . . I don't know how much I'm supposed to tell you exactly."

"What's one more off-book lesson?" I ask hopefully, but Lucio shakes his head slowly as he toys with his tattoo.

"I can't betray Aidan's trust."

It's hard to argue with a statement that honorable. "Aidan sure seems like he has a lot of secrets." I take the last bite of my taco.

"He does."

"Do you realize that I don't even know which building his lab is in?"

"I'm sure he'd tell you if you just asked."

I shrug. Finally, I say, "Do you ever think about giving it up?"

"Giving what up?"

"Luiseach-y-ness," I say, not sure if there's a luiseach word equivalent to *humanity*. "You know, becoming a normal person. Like Victoria did."

Well, sort of like Victoria did. I'm not sure I would call her *normal* exactly. But then, I wouldn't have ever called myself normal, even long before I knew I was a luiseach. I never quite fit in with other kids my age, as evidenced by the fact that the T-shirt I'm wearing today is older than I am, dug up from a bin in the back of a vintage shop while everyone else I went to school with bought their shirts from Old Navy or H&M.

"Are you crazy?" Lucio asks.

Still thinking about my fashion sense, I shrug. "It's entirely possible."

Lucio clearly isn't thinking about clothes as he continues. "Giving up your powers doesn't make you feel *normal*. It hurts. It's like splitting in two."

"Splitting in two?" I echo, remembering that Victoria said Aidan required her to give up her powers in order to place Anna into our house back in Ridgemont, like what she gave up created some sort of power surge.

"Anyway," Lucio adds, "if the work Aidan's doing in there turns out to be right, we're not going to be helping spirits move on for that much longer."

"But then what would our job be? Isn't that pretty much the point of being a luiseach—how else do we maintain the balance?" I imagine all the luiseach in the world finding themselves suddenly unemployed, forced to apply for normal jobs like normal people, trying to figure out how to put "exorcising demons" on the special skills section of their résumés.

"What our job would be is kind of beside the point."

"Then what *is* the point?"

"Aidan thinks we're going extinct." Lucio sounds almost matter-of-fact about it.

Before I can ask *What do you mean, extinct?!*, the music around us gets suddenly louder. The kids playing around the fountain run to their parents, who are lining the sides of the street.

"A parade!" Lucio grabs my hand and hops up, pulling me along beside him.

There's plenty of space by the side of the road to see the parade—if that's what you want to call it. It's more like a traveling party. A few dozen people dressed in bright clothing slowly walk down the street. Some dance, while others just walk and wave. A band composed of mostly trumpets and a large drum follow the group, providing the marching theme.

"I knew this was coming up, but I didn't know it was tonight," Lucio shouts over the music and shouting spectators. Almost everyone in the parade has a brightly colored mask like the ones I've seen in pictures of Day of the Dead celebrations in Latin American history class. Traditionally Day of the Dead is a chance for family and friends to pray for and remember people who have died. I'm pretty sure it usually falls around Halloween. But I guess no one around here is going to let the time of year stop them.

"What's going on?" I ask.

"A local celebration," Lucio answers. I smile, suddenly so happy he brought me here. I shift my weight toward him, leaning comfortably on his arm.

"There's something else you should know about the darkness." Lucio looks at me seriously.

"What?" I shout back over the band.

"It's changing. Growing." He pauses, taking a second to think. "Something has changed. I don't think it's just spirits fighting to stay on Earth and eventually turning dark. I think there's something else going on." As Lucio continues, the music of the parade fades into the background, and it feels like I can't hear anything but the words coming out of Lucio's mouth. "It's *organized* somehow."

"Organized?" I echo. Then I realize the music actually has stopped. But the night doesn't remain quiet for long. Before Lucio can tell me anything else about the darkness, a scream breaks through the silence. We both look over to see one of the trumpet players collapsed onto the street, clutching his chest. A few of the local women rush to try to help him.

That's when I see a dark, shadowy figure on the other side of the street, crouching on all fours. Its face lights up as a horrifying smile spreads across its face, revealing row after row of sharp white teeth. Whatever it is, it's *happy*. I grab Lucio's arm.

"Look!" I point. Lucio squints.

"What?"

"Can't you see it?"

"See what?"

"I think it's a demon!" It *must* be a demon. Only a demon would look that pleased at the sight of someone else suffering.

"A demon?" Lucio echoes incredulously. "You can *see* it?" The commotion in the street grows as the man on the ground writhes in pain. A woman, probably his wife, wails in agony. But I force myself to look away because I don't want to lose sight of the demon. I can see it more clearly now, as though my eyes had to adjust, the way they get used to seeing in a dark room. Suddenly it takes off, running toward a back alley.

"Come on!" I grab Lucio's arm and give chase.

"I can't see anything!" Lucio shouts as we cross the street, pushing our way through the crowd. As we pass the dying man, his spirit is released from his body. The demon may have killed this poor man, but he didn't possess him, so at least I can help his spirit move on. I reach out and send it on its way.

Instantly the body it left behind bursts into flames. The people around the fire run away in horror. Smoke fills the air so that it's difficult to see even a few inches in front of me, but I don't slow down.

I saw where the demon was headed, and I'm determined to follow.

CHAPTER SIXTEEN
The Hunt

The quaint fishing village I was romanticizing just a few minutes ago has turned dark and sinister as we enter the back alleys. Gone are the cute kids running around, the glowing lights, and the happy faces. The alleys are like a labyrinth of shadows and corridors as we give chase.

"Where is it?" Lucio cries. "Can you still see it?"

"There!" I point toward the creature as it ducks around a corner. We run after it, not pausing to consider whether chasing a nightmarish demon down a dark alley is actually a good idea. Or at least I'm not thinking about it; maybe Lucio is. But I doubt it. He's not slowing down either.

As we get closer, the demon comes into focus. It's a dark color but not black, more like the color of dark, rusty water. It runs on all fours like a goat, complete with hooves, but it sprints along the cobblestone alleys with ease. A real goat would slip and slide across a surface like this.

We round another blind corner. We are getting closer to it. I don't stop to think it might just be letting us get close, leading us somewhere. Suddenly a shabbily dressed man stumbles out of one of the shadows and crashes into Lucio, barely missing me as well. Lucio and the man fall to the ground, and the man groans in pain. I don't look back because I don't want the demon to hide in one of the shadows while I'm not looking.

It takes a sharp left and enters a room off the alley. I slow down and cautiously look inside. The room is covered in pale green tile, and mold is growing in the corners and on the ceiling. An old, dirty fluorescent light hangs from the ceiling, flickering over a few pieces of garbage on the floor.

We're not alone. A woman sits in the middle of the room. She looks exhausted and her face has that same blank stare I sometimes saw on Mom's face when the water demon possessed her.

I can see the demon clearly now. Its fur seems to be soaking wet, but I don't think it's sweat or water because it reeks like it's been doused in gasoline. It has a short, pointed tail and horns that twist up behind its face, which is more human than goat, although its eyes glow yellow. It takes one look at me and leaps toward the woman.

She opens her mouth to a disturbingly unnatural size and easily swallows the demon's head. The rest of its body flails about, forcing itself inside this woman, kicking off the sickly green tile below it. First the front legs and eventually the back legs, so only the tip of the tail is hanging out of her mouth. She turns her focus on me, smiling after she consumes it.

Lucio bounds into the room. "Where'd it go?!" He pants heavily. All I can do is point at the woman. She stands and walks toward us. I reach for the knife in my back pocket, only it's not there.

The woman's grin grows larger as she approaches us. Maybe this *was* a trap. We need to run.

"Run," I whisper loudly, backing into the alley. I pull Lucio's arm, and in an instant we're going as fast as we can. Only we're not the ones giving chase this time. Much to my surprise, the possessed woman doesn't follow us for long, though. Instead, she stops and laughs, a high-pitched cackle that echoes through the narrow walls of the town's back alleys and makes my skin crawl.

We run through the maze of alleyways at top speed. As we round one of the corners I catch a glimpse of a man lurking in the shadows, wearing a long black coat and black hat, surrounded by darkness.

It doesn't take us long to kick-start Clementine awake. We jump on, and Lucio gases it. Soon we're climbing the hill we descended earlier. I hang onto Lucio as I look back at the town—not so cute and peaceful anymore.

Things don't calm down much when we get back to campus. Before Lucio can even bring us to a full stop, Aidan bursts out of a stucco building directly across the courtyard from the mansion. I can tell Lucio's eager to fill Aidan in on what happened, but Aidan doesn't want to listen right now. Instead, he scolds Lucio for taking me off campus. I hear phrases like *You know it's not safe* and *Do I need to remind you what's at stake?* Lucio argues that we stayed on Llevar la Luz land, but my brain tunes out most of it because it's still stuck on what happened back at the town, on that poor man the demon killed, on the sound of that horrible laugh as we ran away, and on the man in black. Why did he look so familiar? Was that the same man I saw at the airport back in Washington?

The sound of Lucio's voice saying my name breaks through the thoughts racing around my brain. "Sunshine, you have to tell him." I look up and see Aidan and Lucio staring back at me.

"Is it true?" Aidan asks.

"Is what true?"

"You can see spirits, both light and dark?"

"Yes. It's true." I answer, exhausted. I know Aidan wants to hear every detail of what happened tonight.

"Let's go inside." Aidan turns to lead the way into the house. Lucio follows, and I notice something on the ground, not far from where we're standing. My rusty old knife. It must have fallen out of my pocket when I got on the motorcycle earlier. I quickly bend down and put it back where it belongs, relieved to feel its weight in my pocket again.

For the next two hours we sit at the kitchen table, and Lucio and I tell Aidan about everything that happened. Aidan takes notes and asks questions, but in typical Aidan fashion, he gives us little in return.

Eventually, as the two of them discuss the description of the demon I gave them for a fifth time, I begin to fall asleep right there at the table. Aidan finally excuses us so we can get some sleep. But I'm pretty sure that no matter how tired I feel, I won't be getting much sleep tonight.

I Find the Protector

I see him across the crowded coffee shop. I think I would have recognized him even if that woman hadn't told me what he looked like. He has that same far-off look so many protectors have, as though being out here in the world interacting with people doesn't come nearly as naturally to him as burying his head in a book.

There are a stack of open books in front of this boy. As he reads, he fingers a camera on the table with one hand, gripping his coffee mug with the other. He doesn't take a single sip, as though he's forgotten why he's holding it at all. Instead, he puts the cup down and starts making frantic notes, like he's hoping if he just writes quickly enough, he'll get to his answer that much sooner.

Poor boy. Even from here he's trying to help her. Hoping his research might reveal all the solutions they haven't yet found. He looks profoundly unhappy. Which should make this a whole lot easier.

Like most luiseach, I'm aging slowly: no one who saw me would guess my real age. (Which is decades younger than Aidan, in any case.) And I'm short, shorter than the average female, which should work to my advantage.

Humans never quite stop associating height with age. When elderly people begin shrinking, humans treat them like they're younger than they are. I can easily pass for a college student, just a few years older than that boy. I had the forethought to dress the part. Rather than my usual vintage clothes, I bought two pairs of jeans, several graphic T-shirts, and a puffy down jacket that makes me look like a marshmallow from nearby chain stores—nothing one-of-a-kind. Now I pull my hair down from its tightly knotted bun, letting my curls fall across my face. I concentrate on softening my expression: unfurrowing my brow, unsquinting my eyes, relaxing my jaw. Like I haven't a care in the world.

That woman told me his name.

Of course, I have to pretend not to know it now.

Have to pretend I'm sitting down beside him only because there are so few vacant seats in this shop.

Have to strike up a conversation because I'm new to Ridgemont—just transferred to the university a couple of towns over, and rents were so much cheaper here than close to campus, but it's hard making friends when you live so far away and you're majoring in such a specialized subject.

A subject, I have no doubt, that will grab this boy's attention.

It shouldn't be so easy, but it is. I tuck my hair behind my ears, roll my shoulders into a schoolgirl-ish slouch, and smile slightly as I ask, "Is that a Nikon F5?"

CHAPTER SEVENTEEN
My Ghost

I haven't had a decent night's sleep since I arrived here. Each night I go to bed exhausted from the day's work, certain that *tonight* I'll finally crash into a deep, dreamless sleep. I imagine I won't wake up until Aidan is banging on the door, insisting it's time to get started for the day. But that never happens. Not even close.

The nightmares that started on my first night here haven't stopped.

The woman holds my infant form tenderly, humming a sweet sort of nonsense tune. Her grip turns tight; her fingers are like rods of steel digging into my sides, my neck, my legs. I try to scream, but she's squeezing me so tightly, I can't even get out a pathetic, baby wail. I'm so small that she can wrap her hands around my entire rib cage. It feels like she's going to break every bone that protects my heart. It feels like she's going to keep on squeezing until her fingers go right through me.

I wake up gasping in the darkness. This isn't the first time my dreams have carried over into my waking life. I spent night after night dreaming of Anna in her wet dress back in Ridgemont.

But when I dreamed of Anna, I was living in a haunted house. She left her wet little fingerprints all over my stuff; she laughed and played and whispered in my ear.

I get out of bed and head for the bathroom. I can feel the cool air coming from the crack beneath the nursery door, smell my birth mother's perfume from the master bedroom down the hall. I close my eyes and picture the forgotten furniture downstairs, covered in sheets and decaying in the humid air.

When Anna was haunting me, at least it was fun from time to time. I mean, don't get me wrong: I was terrified and confused and overwhelmed, but I was also playing Monopoly and checkers with a little girl who liked my toys and laughed when she won. There's nothing *fun* about this house. It's so humid that sometimes it looks like the walls are crying.

I miss Anna. She's probably moved on by now, right? I know that Victoria's letter said her spirit still had work left to do on Earth, but it's been weeks since I destroyed the water demon who killed her. She knows better than anyone the risks of lingering too long.

Lucio mentioned once that you could seek spirits out if you knew about their lives before they passed away. I know a lot about Anna's life: I know where she lived and how she died and that her favorite toy was a stuffed owl that matches the one in the nursery across the hall.

I swing my legs over the side of the bed. It takes all my strength to open the window wide with the vines pressing heavily from the other side. The plants crack and rip as the window ascends. I stick my head outside and close my eyes.

Concentrate. Just like Aidan always tells me to.

I picture the inside of Victoria's house, its plush, pastel-colored furniture, a stark contrast to her dark clothes. I picture Anna's face—not the little girl in the wet dress I saw in my dreams, but the pictures on Victoria's mantel—the pretty girl with the nearly black eyes that matched her mother's. If I can pull her near, now that I'm more experienced, will I be able to see her? Will I want to see the Anna who was drowned in her own bathtub? Goosebumps blossom on my arms and legs.

"Anna!" I say out loud, careful not to shout—Lucio is asleep in his room below. "Anna?" I repeat, a question this time.

Softly, like it's coming from miles away, I hear the laugh I know so well.

Then, as quickly as it came, the sound disappears, like a connection that's been broken, a call that's been dropped. I concentrate once more.

"Please." I hold my arms out in front of me, like I think if I just reach out far enough, I'll be able to grab her and pull her close.

No such luck.

Then I have an idea.

I run into the hallway and throw my weight against the nursery door. Just like my first night here, this room is a pleasant few degrees cooler.

But I'm not here to enjoy the weather. Even in the darkness I find what I'm looking for almost immediately. I grab it, its fur soft and cool under my fingers. I close the door behind me and go back to the window. This time, when I reach my arms out in front of me, I'm holding something Anna will recognize.

I close my eyes and concentrate, thinking of the sound of her voice saying *night night* and of her footsteps pattering on the floor above me. I even think about our bathroom on the night the demon arrived. The sound of her voice when she begged for her life.

I open my eyes and I can see her. She is *all* I can see—her long, dark hair and her pale skin and her dark eyes. "You're dry," I say dumbly. Every time I saw her before—and then it was only in my dreams—her hair was wet, her clothes dripping. Whenever she touched anything in my room, wet fingerprints were left behind. She nods but doesn't speak, and I understand she's been dry ever since the water demon was destroyed.

"Are you ready to move on?" I ask, holding out the stuffed owl that matches hers.

She shakes her head.

"Don't you *want* to move on, Anna?" I sense her answer immediately. I smile, relieved. Until she adds, *But not until the time is right.*

"What does that mean? It's too risky to stay here." If anyone knows what's at stake when a dark spirit manifests, she does. "You have to move on," I say fiercely. "Please let me help you." My hands are trembling, so the owl is shaking in my grip. It looks like it's about to take flight. In a second it does. I mean, it's floating up away from me.

"How are you doing that?" I ask. The last time I saw a stuffed owl fly, it was Dr. Hoo in my bedroom, his wings flapping so hard they lifted my hair in the breeze. But that was when the water demon was there too.

"Please!" I shout at her, not even bothering to try to stay quiet. "Let me—"

But before I can finish, the owl falls abruptly to the ground. I can see the ground now. I can see everything. Everything except Anna, who's vanished.

I run out of the bedroom and down the stairs, opening the heavy front door. The moist night air covers me like a blanket as I go around the side of the house and pick up the owl, one of its wings stained brown with mud where it hit the ground. I hold it up, ready to flex every single muscle in my body, ready to concentrate in order to bring her back, but I can't concentrate because I just noticed a tiny beam of light coming from the window of one of the stucco buildings across the courtyard.

The building Aidan angrily emerged from as Lucio and I returned from the fishing village. That must be the building where he does all his work.

CHAPTER EIGHTEEN

A Dark Discovery

Before heading upstairs to bed tonight, I managed to pull Lucio aside and ask him the question I hadn't had the chance to ask before: "What did you mean, Aidan thinks we're going extinct?"

"Well, not you and me personally. But the *species*. Which I guess is sort of you and me personally, if you're the last luiseach to be born, right? He thinks that's your destiny—you're the last luiseach."

I wrinkle my nose. *The Last Luiseach* sounds like the name of a movie, and not one I want to have a starring role in. What will happen to humanity if luiseach go extinct? I remember what the water demon almost did to my mother. What it succeeded in doing to Anna and her father when there wasn't a luiseach to save them.

Will the rest of humanity suffer the same fate? With no one around to exorcise them, will the entire world be blanketed in dark spirits? I close my eyes and imagine such a world: humans running away, as though it's possible to hide from a demon. People dying, their spirits trapped here on Earth. Will this be the result of the growing darkness Lucio was telling me about?

"But *why* does he think we're going extinct?" I asked. If I really am the last luiseach, then someday I'll be here on Earth all alone after the rest of the luiseach are gone. A single person trying to do the work that a whole species used to manage together. "He wouldn't just let the planet descend into chaos. That must be what he's working on in his lab at all hours."

"You should ask him yourself," Lucio said.

No time like the present, right? In my bare feet and pajamas— worn-out sweatpants and an old T-shirt—I make my way across the courtyard.

I stop and carefully lie the stuffed owl down on the house's front porch. I won't give up until I get Anna to agree to move on.

Even at this hour the air is thick with humidity, as warm as a touch on my skin. The building where Aidan does his work is in surprisingly good shape. In the moonlight I can see that there's no dust on the floor, which is covered with enormous, cream-colored tiles. I hear footsteps clicking above me, and I head toward the stairs on the far right, even though there are no windows along the staircase so after the first few steps it turns pitch black. I cross my fingers and hope there aren't any missing steps that need to be hopped over.

I nearly fall flat on my face when I get to the top of the stairs and bite my lip to keep from crying out. I hear noises coming from down the hall. Blindly I head in the direction of the sound, but soon my steps become heavy, labored. The air feels thick, like walking through quicksand. I can barely put one foot in front of the other.

And the temperature is plummeting.

I manage to make it to the open doorway all the way down the hall. There's a circle of light coming from inside, where Aidan has a flashlight perched on a cold-looking metal table, the sort of surface you'd expect to see in a doctor's office or a morgue. Nothing else in this room looks like I expected; it doesn't bear even a passing resemblance to my high school's chem lab. Just shelves with books, hundreds of newspaper clippings tacked to the wall, and a large map of the world with four spots circled in red and what looks like dates next to them. There aren't any beakers of fluid bubbling up in the corner, no microscope so Aidan can study specimens through its lens.

But there are *specimens* in there.

The room is filled with spirits, but I can't see them like I usually can. They're worked into such a frenzy, so upset for some reason that they swirl the room in a blur. I think there might be dozens of them. Hundreds of them? I remember the chill I felt when I first arrived here, the presence of spirits so close and yet unable to touch me. Now, from the doorway, I can hear their voices drifting in and out of my head.

I sink to the floor. I've never heard such agony. They're *begging* for my help, begging to be set free. Pleading with me to help them move on, beseeching Aidan to stop what he's doing to them. Flashes of their lives and deaths spring up behind my eyes, as vivid as images on a movie screen: a man throwing a ball for his beloved dog, a woman rocking her baby to sleep, a toddler taking his first, uncertain steps. Then, a hospital heart monitor flatlining, a car skidding across the meridian, a pair of eyelids dropping heavily and permanently shut.

I press my hands to the sides of my head, like I think I can squeeze them out.

I'm shaking so hard that my teeth are chattering, making it almost impossible to get the words out. My heart is pounding so fast I can't even feel each individual beat; instead, it feels like my heart is humming, just like the woman hummed in my nightmare before she tried to kill me.

I manage to curl into a ball, trying to keep myself warm, rocking back and forth like a crazy person in a padded room. Mom wanted me to come here so what happened in that parking lot would never happen again.

What would she say if she could see me now?

CHAPTER NINETEEN
Behind Closed Doors

Aidan must hear me because he turns to see me crouching in the doorway. He's at my side almost before I take my next labored breath. He lifts me up and carries me into the hallway with one arm, slamming the door to that room shut with the other.

I had no idea my mentor/father was so strong. I feel like a baby in his arms. And not the helpless kind of baby I feel like in my dreams. This feels like something else entirely. This feels warm, familiar, comforting. *This* must be why little kids are always begging their fathers to pick them up, carry them, give them a piggy-back ride. In Aidan's arms I feel safe.

Gently he lays me on the ground in the hallway and presses his hand to my forehead, like a mom checking whether her child has a temperature. Soon my teeth aren't chattering and my fingertips aren't blue with cold. My heart slows until it feels normal again, one beat after another, steady and strong. *Ba-bum. Ba-bum. Ba-bum.*

But it doesn't feel like it did that day at the hospital. Aidan helped all those spirits move on then. This time I can feel the spirits are still trapped on the other side of that door, here on Earth.

As soon as I open my eyes he takes his hand away from my head, like he doesn't want me to see him touching me. "What are you doing here?"

"What am I doing here?" I shake my head, still slightly out of breath. "What are *you* doing here? In there?" I point weakly toward his lab.

"That's my work," he says simply, as though that's enough to explain anything.

"Your work is *not* helping spirits move on? Isn't that completely at odds with the whole maintaining-the-balance thing you said was so important?"

He shakes his head and backs away from me slightly, still crouching on the floor like a frog. "Of course not." His voice sounds completely normal, as though he wasn't just tormenting a roomful of spirits desperate to move on. As though his daughter/mentee hadn't just nearly passed out in front of him.

"How can you say that?" I press my hands onto the cool floor and push myself up into a seated position. I cross my legs beneath me and straighten my spine. It's hard to be taken seriously when you're still in your pajamas. Especially when your pajamas include a T-shirt with a picture of a Care Bear. "What am I doing here?" I ask finally, even though Aidan asked me the very same thing just seconds ago.

"You tell me. You're the one who came to my lab."

"Your *lab?* Is that what you call that torture chamber?" Aidan doesn't answer, so I keep talking. "I don't mean *here,* in this building right now. I mean here on this campus, in this country, a zillion miles away from my mom and my protector and everything and everyone I've ever known."

"You're honing your skills."

"Why do I need to get better at helping spirits move on if your work is all about *not* helping them move on?" Frustration is making me nearly as hot as I was cold before. In my head I can still hear the faintest cries from behind the closed door, and I can hear Aidan's voice answering them loudly: *No. Not yet.* I shudder. Anna said the same thing to me earlier tonight.

"What do you mean *not yet?*" I ask, as though he said the words out loud.

"I mean I'm not going to help them move on right now."

"But why?" I ask. "If you wait too long, they'll go dark, one right after the other. Just like the demon who killed Anna. Just like the demon I saw tonight."

I push myself up to stand, using the rough stucco wall behind me to steady myself. "You're *torturing* them. These spirits came to you for help, sensing the presence of the nearest luiseach. They *want* to move on." Unlike Anna. In my head I recall her sweet voice, *Not until the time is right.*

"I can't help them, not yet. My work—"

"I *know* what happens to spirits who linger on Earth too long," I shout, the anger in my voice surprising even me. *This* is what Lucio meant on my first night here when he said one of our spirits had escaped. The one he's looking for, on the verge of going dark—it came from this lab. "The spirit of even the kindest person can turn dark. Can turn into a demon, just like the one who killed Anna and her father. The one who almost killed my mother." I look at Aidan meaningfully.

"I would never have let anything happen to Kat," he says softly.

"It sure didn't look that way," I mumble. "And whatever your work is, how could it be more important than whether my mom lives or dies? Your work isn't more important than making sure that all of those spirits in there move on before they have a chance to escape and hurt someone else."

"Yes," Aidan says firmly. "It is."

Despite the fact that not a single hair on his head is out of place, Aidan looks like a mad scientist. Someone who uses innocent people and spirits as his guinea pigs. Even if my frizzball is a mess and my clothes are wrinkled from hours of restless sleep, *he's* the crazy one.

I stand and cross the hall, placing my hand on the door to his lab. I plant my feet firmly on the floor, then close my eyes and concentrate, trying to reach out to just one of the spirits on the other side of the door. I stretch my arms in front of me as though I think I can grab hold of them one at a time and help.

I should be able to do this.

I should be strong enough after everything I've learned.

I was strong enough to bring Anna to me.

A dozen voices fill my brain at once, but this time I'm able to pick out a single voice among the others. It's not a spirit's voice, but Aidan's firmly shouting *No.* He pulls me away from the door before I collapse all over again.

"Lucio told me your theory," I declare, opening my eyes. "You think luiseach are going extinct!"

Aidan nods calmly. "I do."

"So shouldn't we help as many spirits move on as possible while we're still here?"

He shakes his head. "Think about it, Sunshine," he says, patient as the best teachers have to be. "How will spirits move on when we're no longer on this planet to help them?"

A lump rises in my throat. "I don't know," I whisper.

"Neither do I," Aidan admits, his voice as even as ever. "But I'm determined to find a solution."

He opens the door to his lab then quickly closes it behind him. I stand in the darkness, shocked that he's just left me here, but then the door opens again, bringing a beam of light along with it. Aidan holds his flashlight out in front of him.

"Take this and go back to the house," he says.

"Are you sending me to my room?" I ask. Like he's a strict father, punishing me for sneaking out of the house in the middle of the night. Is he going to try to ground me next?

Not that there's anywhere to go around here.

CHAPTER TWENTY

Girl Talk

I trudge back to my room with the stuffed owl in one hand and Aidan's flashlight in the other. No. Not that this room feels like *mine,* but it's the room with the bed that I sleep fitfully in. I feel ridiculously, absurdly, enormously homesick. Homesick for *Ridgemont,* not Austin, something I never really thought would happen. But they say home is where the heart is, and I guess my heart is in Ridgemont now. That's where Mom is. And Nolan. Maybe even where Anna returned to after she left me behind.

I want to try to pull her close again, but I'm not strong enough after what happened across the courtyard. I wish Nolan were here. Wish I could share all of my questions with him. If anyone can make sense of Aidan's senseless experiments and if anyone might be able to answer his answerless question—how will spirits move on without luiseach?—it's Nolan. Or, at least, he'd be able to do the research that will get us closer to the answer. Maybe he'll be able to figure out what Anna's waiting for, what the *right time* means. Maybe Nolan will be so intrigued by figuring all of these things out that he'll forget he's mad at me and that we haven't actually spoken since I left Ridgemont.

I reach for my phone. There's no reception in here, but I've been able to talk to Mom a few times by pacing the campus, holding the phone out in front of me until the bars in the upper right-hand corner go from zero to something, anything higher. I make my way out of the bedroom and to the stairs, almost tumbling down them altogether. I tighten my grip, suddenly terrified I might drop my phone, that it might shatter into a thousand pieces and my only link to the outside world would be broken.

Not that it's much of a link because there's no signal on the first floor either. I open the door and head outside. Dawn can't be too far away; the tiniest pricks of sunlight are edging their way up into the sky. I pace back and forth, desperate for cell service.

I don't want to take a single step toward the building where I know Aidan is tormenting spirits, so I head around to the back of the house.

Still no signal. I keep walking, into the jungle beyond the garden. I must be about fifty yards from the house, halfway up the hill with the playground on top by the time I'm finally able to make a call.

Ring. Ring. Ring. There's no answer. Maybe he's still sleeping. I glance at the clock on my phone. Of *course* he's still sleeping. It's four in the morning back home. Maybe my call woke him up. But maybe once he saw who the call was coming from, he hit *ignore*. Maybe he doesn't want to talk to the girl who gets sick when she touches him.

But I need to talk to him! I need him to whip out his protector super-sleuth skills so we can find some answers. But then . . .
am I just *using* him? What is he getting out of this friendship?
Being a protector suddenly seems ridiculously unfair.

After the fifth ring, his voicemail picks up. How can I ask
him for help when I've hurt him? I still haven't found an answer
when the telltale beep lets me know that it's too late to hang
up—his voicemail has already started recording.

"Um, hi," I say. "It's me. I mean, it's Sunshine. I was just
calling because—" Because why? Because I'm confused and
alone and homesick? "Because there's some really weird stuff
going on down here. In Mexico. That's where I am now. And
I thought you might be able to . . . help. If you want to. You
don't have to, you know, just because you're my protector. It's
just that"—I take a deep breath, surprised to feel a lump rising in
my throat—"Aidan thinks that luiseach are going extinct. He's
doing these . . . experiments. I don't understand any of it. And
I'm not getting any better at handling multiple spirits. It's all just
a big"—I bite my lip, searching for the right word to describe just
how bad it is—"a big *clustercuss*, you know? I mean, I know you
don't know, because we haven't talked in a while." The words
I've been thinking for so long tumble out of my mouth before I
can stop myself: "I wish you were here because—"

Beep. Nolan's voicemail cuts me off. Not that I knew exactly
what I was going to say after *because* anyhow. A bird coos in the
trees above me, and I slap at the mosquitoes that are threatening to eat me alive. Still, I don't want to leave the forest yet. I
want to take advantage of my link to the outside world while
I'm standing in the one place in Llevar la Luz with a decent cell
phone signal.

So I call my mom. Just hearing her say *Hello* makes me feel better. When Nolan didn't pick up, it felt like my life back home was even farther out of my reach than it already was.

I can hear the beep of machines in the background, and I know she's at the hospital, working the overnight shift. I close my eyes and imagine her walking down the brightly lit halls of the neonatal unit, her pink pastel-colored scrubs bringing out the red in her hair.

"Sunshine!" Mom exclaims when she hears my voice. "I haven't talked to you in days."

"Sorry," I answer. "The service here sucks. And"—I pause, biting my lip—"I've been busy."

"I guess that means you're learning a lot." She's trying to sound casual and nonchalant, but I can detect the edge in her voice. She doesn't want to hear that I still can't manage even just two spirits on my own, let alone that I was face to face with a terrifying demon only hours ago. And no matter how much I want to tell her, no matter how much I want to sink to the ground and cry until she swears to rescue me from this terrible place, I can't do that to her. I can't make her even *more* worried than she already is.

"I *have* learned a lot," I answer, hoping Mom can't recognize the false brightness in my voice the way I did in hers. "Aidan is really nice." That's sort of true. I mean, he may be imprisoning spirits, but he also carried me across the hall from his dastardly lab and held me until I felt better.

"I'm so glad to hear it." Mom sounds so relieved that it even makes me feel calmer.

"I miss you, though." The lump that appeared when I called Nolan rises even higher in my throat.

"I miss you too, baby," Mom answers. "So much."

"Up to the moon and back?" I ask, an old game of ours.

"No," Mom says. "Moon's too close. I miss you to Mars and back."

"I miss you to the sun and back."

I hear her name being called from somewhere on the other end of the line.

"I'm so sorry, sweetie. I've got to go."

"Okay." I bite my lip to keep from crying. "I love you."

"I love you too. To the moon and the sun and Pluto and around the world and back again."

After she hangs up, I take a deep breath and turn around, knowing the mansion is just beyond the trees in front of me. I'm not ready to go back there, not yet. I just want a few more minutes of reaching out to people in the real world. I mean, it was nice to hear a familiar voice when Anna arrived, but that's not exactly the kind of girl talk that makes a person feel like she's on the right side of *normal*.

So I dial Ashley's number, even though she's definitely sleeping. If I'm right about what time zone I'm in, it's the same time in Austin as it is here. Ashley will pick up; she sleeps with her phone under her pillow even though her parents have begged her not to—she doesn't want to miss out on anything.

"Sunshine!" she shouts groggily. "I haven't talked to you in ages!"

"I know. I'm sorry. There isn't good cell reception where I am."

"Where are you?" she asks, and I remember Ashley thinks I'm still in Ridgemont. I look down at the moist dirt staining my sneakers. I can't tell her the truth. Or, anyway, I can't tell her the *whole* truth.

"I'm in Mexico," I say finally. "I, um, I found my birth father, and he brought me down here—he lives here—so we could . . . get to know each other better."

"What?" Ashley sounds wide awake now. I imagine her sitting up in bed, her straight blonde hair just as perfect at the crack of dawn as it was when she fell asleep last night, not a hint of frizz anywhere. "You found your birth father? I didn't even know you were *looking* for your birth father."

"I wasn't. I guess he found me."

"Are you okay?" Ashley sounds so kind and loving and concerned that I actually sink down to the ground in gratitude, even though it means literally sitting in a pile of mud. Finally I let my tears spill over.

"I'm kind of okay. I mean, he's nothing like I ever thought he would be. He's . . ." There's no word for what he is, so I say, "He's odd."

"Has he told you why he gave you up?" she asks gently.

"Not exactly," I answer honestly, sniffling. "I think he thought it would be better for me somehow."

"That's good, right?" Ashley offers gently, and I nod. I never thought of it that way, but maybe she's right: it was *good* of Aidan to give me up.

I shake myself like our dog Oscar after a bath. "Can we please talk about something normal?" I beg. "Let's talk about you. Tell me the latest between you and Cory Cooper."

"Oh my gosh, Sunshine. We totally broke up."

"What?" I yelp. "Last I heard you were so excited to kiss him on New Year's Eve!"

"I was," Ashley concedes. "But it turns out having a boyfriend isn't all it's cracked up to be."

I shrug. "I wouldn't know."

"Maybe not yet." I can practically hear her smiling. "But you're going to."

"What makes you so sure?"

"Haven't I always told you I'm wise beyond my years?"

I shake my head. "I literally don't think I've ever heard you say that."

"Well, maybe I haven't said it out loud, but I *think* it all the time."

I laugh out loud, and on her end of the phone—all the way in Austin, Texas, in her pretty room where we used to have sleepovers and movie nights and study sessions—Ashley does too.

CHAPTER TWENTY-ONE
Helena

By the time Ashley and I get off the phone—we don't so much say good-bye as my phone drops the signal and, no matter where I wander, I can't seem to get it back—the sun is high and hot, beating down mercilessly through the trees. I head back toward the mansion. When I finally reach what was once the backyard garden—now overgrown with jungle vines—the sky is so blue and cloudless overhead that it looks fake, something out of a movie set instead of real life. Sweat drips down my forehead and gets into my eyes. Everything goes blurry.

I hear Lucio shouting my name, circling the mansion. (Which could take a while. I mean, it *is* a mansion.) I head in the direction of his voice.

"Where've you been?" he shouts when he sees me. "I was worried sick."

Worried sick? Guess I'm not the only one who goes around using expressions usually reserved for people at least twice my age. But then I guess that's a luiseach thing. We're drawn to things not quite our age—my vintage clothes, Lucio's old-fashioned language. Even Aidan's formal way of dressing is a remnant from an era when people dressed differently.

Sometimes I forget the three of us actually have something in common.

"You're not the boss of me," I answer, only half-joking.

Lucio doesn't laugh. "You can't just wander off," he says solemnly. He rubs the tattoo on his right hand.

"Why not?"

"It isn't safe." He stamps at the ground like a racehorse just itching to start running. Like he has all this pent-up energy just waiting to get out.

"I thought the whole point of bringing me here is because it *is* safe."

"Llevar la Luz is safe," Lucio answers. "But outside our borders . . ."

"There's a dangerous demon and another spirit on the verge of going dark," I supply. Instinctively I reach for my back pocket, then remember I'm in my pajamas. The weapon is still tucked beneath my pillows. I feel kind of naked without it, so I fold my arms across my chest.

"Well, that too," Lucio answers mysteriously.

"What do you mean?" I ask, but Lucio shakes his head, not willing to reveal any more. "Maybe we should take a day off," I try. "Don't luiseach get weekends off? Vacation days?"

"National holidays?" Lucio suggests. "Summer Fridays?"

"Exactly!"

"Come on." Lucio grins, leading the way around the house. Much to my surprise, he doesn't head for the front door. Instead, he keeps going, across the quad and behind the building where I nearly passed out a few hours ago.

Lucio leads me to a circle of benches behind the courtyard, set in the middle of an overgrown shady grove. Most the benches are overgrown with vines and covered in fallen leaves, but around one of the benches someone has made an effort to pull back the vines and clear a path. This place must have had a groundskeeper once, but now there's only Lucio.

The spot looks cool and inviting, and in front of the bench is a jug of lemonade and two glasses. I scratch at my fresh mosquito bites—courtesy of early-morning phone calls in the jungle—and tug at my Care Bear T-shirt. I wonder how long Lucio's been looking for me—the ice in the jug has melted down to almost nothing.

"What's all this?" It's the kind of thing that would make Ashley squeal with delight—a handsome boy setting up a lovely picnic for two.

"*This* is my favorite spot on all of Llevar la Luz," Lucio answers. "When I was little, it was my go-to spot for a game of hide-and-seek."

"Couldn't they always find you if you hid in the same place every time?"

"No one ever seemed to catch on."

I try to imagine what this place must have been like before the rift: a hive of activity, luiseach students and mentors and protectors scattered across the quad, scrambling from one building to the next. Luiseach children playing tag and hide-and-seek. Back then the buildings weren't dilapidated. They were in such good shape that they practically shone in the sunlight, and hot water came right out of the tap. Each building had air conditioning turned up so high that, despite the heat outside, everyone wore sweaters to work, class, and wherever else they were going.

"I thought you might want to talk about what I said the other day. I'm sure you have questions. You know, about our species going extinct."

"Oh that," I joke. "I almost forgot about *that*." *Questions* is an inadequate word for the thoughts running through my head. *Questions* are what you have in math class when a geometry proof doesn't make sense. There should be a bigger word than *questions* that's specially reserved for times like this.

Although I'm not sure anyone has ever experienced a time like this before.

"I followed Aidan to his lab this morning," I confess. In this humidity the temperature barely drops when you go from sunshine to shade. But when Lucio sits on the bench, I drop down beside him. This bench is small, meant for two. It's easy to imagine teenage luiseach-in-training meeting here for secret rendezvous when their mentors weren't looking. Lucio and I sit so close that our knees touch. Through my mud-splattered pj pants I can feel the heat coming off his skin, but I don't move to avoid it. It's nice to be around a boy I can sit close to for a change. If Nolan were here, I'd be struggling to not get sick.

Seriously, Sunshine, I command myself, *Stop comparing Nolan and Lucio!* Now's not the time for those kinds of thoughts anyway.

"Aidan thinks spirits need to learn to move on without luiseach help," he replies.

I lean back and stare at the leaves on the tree branches above us. *That's* why he wasn't helping them. He was trying to force them to do it on their own. Trying to answer his own question: *How will spirits move on when we're no longer on this planet to help them?*

A chill runs down my spine as I remember what I saw. What I *felt*. "He was torturing them," I whisper.

"I know it's hard to watch." Another word that feels wrong. Chemistry tests are *hard*. This is . . . I don't know what this is. "But if Aidan is right, it changes everything. It's the first step in proving humans can learn to move on without us."

"Because I'm the last luiseach," I say softly. How I hate the sound of that.

Lucio nods. "If human spirits are capable of moving on by themselves, then your birth—and the lack of luiseach births since then—isn't the calamity that Helena thinks it is."

"Helena?"

He claps his hand over his mouth so hard the bench shakes beneath us.

"Lucio," I prompt, growing hotter despite the cool glass of lemonade in my hand. I turn from gazing at the leaves to face this dark-haired boy and square my shoulders. "Who is Helena?"

Lucio sets his jaw. This boy may feel sorry for me, but his loyalty is to Aidan, no doubt about it.

"Helena was your mother," a deep voice answers from behind us. I jump in surprise.

Suddenly I can smell her perfume and see the strands of hair left behind in her brush.

I stand and see Aidan walking toward us. "*Was?* Is she . . . gone?"

"She left Llevar la Luz a long time ago." His voice gets louder with each step he takes. "But I don't think that's the kind of *gone* you were getting at. She leads the luiseach on the other side of the rift." He reaches into his pocket for a perfectly white handkerchief to wipe invisible sweat from his brow. "And she's wanted to eliminate you from the day you were born."

"To *eliminate* me?" Aidan can't possibly mean what it sounds like he means. I'm not the kind of person another person would want to *eliminate*. I'm not evil or powerful or anything at all really. I mean, I know I'm not normal, but I'm not . . . I don't know. I'm not *enough* to warrant elimination, right? "Just to make sure I know what you mean"—I gulp—"you're saying she wants to *kill* me?"

"Yes," Aidan confirms with a terse nod. "And she won't rest until she succeeds."

I step backward away from them, tripping over a root from one of the trees surrounding us. I gasp as I fall forward, flinging my arms out in front of me. The glass I'd been holding goes flying, lemonade and all. It lands in the dirt at Aidan's feet, shattering into what looks like a thousand pieces, kind of like what's happened to my life ever since I turned sixteen.

Kindred Spirits

This is harder than I thought it would be. Our first day together the boy barely looks up from his book, and on the second day, when I find him sitting in the exact same spot with the exact same book—just turned to a page much closer to the end—he's so absorbed in his studies, I'm not sure he even recognizes me from the day before.

He's trying to find out more about his role as her protector. He's trying to see whether he can protect her from this many miles away.

On the third day I try another tact. "Got a thing for ghosts?"

This time he practically snaps to attention. Finally. "What?" he asks.

"Your book," I prompt, gesturing toward the ancient-looking tome spread out on the table between us, the one he's been reading over and over since I first saw him. "I recognize it."

"You do?" he asks dubiously. And he's right to be dubious. The book he's studying is more than a century old, and although he doesn't know it, there are only two copies in existence. One is mine, and the other belonged to a friend of Aidan's named Abner Jones, who taught paranormal studies

at the nearby university from which I'm pretending to be a student. Aidan must have used Abner to give this boy the book. Which gives me an idea.

I slouch and let my hair fall across my face like I'm embarrassed. "That's why I'm here," I say shyly. "In Washington, I mean."

"I thought you were in school at the university a couple of towns over," Nolan supplies, and I nod. At least he's been listening enough to retain that bit of information.

"Yeah, but there's a reason I chose this school. Years ago there was a professor there. His work was kind of"—I pause as though I'm searching for the right word—"controversial. In some circles he was lauded as a genius, in others laughed off as a quack. But the university agreed to let me go through his old papers and books and files as research for my thesis."

"What's your thesis about?"

I take a deep breath and sigh heavily, like I'm debating whether or not to confide in him. Finally I bite my lower lip and say softly, "It's about ghosts."

Nolan shifts from a slouch; now his spine is straight as an arrow. "Ghosts?"

"Not just ghosts," I say quickly, like I'm trying to cover up my own foolishness. "You know, the paranormal. Spirits. What happens to us after we die. That kind of thing."

The more I say, the more excited Nolan looks, like we have a special connection he's never had with anyone before. Well, with almost anyone.

"This professor," I continue, "his name was Abner Jones."

"You've heard of Abner Jones?"

"You've heard of Abner Jones?" I echo incredulously. And then I grin like I think Nolan might be a sort of kindred spirit. And from the look on his face, I can see the boy feels the same way.

But then, just for an instant, he presses his lips together solemnly. As though perhaps he's thinking of the last girl he spoke of such things with.

CHAPTER TWENTY-TWO
Extinction

A idan wraps his fingers around my arm and pulls me gently to sit down. Lucio's footsteps fade into the distance as
he makes his way back to the house, giving us some privacy.
Now this shady little refuge feels less like the perfect place for a
romantic picnic than it does like a hiding place. I look around,
darting my gaze this way and that, staring at the back of the
building where Aidan keeps his lab, at the trees above our
heads. In front of us is a stone sculpture that looks like it used
to be a fountain but has long since gone dry. Beyond that a
half-circle of single-story stucco cottages, crumbling under the
weight of the vines growing up around them like long, heavy
arms.

Aidan said he brought me here to keep me safe. I should have
known better than to think he wanted to keep me safe from
dark spirits. A dark spirit can't destroy a luiseach.

He was trying to keep me safe from the woman who gave
birth to me. Lucio said I was only safe on the grounds of Llevar

la Luz. This entire campus is some kind of hiding place. No wonder he was so mad at Lucio for taking me off campus.

"So when you said someone might use multiple spirits against me?" I wipe sweat from my cheeks. This sounds more like something out of a Greek myth than real life. "What about the nursery?" I don't know much about Aidan, and I know even less about Helena, but one of them must have been responsible for that cozy white room with its subtle touches of pink.

"Let me explain," Aidan begins calmly.

How is my mentor/father always so composed? (And why couldn't he have handed some of that composure down to me in his genetic bag of tricks? *Composed* would come in handy right about now.)

"Long before you were born, luiseach birth rates were dwindling."

I let my head drop into my hands, wishing (again) that Nolan were here. All of this is just too much to absorb at once. I need Nolan sitting calmly on one of the other benches, taking careful notes in his messy boy handwriting so we can go over all of this alone together later.

"Your mother and I believed—"

"Don't call her my mother," I interrupt hoarsely, looking up. "My mother is Katherine Griffith, and she would never let anyone hurt me, let alone try to *eliminate* me herself."

Aidan reaches for the pitcher of lemonade on the ground below us and pours some into the glass Lucio left behind. He hands it to me and I take a sip.

"With our shrinking gene pool, fewer and fewer luiseach were being born, yet the human race continued to grow. Helena and I knew that in a few generations the situation would become dire: there would no longer be enough luiseach on Earth to help all human spirits move on, to fight against dark spirits when necessary, to exorcise demons when they arose. But we weren't hopeless, like so many of our brethren. We believed we might be able to produce a child strong enough to help matters."

"Because you were two of the most powerful luiseach ever, right?" They just assumed their offspring would be as special as they were.

"No," Aidan says carefully. "We weren't counting on genetics alone."

"Then how?" I ask, my voice shaking. I'm not totally certain I want to hear the answer.

"When Helena was pregnant," Aidan explains, "we conducted . . . experiments, trying to make the child in her womb even more powerful."

I almost drop my glass of lemonade all over again. This is the creepiest thing I've ever heard, and given what's happened to me in the last six months, the bar on what I call *creepy* has been set pretty high.

"What kind of *experiments*?" I ask carefully.

"We exposed you to spirits practically from conception. Throughout her pregnancy, before Helena helped a spirit move on, she held it close so that it touched you as well. She pulled as many spirits to her as she could, spirits from miles around, every chance she got. Even in her third trimester, when her belly had grown so big that she could barely move," Aidan pauses, almost smiling at the memory, "Helena was still exorcising demons, going on missions normally reserved for those in top physical shape."

Aidan continues, "We believed we could create a luiseach powerful enough to handle multiple spirits at once, who could serve spirits from miles around." His voice rises, as though he's reciting words he's said a thousand times before. He has no idea that he sounds more like a mad scientist to me than ever, like someone from a horror story: Dr. Frankenstein or Dr. Jekyll, men who messed with life and death and suffered the disastrous consequences. "If our experiment was successful, we decided, we would do the same thing to every other pregnant luiseach until our dwindling numbers were no longer a problem. Your mother and I were far from the only luiseach trying to procreate at the time. On this campus alone there were three other pregnant luiseach."

"But I'm *not* powerful like that." I press my legs into the bench beneath us, feeling the sweat on the backs of my knees. No wonder he didn't take the bait when I suggested a protector might be able to help us figure out why I'm so sensitive. No wonder he could calmly say "interesting" the first time I absorbed a bit of a spirit I helped move on. He's known *why* I'm different all along, even if he doesn't know how to fix it. "Just the opposite." I shudder with the memory of what happened this morning.

"I know," Aidan answers. "I've suspected for a long time that your strengths would lie elsewhere."

"What do you mean, for a long time? I haven't even been a luiseach for a long time."

"You've been a luiseach all your life."

"You know what I mean," I counter, exasperated. "I've only been able to sense spirits since I turned sixteen, right?" Aidan nods. "That was barely six months ago."

"Do you remember what happened on New Year's Eve?"

"Of course," I answer. *How could I forget?*

"I was observing your every step." Victoria told me that my mentor had been watching me, but hearing Aidan admit it out loud sends a chill down my spine. "I felt it when you gave up hope."

"Then why didn't you help me?" I ask.

"If I'd helped you, you'd never have dug deep enough to find the hidden stores of strength you didn't know you had."

Yep, Aidan would have been the kind of father who'd have thrown me into the deep end of the pool to teach me how to swim.

He continues, "The weapon Victoria gave you took longer to manifest than I would have liked."

"It took longer to manifest than I would have liked too," I mumble, remembering what happened that night: the roof disappeared from above our heads, the rain beat down until I was drenched. I'd begged the weapon to manifest, begged it to turn into whatever it needed to turn into to save my family.

"You couldn't concentrate," Aidan continues. "You may not realize this, but you bounce back from a spirit's touch quickly: your temperature rebounds almost immediately, your heart rate slows to a normal pace." I shake my head; it doesn't feel like I bounce back quickly, especially lately. Aidan continues, "At first I was certain you'd make short work of that demon. I didn't understand what was taking you so long."

"I was trying," I say miserably. "It was a little hard to concentrate when so many people's lives were at stake."

"Exactly!" Aidan snaps his fingers. The sound is sharp, echoing against the trees, causing a bird perched on a branch above us to take flight. "You were distracted by your concern for Katherine, for Nolan, even for Victoria and Anna—and you barely knew Victoria and Anna. When most luiseach face a demon, the rest of the world fades into the background. They are able to concentrate entirely on the task at hand. But you . . . I didn't understand it until I began working with you here."

"Understand what?"

"How sensitive you are. For you, the rest of the world doesn't fade away. Instead, you feel the emotions of the spirits that touch you."

"Why?"

"I don't know," Aidan admits. "Perhaps because Helena held spirits close for so long when she was pregnant with you, you don't know what it feels like not to absorb their stories."

I take a deep breath, trying to fit all of these pieces together. Their experiments made me weaker, not stronger. Just like all the characters in those mad-scientist stories, they opened me up to more risk. "So when I was born, Helena could tell right away that I would be"—I search for the right words—"abnormally connected to the spirits that touch me? She realized that your experiment was a failure, and she was so upset that she wanted to get rid of me altogether?"

Aidan shakes his head. "Your moth—Helena," he corrects himself, "would never be so irrational."

"Yeah, she sounds really levelheaded," I mumble, looking at my feet. I kick the ground, knocking my lemonade over, sending a tiny splatter of mud into the air. It sticks to Aidan's khaki pants, the first time I've ever seen him wear anything that wasn't perfectly clean.

"Our experiment went awry," he explains, and I look up at my mentor/father's face. His expression is serious, somber. *Sad.* "When you were born—" He pauses, like this is the part of the story that's hardest for him to say out loud.

What now? What could be worse than what he's already said?

"Helena was in labor for more than twenty-four hours. Our doctors and midwives were attending to her all along, but she refused all aid. She was certain you'd come in your own time. And she was right. At precisely 7:12 p.m., Central Standard Time, August fourteenth, there you were, screaming your head off like a wild thing."

He smiles, so I do too. It's the kind of story most kids given up for adoption never get to hear. But then his smile vanishes.

"Your screams were so loud that we didn't hear it at first."

"Hear what?" I whisper.

Aidan hesitates. Softly he finally says, "It started with one woman. A wail of agony like nothing I'd heard in all my years. And then another woman joined in, then another, like some kind of macabre chorus."

He takes a deep breath. "Within seconds they were pounding down our door with the news: each pregnant luiseach on the property had miscarried."

I look out at the crumbling cottages in front of us, tears beginning to fill my eyes. Did some of those women live here? Were they in these buildings when something inside their bodies snapped unexpectedly? Did they run from their homes desperately, their hands pressed to their centers like they thought they could hold their babies in from the outside?

Reluctantly Aidan adds, "But that was just the beginning."

"The beginning of what?" I ask, sitting on my hands to keep them from trembling. I imagine woman after woman pounding desperately on the enormous door of the mansion.

Aidan doesn't break my gaze as he explains. "The news poured in from across the globe. By ten o'clock that evening we'd heard reports of miscarriages in places as far-flung as

Eastern Europe and Australia, like a terrible shockwave sent 'round the world, some kind of collective falling down the stairs. Some mothers didn't just miscarry—at least two women went into early labor and did not survive their ordeal."

Their ordeal? He means that they *died*, right? The same way he meant *kill* when he said *eliminate*.

"I did all that, just by being born?" I stand and turn my back on Aidan, looking around desperately. Maybe if I can just put enough distance between my ears and Aidan's words, it'll be like I never heard them at all.

"It wasn't your fault," Aidan says firmly. He stands and grabs my arm like he can tell I want to run. "It was *our* fault. Your birth released a surge of unexpected energy that sort of jostled the spiritual plane. Helena was horrified."

"Who wouldn't be?" I manage to croak. There's a lump the size of a boulder lodged in my throat. Aidan is right about how sensitive I am. I never met the luiseach who died that day, but I feel like I'm mourning them. Crying for them. My tears get all mixed up with the sweat on my face, and when I lick my lips, all I taste is salt.

Of *course* I wondered about my birth parents over the years, no matter how happy I was with Kat. I always thought they must have had their reasons for giving me up. But I never could have imagined . . . *this*. Never imagined I was just the product of some kind of test in breeding.

"We gathered all of our people together and struggled to decide what to do next. Less than an hour after Helena gave birth, she stood beside me in the foyer of our home and debated. At first she wanted to imprison you, observe you like an animal in a cage, study you like a science experiment gone awry."

"At first?" I echo. I imagine them sitting in the room to the left of the stairs, the furniture uncovered to reveal plush velvety chairs and benches. The chandelier would have been back in place, hanging down from the ceiling, flooding the room with light. Maybe they passed my infant body around the room, a dastardly game of hot potato.

"But then your mother's second in command, a woman named Aura, suggested we destroy you. She believed your birth had released something truly evil. That by exposing you to dark spirits when you were so vulnerable, we'd released the darkest of dark spirits. A darkness that could actually kill a luiseach."

Months ago Nolan and I learned that a luiseach's spirit—unlike the spirits of mere mortals—could not be *taken, damaged, or destroyed* by a ghost or a demon.

Until, apparently, I came along.

"You can imagine what happened after that," Aidan says.

"No," I answer wearily. "I can't."

"This idea spurred panic," Aidan supplies. "Everyone rallied to Aura's side."

"Including Helena." I expect it to come out like a question, but it doesn't.

"Yes," Aidan nods heavily. "I couldn't believe it. Helena and I had been partners throughout our marriage, running this campus together, training young luiseach together. But now she could only see what we'd done—what our science had done. Within minutes of Aura's declaration Helena agreed that the only way to undo the harm we'd done was to eliminate it altogether. She thought that no luiseach would be safe to procreate while you drew breath. That eliminating you could undo the surge of power we'd released. It was as though all the conversations we'd had over the previous nine months had never happened. She insisted that luiseach must continue as they always had, even with our dwindling numbers—helping spirits move on one at a time, exorcising those we didn't get to in time."

"What did you think?"

"I saw our circumstances differently," Aidan continues, raising his voice like he wants to make sure I'm listening. "I thought perhaps the surge of energy released when you were born was something else. A tragedy, yes, but not one without purpose."

"What did you think it was?" I ask, turning around to face him.

"The next step on the evolutionary scale. Like the big bang or the asteroid that killed the dinosaurs."

"That's why you think luiseach are going extinct? You thought I set an asteroid in motion?"

"Not exactly." Aidan turns to face me and takes my hands in his. "I thought you *were* the asteroid. I thought you would be the luiseach to end all luiseach."

CHAPTER TWENTY-THREE

The Middle of Everywhere

Spirits behave differently this close to the equator. What about the rest of us? Is the air different here? Like, if it's thinner up at the North Pole, is it *thicker* down here? Because no matter how many times I try to take a deep breath to calm myself down, it feels like the oxygen can't get in. I try to imagine exactly where we are on the map: somewhere north of Mazatlan, deep in the jungle, in the middle of nowhere. Come to think of it, we're actually in the middle of *everywhere*: close to the equator, almost perfectly centered between the north and south poles.

"I handed you to Victoria so she could take you up to the nursery," Aidan continues, releasing my hands. "I knew you couldn't understand what was happening, but I didn't want you to hear us arguing about your fate."

"Victoria was there?" Aidan nods. Somehow the idea of my old teacher carrying me up the stairs to that breezy room is comforting.

"It seemed like we argued forever, but it can't have been more than an hour. The sound of your cries floating down from the second floor finally ended the argument."

"How?"

"You were hungry, and your mother—Helena," he corrects quickly, "refused to feed you. It was then that I knew there was no changing her mind." His gaze drops to the ground, as though he can't look at me when he says, "So I gave in. I offered to take care of the matter myself. I insisted on . . . finishing the job."

Finishing the job. As though murdering your own child is just a workaday task, like taking out the garbage or doing the dishes. Despite the shade from the trees above us, my skin feels like it's burning.

"But you didn't finish anything."

"No. Victoria brought you to me, and we drove for hours. I didn't have a car seat, so she sat in the back with her arms around you. I wanted to get you as far away as possible, but we didn't have time enough to go far. I didn't have anything to feed you, but you stopped crying when Victoria started playing with you."

"She played with me when I was just born?"

He nods. "Luiseach are different from humans at birth. They can see clearly, form memories, even respond to what's going on around them. She brought a toy from a nursery. Some sort of stuffed bird. She made it look like it was flying over your face. You were riveted."

"An owl." Victoria must have put the stuffed animal back when they returned here. Years later, when her own daughter was born, she must have remembered the comfort that toy gave me and bought an identical toy for Anna.

Ashley always thought I was weird for keeping a taxidermied owl in my bedroom. Now I know that some part of me was trying to replace the toy I loved.

"I sped every mile of the way," Aidan continues. "You fell asleep as we crossed the border into Texas. You were still asleep when we left you at the hospital. We drove back, stopping in the jungle to dig a grave so we'd be covered in mud when we returned. So everyone would believe I'd done what I said I'd do."

"You lied to Helena, to everyone."

"Yes."

"Because you thought I was the luiseach to end all luiseach." That sounds even more ominous than *The Last Luiseach* did.

"Not entirely," Aidan shakes his head in surprise. "True, I didn't agree with Helena, and I still don't. I don't believe luiseach can continue working as we have before. There simply aren't enough of us left to do it—even before you were born, that was the case," he clarifies quickly. "But that's not why I didn't eliminate you."

"Then why?"

"I didn't eliminate you because you were my baby."

"Oh," I say softly, shifting my weight from one leg to the other awkwardly.

"There was no scientific explanation for the way I felt about you," he continues. "Mothers experience a release of hormones after they give birth to help them bond with their babies. I experienced no such thing, and yet I was even weaker than Helena. How could I kill a helpless creature looking up at me with my own eyes?"

"Not just a science experiment?" I bite my lip to try to keep myself from crying (more), but the tears overflow anyway.

I finally understand what Aidan meant when he said he didn't abandon me: he gave me up to *save* me.

Later, after I've taken a shower and gotten dressed—a T-shirt decorated with Audrey Hepburn's face instead of Care Bears, jean shorts with the knife tucked safely into a back pocket—Aidan is waiting for me in the kitchen, standing at the stove over a pot of soup. He's changed into a fresh pair of khakis and a white button-down. He fills a bowl for me. I sit down and begin eating, surprised by how hungry I am.

After a few spoonfuls, I ask, "Helena found out, right? That you didn't . . . eliminate me?"

Aidan sits in a squeaky wooden chair across from me. "It didn't take long for Helena to discover what I'd done."

"How did she know?"

"Helena believed that killing you would undo the surge we'd released when you were born. A year went by, and no luiseach became pregnant. Even with our dwindling numbers, a drought like that was unprecedented. When Helena confronted me, I couldn't lie to her."

"Why not?"

He smiles. "I was never very good at lying to the people I loved. It was a miracle I was able to keep it from her for as long as I did."

I blush, just like any teenager might when her parents talk about loving each other. Ashley always hated it when her parents got lovey-dovey in front of her. *Eww, gross*, she'd moan, acting like she might throw up.

"Helena was furious," Aidan continues. "She insisted that with you alive, our extinction was inevitable, and I couldn't disagree. She demanded I tell her what I'd done with you, insisted she would find you and eliminate you herself. When I refused, she left."

"And that was the beginning of the rift?"

He nods slowly, like moving his head up and down hurts. Helena didn't just leave this *place*. She left *him*. "One by one, as the years went by and no more luiseach were born, those who stood by my side joined her. I could hardly begrudge them their choice," he concedes wearily. "They're frightened about our future, frightened of what our extinction will mean for the human race."

I lift another spoonful to my lips. "So Helena isn't the only luiseach who wants me eliminated?"

Aidan shakes his head and slowly answers, "Lucio and I are the only remaining luiseach who want you alive."

I drop my spoon with a clatter. Tomato soup splashes across the table, onto my T-shirt and even onto Aidan's white button-down. I really shouldn't be allowed to eat brightly colored food like tomato soup and cherry pie and grape juice. But Aidan doesn't seem to notice. At least, he doesn't seem to care.

"That's why I brought you here," he explains. "Once you passed your test, it would only be a matter of time before she found you. She'd be able to sense you now that your powers had been awakened. All luiseach parents can after their offspring turn sixteen. But she and her people cannot step foot inside this compound, not after the way they abandoned it. It's part of the magic that protects this place. They would need the express invitation of someone who still lives here—yours, Lucio's, or my own."

This place isn't just a campus. It's not even a hiding place. It's a *fortress*.

And everything—whether I live or die, whether humanity survives after the extinction of the luiseach—hinges on what I saw in Aidan's lab this morning. Whether or not those spirits can move on by themselves.

"Has a single spirit been able to do it?" I don't have to explain what *it* is.

"No." His voice drops an octave. "I've been trying for sixteen years, and it's never happened."

"Sounds like the other side of the rift has the upper hand."

He nods. "But just after you passed your test, something happened that never happened before."

"What?"

"One of the spirits escaped. Lucio's been tracking it, but—"

"I know," I say. "He told me. It's on the verge of going dark. That shouldn't happen. Not here."

"Exactly," Aidan says, snapping his fingers.

"How can you sound so happy about it?" I shudder, thinking of Anna's spirit refusing to move on. Of the demon that nearly destroyed her.

"Because it means that the spirits are behaving differently."

"Do you know why?"

"I don't—not exactly," Aidan concedes. "But I do have a theory."

I lean back in my chair even though the wood digs into my shoulder blades. "Something tells me I'm not going to like your theory."

Aidan smiles, raising his eyebrow. His cat-green eyes, mirror images of my own, don't blink when he says, "I think the difference is *you*. I've wondered for years what your gifts might be, what skills you might possess. I've always believed it would be your destiny to change everything."

"So then you think Helena was right. Maybe I *am* dangerous somehow."

"No," Aidan says firmly. "But I no longer think I can teach spirits to move on by themselves. However, I'm beginning to believe *you* can."

It's a good thing I'm not eating anymore because I think I would be choking right now if I were.

Most dads just want their kids to get good grades, go to college, that kind of thing. My mentor/father wants me to change the world.

CHAPTER TWENTY-FOUR
Failure

The next day at dawn, instead of taking me back to the play-ground, Aidan leads the way to his lab. Remembering what happened the last time I was here—can that really have been just a day ago?—I climb the steps slowly, shaking as I put one foot in front of the other. If Aidan notices my nerves, he doesn't say so, but clearly Lucio does notice, because he reaches up—he's one step behind me on the stairs—and slips his hand in mine. His grip is reassuring. *You can do this*, it says.

I'm not so sure. Aidan's lab is filled with dozens of spirits.

I squeeze Lucio's hand back.

Both Aidan and Lucio carry enormous flashlights, but the thin beams of light do little to break up the darkness. It should be a million degrees in the long, windowless hallway at the top of the stairs, but it's so cold that I can see my breath.

Before we reach Aidan's lab, I finally find my voice.

"What do you want me to do?" I ask. "How can I help them move on without actually . . . *helping* them move on?"

Aidan turns to look at me. "I'm not sure," he answers honestly. "Start by reaching out for them, one at a time. Try to communicate with them."

"And then what?"

"Then, we'll see."

We'll see. Not exactly the certainty I'd been hoping for. I wanted Aidan to tell me he had a plan, to reassure me that no matter what happened, everything would be okay. To promise he'd get me out of there before my heart starts beating too quickly, before my temperature drops too low.

Instead, he steps forward and opens the door.

I get another glimpse of the lab (it seems like more of a research library) before the spirits hit me like a stiff breeze, as forceful as a slap against my skin. Once more, flashes of their lives and deaths spring up before my eyes. At least this time I'm prepared for the images filling my field of vision: a man throwing a ball for his beloved dog, a woman rocking her baby to sleep, a needle filled with the cancer treatment that stopped working, a man's hand clutching his chest as his heart went into cardiac arrest.

And again I hear their voices. Begging me for their freedom. Pleading with me to help them move on.

Try to communicate with them.

"I can't help you!" I shout between chattering teeth. It's the truth. Even if Aidan hadn't told me not to help them move on, I'd be useless. There are so many of them and only one of me.

"I'm sorry!" I shout as image after image flashes before me like a strobe light gone haywire. My legs feel like they're made of jelly. How am I still standing upright? I become aware of pressure on my shoulders. Lucio must be holding me up from behind. When I slump against him, I feel that each of the muscles in his body is clenched. He's fighting the urge to help these people move on.

"Concentrate," Aidan's deep voice practically growls.

"I'm trying," I whisper. Tears are slipping out of my eyes. My face is so cold that the liquid freezes before it hits my chin.

Please, the spirits plead. I can't tell whether I'm speaking out loud or just in my head when I tell them I'm sorry.

I would if I could.

I'm supposed to be stronger.

But maybe I just made them stronger.

Strong enough to escape Aidan's lab and turn dark.

Strong enough to blanket the entire world in darkness.

I was supposed to be a super-luiseach who could help spirit after spirit move on all at once, like some kind of mystical assembly line. Instead, I'm an experiment gone awry, just like the other luiseach thought.

"You'll never succeed if you can't tune them out," Aidan commands. It sounds like his teeth are clenched. Maybe he's also fighting the urge to help these spirits move on. "Listen to only one of them at a time."

"I can't," I cry, gasping for breath.

"Your ability to feel all of them at once weakens you. You can't focus," Aidan says firmly. "You must learn to control it. Everything but the task at hand should fade into the background."

I try to shout back at him, but I can't. Because I can't speak. I think my mouth has frozen shut. My heart is beating so fast that if it were hooked up to one of the machines in Mom's hospital, instead of one beep after another, it would emit one long, endless wail. I close my eyes and imagine I hear it keening.

No. Not imagine. I *can* hear it. A high-pitched wail that nearly drowns out every other sound.

I don't figure out what the sound is until Lucio drags me from the lab, slamming the door shut behind him. Aidan is shouting in protest, and even in my weakened state, I can tell that this is probably the first time Lucio has ever knowingly disobeyed him.

"They were killing her!" Lucio shouts.

My eyes are still closed. But now all I see is darkness.

Aidan's voice: "Don't be absurd. You know as well as I know that they *can't* kill her."

"Her body was going into shock," Lucio counters. "She's ice cold. We're miles from the nearest hospital."

"And what would you have told the doctors? That despite the tropical climate, this girl managed to develop hypothermia?"

It's the kind of thing I would say, the kind of thing I have thought more than once: *human doctors are useless for paranormal problems.*

"I would've come up with something before I let her freeze to death!"

It's so hard to hear them that it sounds like this argument is happening miles away from me. Lucio folds me into his warm arms. I know he's not taller than I am, but right now he feels like a giant. A strong, friendly giant. Like Fezzik in one of Mom's favorite movies, *The Princess Bride.* When I get home, we'll have a movie night. She'll make popcorn, and we'll watch that movie together, arguing over which of us is hogging the blanket just like we used to.

The last time Mom made popcorn was on New Year's Eve. When it wasn't Mom making the popcorn at all but rather the water demon that had taken over her body.

Maybe normal things like movie nights aren't part of my life anymore.

I'm aware of Lucio's hands rubbing my arms, up and down, up and down, trying to heat up my icy skin. Eventually Aidan's arms wrap around me alongside Lucio's, and I feel my body begin to thaw.

I open my eyes. That's when I discover what that wailing sound was. My mouth wasn't frozen shut after all. When I finally understand why Aidan and Lucio sounded like they were arguing from miles away: I was straining to hear them over the sound of my own voice.

This whole time I've been screaming.

CHAPTER TWENTY-FIVE

Elimination

"I'll draw you a bath," Lucio offers later. *Draw you a bath.* A phrase that doesn't exist outside of old novels. Except, apparently it does for me.

Lucio fills the tub in the bathroom on the second floor until it's nearly overflowing with warm water.

"You should let it cool down a little before you get in," he says, lingering in the doorway. "Too much heat might be a shock to your system."

I nod. I haven't said an actual sentence since we got back to the house. My throat is so hoarse from screaming that I'm not sure what I'll sound like.

"I'll leave you to it," Lucio says, shifting from one foot to the other awkwardly, like he's feeling shy.

"Lucio?" I manage to croak before he walks away. He turns back to face me.

"You said you've lived in Llevar la Luz all your life, right?"

Slowly he nods. I think he knows what I'm getting at.

"You would have been one year old," I say finally.

He nods again. "I remember the sound of them screaming," he says.

"The women?" I prompt. "When they miscarried?" Lucio hesitates, and I add, "I can handle it. I promise."

He takes a deep breath. "I've never heard anything like it since. Not until today," he adds, gesturing to my neck. To the raw, red, exhausted throat beneath. "I crawled into the living room downstairs," he continues. "My parents thought I was sleeping." I imagine Lucio crawling, following the sound of arguing voices. Hiding behind one of the enormous antique chairs. "When my mom saw me crouched in a corner, she carried me back to my room, even though I kicked and screamed bloody murder."

I smile. "Sounds like you were a real angel."

"Let's just say I had a strong sense of self from an early age."

"Right."

"But my mom never lost her patience with me, not even that night, with everything that was going on. She put me to bed and sang to me until I fell asleep." He smiles softly at the memory, then swallows it away. "But I didn't stay sleeping for long. That night I had a nightmare that would recur for weeks."

"What did you dream?"

He doesn't answer right away, like he's not sure he should tell me.

"Say it," I plead. Steam rises from the bathtub behind me.

"I dreamed about Helena squeezing a tiny baby so tight, it was like she was squeezing the life out of her. I dreamed she was trying to kill you."

I shake my head. "Aidan said he was the one who offered to do it."

Lucio shrugs. "I know. But I was a baby. I probably heard one thing and imagined that I saw another, you know?"

"Sure."

"Anyhow, I have to go."

I nod, knowing that in a few minutes I'll hear the familiar roar of Lucio's motorcycle, Clementine, taking off the way it does every day as he tracks the missing spirit.

"Any luck?"

Lucio shakes his head. "Not yet."

"But it still hasn't turned dark, right?"

"I'm not sure," he admits. Before I can say anything—and I was about to say something along the lines of *What do you mean you're not sure? Does the demon we saw have something to do with all this? Is it here to help turn the lost spirit dark?*—Lucio says, "It looks like your bath is the right temperature now." He gestures to the tub behind me. I glance at the still water and am suddenly aware of the ache in my muscles, more intense than anything I've felt before. I guess I never had to work as hard as I did today.

"Thanks," I say as Lucio closes the bathroom door behind him. I listen to his footsteps fade as he walks through the hallway and down the stairs. Then I undress and sink beneath the warm water until my own splashing is the only sound I can hear.

It's the first time I've taken a bath since I learned how Anna died.

After my bath, I change into sweatpants and a sweatshirt I stole from Mom months ago. I grab the owl from the nursery and stick my head outside the open window in my bedroom. I try to concentrate. Try to focus. But instead of Anna, when I close my eyes, the same images I saw in Aidan's lab play out in my mind's eye.

Aidan is right. I can't focus. Because all I can see is the lives led by the spirits I couldn't help.

If I can't even help the spirit of one little girl move on before she turns dark, how will I ever help all of them?

I slam the window shut. Well, *slam* is a bit of an overstatement. My muscles are about as useful as rubber at the moment, so it's more like I struggle to get the window about halfway shut and then give up, leaving the stuffed owl on the windowsill. *Eliminate.* Quietly I say the word out loud. Then again, louder this time. Helena isn't the only one trying to eliminate something. Aidan wants to eliminate the need for luiseach. And he thinks I might be the key to that elimination. Just like *The Last Luiseach* and *The Luiseach to End All Luiseach*, it sounds like the name of a movie, a summer blockbuster: *The Eliminator.*

Lucio carried me down the stairs from Aidan's lab and out into the sunlight today. As we crossed the courtyard, Aidan said, "We'll try again tomorrow." My throat was so sore from screaming that I didn't protest, even though I was literally too frozen in place to be useful in his lab today. If Aidan is wrong, then my . . . *elimination* could save the luiseach species so that they could go on protecting the human race like they have for millennia.

I *will* try again tomorrow. Because if we can't eliminate the need for luiseach in Aidan's lab, then . . .

I shake my head. Aidan will never let Helena eliminate me. Will he?

Strange Words

What a stroke of genius it was to invoke the name Abner Jones; the boy seems more than a little in awe of Aidan's old friend. Each afternoon I come to the coffee shop on Main Street bearing news of another revelation from Professor Jones's files. (No matter that I make them up as I go along.) Nolan takes frantic notes, hanging on my every word. He pretends his interest is just academic, like mine, and I pretend to believe him. I pretend that I don't know that he's trying to make sense of everything that's happened to him since he met the girl he's now tied to.

I think the boy will be particularly excited about today's discovery.

"So," I begin my lie, twirling my curly hair around my finger like I'm unsure of myself, "the university said they can't find most of Professor Jones's files anymore. His wife must have taken them when he died or something."

"Or something," Nolan murmurs, trying to hide a knowing grin.

"But they did manage to find a couple of boxes in their archives, and they let me take them. I think they were glad to get rid of them, honestly." I pause and smile. Reminding him that other people don't care about these

things like we do is an opportunity to strengthen our bond. "Anyway, I keep coming across these words in Professor Jones's files that I don't understand."

"What kind of words?" Nolan asks. He shifts in his seat as though he knows what's coming.

"Well, it's strange. I see the words mentor and protector—and obviously I recognize those words—but they're always used in reference to a word I've never seen before: luiseach." I pronounce the word incorrectly on purpose, pretending not to notice the way the extra syllables make Nolan squirm.

"You've never heard that word before, have you?" I ask innocently.

Nolan doesn't answer, so I go on talking. "In one of the professor's notebooks he writes that relationships between luiseach and their protectors are often incredibly intense. Like, their bond is stronger than the bond between parents and their children, between brothers and sisters."

"So it's like a familial kind of bond?" Nolan breaks in.

"Not exactly," I say. "At least, not according to the professor's notes. Sometimes the intensity of their connection can lead to romance." Nolan can't hide his discomfort: he presses his hands onto the table and tosses his hair away from his face and shifts in his chair.

"You're sure the professor's notes said romance?" he asks.

"Definitely," I answer. "He made it sound really intense. Like protectors and their luiseach literally can't keep their hands off each other." I sigh wistfully, resting my chin on my palm. Nolan lifts his hand off the table, flexing and releasing it restlessly. "I have no idea what all of it means, but it sure sounds romantic, doesn't it?"

Nolan leans back in his chair, raising his arms up like he's given up. "I have never been this confused in my entire life," he says miserably.

I blink innocently. "What do you mean? Because of the word luiseach? I'm sure I can find some sort of explanation for that word in Professor Jones's notes. I just need to keep digging."

"No," Nolan answers. "I don't mean because of the word *luiseach*." He pronounces it correctly.

"Then what?" I ask.

Nolan takes a deep breath and closes his eyes. I sense the instant he decides to tell me everything.

CHAPTER TWENTY-SIX

Argi and Jairo

I spend every day in Aidan's lab, every evening soaking in a tub of warm water, and every night tossing and turning with nightmares while Lucio is out hunting the missing spirit and Aidan is back to his lab to write about what happened during the day in his log.

"Does luiseach work always wear you out like this?" I ask Lucio as I take a bite of soggy cereal one morning. (It's so humid here that Cheerios lose their crunch even before you add any milk.) I'm so hot that my skin itches, even though I know a world of cold waits for me in Aidan's lab like a paranormally powered air conditioner.

He shakes his head. "Just the opposite, actually."

"What do you mean?"

"Well, think about how you feel when you help a spirit move on."

I sigh dramatically. "It's been so long that I can barely remember."

"Sure you can," Lucio counters with a smile, and of course he's right. Because helping a spirit move on usually feels *wonderful*.

"All luiseach gain strength from helping spirits move on."

I nod. Luiseach literally means *light-bringer*; I never feel quite so much light as when a spirit has just passed through me to the other side. But now every day at Aidan's lab I'm not just over-whelmed by spirits; I'm also resisting my instincts: all I want is to help them move on, and I can't allow myself to so much as try. I feel like the least sunshine-y version of myself. I don't know how Aidan has done this for so long, though I guess it explains why he seems to be the world's most serious luiseach. It explains Victoria too: by the time I knew her, she had given up her powers and was unable to follow the instincts that had guided her since her sixteenth birthday—so she was a whole lot creepier than she was cheerful.

"After so many days of *not* helping spirits move on, I think my light is about to go out."

Lucio smiles sympathetically. "I know it's hard." He drums his fingers on the table across from me. I watch the white tattoo dance on his finger as he moves.

"What does it say?" I ask finally.

"What does what say?"

"Your tattoo." I point with my spoon. "I can tell that it's words, but I don't know what they are or what they mean."

"They're not really words," Lucio explains. "They're names."

"Whose?"

"My parents." He reaches his arm across the table and spreads his fingers so I can see. "Argi," he says, tracing the letters on one side. "That's my mother. And Jairo," he adds, turning his hand. "That's my dad."

When he says the names out loud, I finally understand something that eluded me before now. How did I not put the pieces together sooner? If Nolan were here, he'd have figured it out ages ago.

Lucio said that his parents were killed for what they believed in, that luiseach on the other side of the rift were interrogating them for information. But Argi and Jairo kept their secret. And now I finally understand that their secret was *me*. They must have ventured outside the borders of Llevar la Luz, where Helena found them and overpowered them, trying to force them to reveal where I was. They died rather than give me up.

"I'm sorry," I whisper, tears springing to my eyes.

"Not your fault," Lucio answers firmly. His hand is still splayed on the table in front of me, and I put my own on top of it. His fingers lace their way through mine. I squeeze. "It was for the greater good." I watch his Adam's apple bob up and down as he swallows. "Our work is more important than two people's lives, even if those two people were my parents."

I blink away the tears trying to work their way to the surface; it doesn't seem right that I should be crying when Lucio isn't. Maybe Aidan is right: my sensitivity is a weakness. I don't think I could be as strong as Lucio. I don't think I could give my mother up for anything.

"I can ask Aidan to give you a day off," Lucio offers. "You don't look so good," he adds, with a grin, trying to make a joke. "Your hair seems to have taken on a life of its own."

I reach up and pat my frizzball. I'm pretty sure it's growing straight out from my scalp instead of, you know, down my back like other people's. "My hair has *always* had a life of its own. I'm pretty sure it regularly goes on adventures that I'm not a part of."

"Like when you're sleeping, it just walks away and heads to the nearest town to party with the locals?"

I nod. "Exactly. Then before I can wake up, it plops itself right back on my head, too tired from living a life more exciting than mine to bother trying to look halfway presentable."

Lucio laughs, but I shake my head, standing up so quickly that my chair falls to the floor beneath me. I shouldn't be sitting here having fun. Not when people like Lucio's parents died to protect me. I decide that there will be no days off and no more complaints about how hard this is. The very least I can do in return is try my best.

"Where are you going?" Lucio asks.

"To work," I answer quickly. I practically run out the front door, hoping Lucio won't follow because I can't staunch my tears any longer and I don't want him to see me crying.

Who am I to be so protected? What is my life up against Lucio's parents or Aidan's or all of these spirits he's forcing to remain on Earth?

I open the door to Aidan's lab, and the spirits take hold all at once.

My teeth are chattering as I finally begin to understand: Lucio doesn't think he lost his parents for any *one* life. He thinks that protecting me—saving me—will save *every*thing. Everyone. And that's bigger to him than a few lives lost along the way.

But only if Aidan is right about me.

I close my eyes. Last night my hot bath was waiting for me the instant I arrived at the mansion. I undressed, my muscles sore from the effort of staying upright. I thought I'd never want to take another bath again after I learned how Anna died, but for the past few days I've luxuriated in the warm water. Before I stepped into the tub, I paused to stare at myself in the mirror. I studied the bulge of my biceps and triceps, the shadow of a six-pack across my belly. I never knew I would be this strong. After all, klutzes like me are rarely athletic, right?

Despite my new muscles, I felt weaker than ever before. Each day, no matter how I beg these spirits to move on, no matter how I plead with them to come to me only one at a time, I can't gain control. They overtake me every time.

I submerged my head under the bathwater, trying to literally drown out the sound of the voice in my head reminding me each and every day that I'm a failure.

Today I know Lucio's parents died because they believed in Aidan's theories, because they believed in *me*.

I open my eyes. I'm sitting on the floor outside Aidan's lab; Aidan is crouching on the ground beside me. He must have dragged me here after I failed once more.

"*Again*," I say, peeling myself off the floor for the umpteenth time. I will do this all day long until the sun goes down and my fingers are blue and my tear ducts have frozen shut. "I'm ready to try again."

CHAPTER TWENTY-SEVEN

Real Luiseach Work

That night, while Lucio is out scouring the countryside for a demon and Aidan is holed up in his lab, I decide to do something productive for a change. I take the stuffed owl down into the backyard. I hold it up to the sky. I must keep Anna from going dark. I *will* keep Anna from going dark. But no matter how hard I concentrate, I can't find her. The tropical air remains warm on my skin; my heart maintains its steady beat.

Maybe she doesn't want to be found, like the spirit Lucio is hunting.

Thunder rumbles in the distance. We're in for a storm. Warm rain begins to fall, drenching my skin and hair. But I don't stop, not even when lightning illuminates the night sky. I stand up to my ankles in mud, my arms aching from holding the owl out in front of me. The rain passes and the sky clears, and all the while, I stand my ground.

I'm in the same spot when Lucio finds me at dawn. Not that I'm still upright. I must have sat at some point, must have hugged the owl to me like a Teddy bear, must have fallen asleep beneath the night sky.

"You're covered in mud," Lucio says.

I shrug.

"Come with me." He puts his hand in mine and pulls me to my feet.

"Where?"

"You'll see."

I shake my head. "Aidan is expecting me," I protest, trying to pull my hand out from his, but his grip is firm. No matter how many muscles I may have built up here in Mexico, I'm definitely not as strong as this guy.

"You need a day off from the lab. Yesterday you looked like you didn't know how much more of this you could take."

"That was before . . ." I begin, trailing off.

"Before what?"

I bite my lip. "Before I realized just how important this work was."

"You mean before you realized my parents died to protect you," Lucio counters bluntly. I don't know what to say, so I just look down. My newly muscled legs are tan, popping out from beneath my homemade denim cut-offs.

"I told you it wasn't your fault."

I shake my head. "It's not that simple."

"Yes," Lucio says firmly. "It *is* that simple. Besides, if you keep going like this, you're not going to be strong enough to make any progress in Aidan's lab anyway."

Lucio leads the way to the playground. I finally understand why it's called that. My lessons may have been hard, but when they were actually successful, they were also kind of *fun*. At least, they were certainly more fun than anything I've been doing since.

"Today you're going to help me do some real luiseach work."

"What's that?"

"You know I've been tracking the spirit that escaped." I nod. "I still haven't found him. But I figure between the two of us, we might be able to get him."

"Between the two of us?" I echo.

"Our combined strength," Lucio explains. "You and Aidan hadn't gotten to this lesson—it's a little advanced, but . . ."

"Desperate times call for desperate measures," I suggest.

"Something like that," Lucio agrees. "Remember when Aidan held your hands and watched you work?"

"Of course," I answer. I also remember the name of the spirit I helped move on that day: Eddie Denfield. The girl he loved was Meghan Waters.

"Well, today we're going to take that one step further."

I raise my eyebrow.

"There's strength in numbers," Lucio explains.

It's worth a try. If it fails, then at this point, really, what's one more failure? But if we succeed . . . then maybe together we'll find not only this one missing spirit but eventually Anna too.

"Okay," I say finally. "Tell me what to do."

Lucio holds his arms out. "Take my hands." His hands are warm in mine. I can feel the calluses on his palms from where he grips Clementine's handles. "Close your eyes," Lucio instructs, and I do. "His name was Michael Weir. He lived in San Antonio, Texas, and taught algebra at the local high school." Lucio adjusts his grip on my hands, and for just a second I see a flash of a man's face.

I gasp, opening my eyes and dropping Lucio's hands. I'm able to see my fellow luiseach standing across from me, and there is no chill, no quickening pulse—nothing to indicate that a spirit is near. "How could I see him?" I ask breathlessly.

"You were seeing what I've seen," Lucio explains. "I've been close to his spirit before, close enough to see the details of his life. Now you need to know exactly what we're looking for so we can combine our powers."

"Does that mean you could see what I was thinking of?"

Lucio nods. "A little girl with dark hair and black eyes."

"Her name was Anna," I supply. "She was Victoria's daughter. I've been trying to get her to move on, but I can't seem to reach her."

"I know about Anna," Lucio says. "And the time isn't right for her yet."

"What do you mean the time isn't right?" I argue. "If we wait too long—"

"This won't work if you're thinking about Anna!" Lucio practically shouts. Even when he told me about his parents, he didn't look this distressed. "We need to think of Michael Weir and only Michael Weir."

"I can't just abandon—"

"This is one of the most important lessons you'll learn. This is an enormous part of how we protect humans—finding spirits before they turn dark. Time is running out for Michael Weir. Do you understand?"

I've never heard Lucio so worked up. Not when he was arguing with Aidan on my first night here, not even when he was worried I might go into hypothermic shock. So I nod. "The best defense is a good offense," I say drily.

Lucio nods. "Exactly."

I take his hands in mine and close my eyes. "Let's try again."

This time, when the image of Michael Weir flashes into my consciousness, I'm ready for it. There are a thousand tiny cuts on his face where the glass from his car window rained down on him. He was teaching his niece to drive, and neither of them saw the tractor-trailer running the red light up ahead. He never had any children of his own, but he loved his niece like she was his daughter. He helped her with their math homework every night. She survived the accident, but she hasn't gotten over it. She thinks her beloved uncle's death was her fault. He died the instant the truck hit their little compact car, and Aidan drew Michael Weir's spirit here almost as soon as it left his body. He trapped it in his lab, where it had time to grow frustrated. To grow desperate. It wanted to linger long enough to tell the girl it wasn't her fault.

But spirits who linger rarely get a chance to actually finish their unfinished business.

His spirit escaped from Llevar la Luz weeks ago and has been trying to get back to Texas. But it's disoriented; it doesn't know which way is north. It doesn't know the difference between night and day.

Everywhere the spirit looks, it sees only fire.

Now I do open my eyes. "We're too late," I say breathlessly.

"What do you mean?"

"His spirit's already gone dark."

Lucio opens his eyes. "How can you tell?"

"I saw fire." Thanks to Victoria, I know that there are different kinds of demons. The demon I defeated on New Year's Eve was a water demon, vanquished by fire. It drowns its victims, taking strength from the energy released when they die. She told me about earth demons, who tend to bury their victims alive.

And she told me about fire demons, who can burn their victims to death, sometimes from the inside out. Suddenly it hits me like a blowtorch to the brain. That man in the parade bursting into flames, the red demon that smelled like gasoline, that was Michael Weir's spirit! Lucio didn't recognize him because he had already turned. I didn't know about him at the time so I couldn't put the pieces together.

"Close your eyes. Concentrate. What else do you see?"

I squeeze Lucio's hands in mine. "I see . . . a village. Or the remains of one. It's already burning." The demon is already so much stronger than it was that night. Now, instead of a single person, it's setting a whole town on fire.

"What does the place look like?" Lucio asks desperately. "Anything to help me identify it."

"Stucco buildings . . . no more than one-room shacks, really. They have thatched roofs, and the jungle vines grow up and around them. But half the roofs are burning now."

Lucio tightens his grip. "What else?"

"There's a wheelbarrow with a name on it. I can't quite . . ." I squeeze my eyes shut, trying to make out the letters before they catch fire. "Lado Selva," I say finally.

Before I know it, Lucio is pulling me down the hill, shouting Aidan's name.

"Lucio!" I shout. "What's Lado Selva?"

"It's the name of a town," he says without turning around to look at me. "It comes from *al lado de la selva.*"

"What does that mean?"

"Beside the jungle. It's a tiny little town in the jungle."

He shouts Aidan's name again as we emerge into the court-yard. But the black SUV isn't out front like usual.

"He must have gone into town for supplies." Lucio throws his hands up in frustration. "He could still be back in time to—"

"Lucio!" I interrupt. "There isn't any time to wait. We have to get to those people *now*."

Lucio runs his fingers along his cropped hair, his tattoo practically iridescent in the sunlight. "I don't know if I'm strong enough—I've never faced a demon in full force."

"Then today's your lucky day," I say, reaching into my back pocket and pulling out the knife. "Because I have."

CHAPTER TWENTY-EIGHT
The Town on Fire

Lucio gasps, "Where did you get that?" He reaches out and holds the weapon, turning it over in his hands.

"Victoria gave it to me. I used it for my test."

"Do you know how rare these are?" he asks.

I shake my head.

"Aidan invented them, years ago. He only had enough power to make five of them."

It's the first time I've heard much about the kind of work he did before the rift, back when he was a respected and powerful luiseach. I wonder what else he created before I came along and changed everything. "He must have given one to Victoria."

"And then she gave it to you."

Lucio places the knife in my palm and closes my fingers over it. "Come on." He grabs a helmet from his handlebars and puts it on my head, smashing the frizzball.

I swing one leg over Clementine and lean against Lucio when he sits down in front of me. I feel the sweat on his back through our T-shirts—his covered in orange and white stripes while mine is bright green—but it doesn't gross me out. Instead, I lean against him, holding him tight. I don't want to face what we're about to face alone.

As the bike's engine roars to life, Lucio looks back at me with concern. "You ready to do some real luiseach work?" I can tell he's not sure we can handle this, but he's determined to try.

I nod. I will help fill the gap in his confidence. My fingertips are tingling, there are butterflies in my stomach, and my breath is coming quick and short. It takes me a second to recognize it, but it's undeniable: I'm exhilarated.

I hold tight as we drive, squinting in the sunlight. I glance around furtively as we ride along, as though I think Helena might jump out at any second, hiding behind the trees with their enormous leaves.

There would be a million places to hide in this jungle.

But the trees around us are empty. Lucio veers to the right so suddenly, I have to dig my fingers into his rib cage to keep from falling. I can feel his heartbeat beneath my fingertips, feel his chest rise and fall with each breath, and soon we are breathing in unison.

I feel the town before I see it. I mean, I feel the heat of a place on fire. The taste of smoke fills my throat. I can barely breathe.

The town appears before us as suddenly as a mirage. The road widens, and there are dilapidated stucco structures on either side of us, not one more than a single story high. The only colors are the brown dirt at our feet, the blue sky above us, and the orange fire in between, climbing so high that it all but blocks out the green of the surrounding trees.

Lucio turns off the bike.

People are rushing from one building to another, trying to douse the flames, desperate to keep their town from burning to dust. Their wretched shouts fill the air, even thicker than the smoke.

"Don't worry," Lucio says suddenly, jumping off the motorcycle. "You're safe here."

I must look at him like he's speaking Japanese—safe, with the flames rising higher and higher and a demon who should not have been able to turn dark in the first place, just waiting to fight us off? I mean, I know that technically a demon can't kill me, but I wouldn't exactly call this *safe*. "I didn't mean *that*," Lucio adds quickly. "I mean we're still technically on land that's part of Llevar la Luz. Helena can't get to you, even here." No wonder the trees we passed were empty. I wonder just how big Llevar la Luz is.

"Do these people know *why* their town is on fire?" I have to shout to be heard over the roar of the flames. We walk further into town. Hot ashes float down around us like snowflakes from hell.

"Not exactly," Lucio answers. "This town has been here for centuries. Its inhabitants have passed down story after story of the strange things going on at the campus in the jungle."

"They know about us?"

"Let's just say that around here they have a deeply held respect for the afterlife."

"But nothing like this has ever happened before," I insist. "You said spirits don't usually turn dark this close to the equator." A hot wind kicks up and swirls around us as the townspeople desperately try to squelch the flames.

"I know. Things are different now."

"Aidan thinks the difference might be me. But what if it's the growing darkness?"

Lucio cocks his head to the side. "It might be. This never used to happen. And like I said, it's become more organized recently. Plus, Aidan has a theory that there's someone, some-*thing* who sensed the rift in the luiseach community and is using that weakness to summon dark spirits." My heart nearly stops. *Organized. Weakness. Rift.*

"This all started when I was born, didn't it?" Maybe it doesn't matter whether the spirits are behaving differently because of me or because of the growing darkness. Maybe one is connected to the other.

Lucio looks at me, knowing I'm not going to like his answer. "Over the last sixteen years Aidan's detected a shift among spirits. He doesn't know what it means yet, but he's certain there's a pattern."

"What kind of pattern?"

"Dark spirits and demons are growing stronger."

I bet Nolan could have helped figure out the pattern. I can only imagine how different all of this would be if he had been here with me since the beginning, performing research for Aidan, trying just as hard as Aidan to find answers. Maybe he would have even found some.

"Can you sense the demon?" he asks. I nod. Lucio stops dead in his tracks. Despite the flames growing ever higher around us, Lucio and I feel a cool breeze coming from down the road.

Lucio starts walking in the direction of the chill, and I follow, placing my feet in the dusty footprints his steps leave behind. Even though he's not much taller than I am, his feet are bigger than mine, and I feel like a little kid every time I place one of my sneakers in the spot where his dust-covered boot was seconds before. Lucio's wearing shorts, and instead of looking at where we're going, I'm watching the muscles in his calves flex and release with each step. He certainly looks strong enough to confront a demon.

When he stops, I practically crash into him.

"In there," Lucio whispers, nodding in the direction of a squat stucco building on our left. It's so small that it can't possibly have more than one room. An icy breeze blows its splintered wooden door open, bringing a wall of smoke along with it, despite the fact that it's the only building in sight that isn't actually on fire. The door bangs against the tiny building with a loud crash as goose bumps rise on my sweaty skin.

"Why did the demon choose this town?" I ask. "These people are completely helpless."

"Exactly," Lucio says. "The same way we gather strength from helping spirits move on, a demon gathers strength from destroying spirits."

Despite the breeze coming from the darkness just a few steps away, I don't think I've ever felt so hot. Somewhere inside a man screams in pain. I grab Lucio's hand, and we head toward the door.

CHAPTER TWENTY-NINE
The Fire Demon

Only the corners of the one-room shack are dark. The curtains around the windows—little more than holes in the wall—have burnt down to ash, letting all the sunlight in.

One human is crouched in a corner of the otherwise empty house—where there might once have been a table and chairs, a bed, an icebox, now there are only piles of soot.

A second human stands in the center of the room, practically bathing in the sunlight. He doesn't look up when we enter. He keeps his focus set on the man cowering in the corner, muttering in Spanish. I don't have to be fluent in the language to understand what he's saying: he's begging for his life.

The man standing in the center of the room laughs at the other man's pleas. He stands perfectly straight, nearly a foot taller than Lucio and me. He's not wearing a shirt, and his flesh is covered in sweat and bright pink, like he sat in the sun too long. He's barely human anymore: the demon's possessing him, just like he did the woman the other night. It's too late for her, but not for this man. Not if Lucio and I act quickly enough.

It's easy to see why the demon chose this man. His muscles ripple beneath his skin. The combination of this human's strength with the power of the demon would make it easy for this demon to overtake everyone else in this tiny village. It could go on a spree, gathering strength from each kill until it's all but unstoppable.

The sound of a woman outside screaming in agony as her home burns to the ground fills the air. Possessed by the demon, the tall man smiles.

He drags the smaller man from the corner into the light in the center of the room. I can't help it: I gasp. The victim's skin is covered in burns. Who knows how long the demon has been toying with him? The skin on the smaller man sizzles beneath the demon's grip, tight around his neck.

My gasp draws the demon's attention. It fixes its gaze on me. The tall man's eyes have turned bright orange, like the demon is burning him from the inside out. Without realizing it, I reach for Lucio's hand and squeeze. "I've never exorcised a demon like this," he whispers.

"Like this?" I echo.

"Already in possession of a human. About to go in for the kill."

I can feel the demon's breath: hot as though he's about to breathe fire like some kind of dragon. But the room is so cold that when Lucio and I exhale, we can see our breath.

Every muscle in Lucio's body is flexed. His eyes are closed and his teeth clenched. He's still looking for Michael Weir, the algebra teacher from San Antonio.

But Michael Weir is gone. What was left of his spirit vanished as it went dark, morphing into the demon. Soon Michael Weir's family and students won't remember him; even his beloved niece won't remember him. She'll throw away every picture of him, wondering why she's smiling in photos with a stranger.

It's too late for Michael Weir. But it's not too late for the two people in front of us. Not yet.

I close my eyes. I draw the spirit of the demon's intended victim close, letting his life wash over me. He has two children, neither older than six. He works on a farm miles away, picking tomatoes that will be shipped to American grocery stores, still fresh from the vine. He walks to work every morning before dawn and comes home each night after dark. The demon has held him in this shack for hours. He's exhausted. But no matter how tired he is, his mouth never stops moving; he never stops begging for his life. He wants to live. He *has* to live.

Suddenly I can see his family wailing with grief, his wife raking her fingers across her cheeks in agony. I know I'm seeing what will happen if he dies.

I perceive the larger man's spirit next, struggling to survive beneath the weight of the demon. This is his house. He works on the farm too. An image of his life flashes before me: he is the fastest picker on the vine, his long arms and legs allowing him to reach farther than any of his coworkers. I can see his dreams: he longs to get away from this place. He dreams of cooler nights and seeing snow for the very first time.

I'm concentrating so hard, I don't notice when my hair catches fire.

"Sunshine!" Lucio shouts as if I'm far away instead of standing right beside him. He grabs me, wrapping my face in his arms and squeezing. I can't breathe. He's trying to smother the flames, but I'm getting smothered right along with them.

As the world fades to black, I'm aware of the sound of laughter. The demon is pleased with itself. I struggle against Lucio's hold as he drags me out of the shack and into the bright sunlight.

"No!" I try to disentangle myself from Lucio's embrace, kicking against the dry ground like I think I can run back into the cottage, even with Lucio's arms around me.

"Sunshine, what were you thinking?" he shouts. He loosens his grip just for a second, but it's long enough for me to take a deep breath. I cough as the taste of burnt hair fills my throat.

"Let me go!" I manage, pushing against Lucio's chest. If we wait much longer, it will be too late to save the two men we left inside. Lucio shifts his grip so his fingers are wrapped around my hair like a human ponytail holder, snuffing out the little fire that remains. I reach up and pat my head; instead of the usual frizzball, my hair stops just above my shoulders. There are patches in the back where it has been singed off completely, like I've been given a buzz cut along my neckline.

"I'm okay," I insist. Lucio's hands are still on me, his fingers grazing the bare spots on my scalp. There are welts rising on his palms where the fire burned him. They look painful, but Lucio and I both know they will heal: demons can wound us, but they can't damage us beyond repair.

"You won't be able to help anyone if you're on fire," Lucio snaps, dropping his hands. "Why weren't you using your weapon in there?"

If Aidan were here, he would say that my sensitivity got in the way again. This time it not only kept the weapon from manifesting quickly; it kept me from using it at all. He would know that instead of focusing on the task at hand, I was thinking about the man with two children and a baby on the way, about the man who had never seen snow.

"We should get out of here," Lucio says. "We'll come back with Aidan."

By then it will be too late. These two men will be gone, and the demon will have moved on to its next victim. We ran away from this demon once before; we're not going to do it again.

I think of the tall man's dreams of snow as I pull myself to my feet. Of his spirit being crushed beneath the weight of the demon as surely as a body can be crushed beneath bricks and mortar as I reach into the back pocket of my ragged denim shorts.

I think of the smaller man's little girl as I put one foot in front of the other.

Of his wife, pressing her hands to her swollen belly, of the way she will scream if he dies as I hold the knife out in front of me.

At once I'm not afraid of the enormous man waiting inside. I'm holding the old knife in front of me like a sword.

"I can do this," I promise Lucio.

I will fight this demon.

I will not let it kill the man at its feet.

I will not let it destroy the man it has taken possession of.

CHAPTER THIRTY

The Storm

Inside the shack the demon takes one hot step toward me, dragging the human behind him. I can feel that the smaller man's spirit is already loosened from his flesh. He's beginning to die.

The knife twitches in my grip, but I hold fast, waiting for it to become whatever it needs to become to save the day.

It stays a knife.

"Sunshine?" Lucio says, no more than one step behind me. The knife twitches again, violently this time, its dull blade ripping a gash in my skin.

Reflexively I open my hand and the knife begins to fall.

"No!" I shout, reaching for it. But before I can catch it, it disappears in front of me with a deafening *crack* that releases a burst of light so bright, it's almost blinding.

Fire. How could we have lost so quickly?

The crack fills the shack again. It isn't fire after all.

It's a bolt of lightning.

The weapon hasn't disappeared—it's becoming a storm.

Clouds cover the shack's ceiling, thick and black like Ridgemont on its dreariest day. The roof dissolves in the fog above us. I jump at the sound of thunder and a flash of lightning, together in perfect unison. I hold my breath.

The rain starts.

This is no mere drizzle. *This* is a pounding, driving rain, accompanied by wind that whips what's left of my hair into my face. The clouds overhead are so thick that the only light left comes from the piercing moments filled with lightning.

Crack, flash. I see the large man drop the smaller one at his feet. Over the wind I hear him shout when the spray touches his pink flesh.

Crack, flash. The large man falls to his knees.

Crack, flash. I fall to mine.

I can actually *feel* the demon moving around inside the tall man's body, holding tighter to his insides, trying to bury itself deeper in his flesh. I sense it so intensely that it's as though it's happening to *me. Crack, flash.* I curl into the fetal position. The pain is like nothing I've ever felt before, like red hot fingers are twisting their way through my intestines. I open my mouth and let the rainwater fill me, hoping it will drip down into my body and cool my insides.

The pain is extraordinary. *Crack, flash.* The man and I are crawling on the ground, our bodies mirror images of agony. Lucio must see me falter, because soon I feel his hands over my own, lacing his fingers through mine, like Mom's hands when I hurt myself as a child: *squeeze my hand as hard as it hurts.*

Crack, flash. The tall man and I fling out our arms, our mouths twisting in so much pain that we can't even scream.

The demon is being dragged through his flesh. It loses hold of his guts and wraps its hands around his kidneys, then moves up to his ribcage, and finally twists its fingers around his heart.

No, I think. *Not his heart.*

Grabbing hold of the heart is how a demon kills the humans it possesses. It squeezes until the blood stops flowing. Or maybe this demon will just set his heart on fire. This demon is determined to get at least one kill in today. His strength is extraordinary.

"We're losing him," I gasp, rainwater running into my eyes and mixing with my tears.

"What are you talking about?" Lucio shouts. "We're soaking this demon! It's not going to be able to withstand this much longer."

No, not much longer. But it doesn't need a lot of time to finish the job.

If the demon stops the heart from beating, this suffering man won't just die; his spirit will be *destroyed.* Over time everyone who knew him, everyone who ever loved him will forget him, as though he never existed at all.

I muster all my strength and get to my feet, gasping for air. The rain is so thick, a person could drown in here, but I manage to take a deep breath and run headlong into the enormous man in front of us. When I crash into him, it feels like crashing into a soaking wet wall.

But it's enough. The impact causes the demon to loosen its grip, though I feel it struggling to regain hold. The wall of a man collapses to the floor, taking me along with him. I scream, feeling the demon's every movement in my own body. I fall away from the man's body, and we are lying on the ground retching in pain. The rain beats down as Lucio runs to help.

Time slows just like it did when I defeated the water demon on New Year's Eve. I stare at the rain: it looks frozen in time. No—it's actually *frozen*, turning from rain into icicles that crash onto the ground around us. Suddenly I know exactly what I have to do. I grab an enormous icicle and plunge it deep into the chest of the possessed man.

At once I feel the demon disintegrate. The man exhales, and a cloud of dark ash floats into the air above us and disappears. The ice melts, splashing across the floor, leaving no evidence of what just happened. The man's chest is smooth and unbroken. Only the demon was stabbed.

"Sunshine!" Lucio shouts. Above us the storm clouds part. The knife reappears and drops, landing with a tiny *ping*. The ceiling is right back where it used to be, the sun streaming in through the uncovered windows. I lie back in a patch of light.

"I'm okay," I pant.

"What were you thinking?" Lucio asks, crouching beside me. He wraps his arms around me. The smaller man has already run out the door of the shack, and beneath me the larger man is unconscious, but I feel his pulse, steady and strong.

"The demon was about to kill him," I explain. "I could *feel* it."

"You actually knew the exact moment the demon went in for the kill?"

I nod. My throat is so raw that speaking hurts.

"Wow. From where I stood, it looked like we were winning— the demon was on the run. But *you* knew what was going on inside that man? You *felt* what the demon was doing?"

I nod again, pressing myself up to stand. Lucio pulls at the bottom of his T-shirt until a piece of cloth rips off. He uses it to bind my hand, still bleeding from where the weapon cut me before it turned into a storm. I'm shaking. I can still feel the shadow of the demon's hands all over me.

Suddenly I can't keep myself from crying.

Lucio holds me as the sobs rattle me to my core. He strokes my hair and kisses my forehead.

Finally I feel strong enough to make a joke. "Is this what you had in mind when you said we'd be doing some real luiseach work today?"

Lucio laughs so hard that I can feel his chest shaking against my own. He drops his arms and laces his fingers through mine once more. We're still holding hands when we emerge from the shack into the sunlight.

The air is thick with smoke, but not a single flame remains. The entire town is drenched. The storm cloud covered all of Lado Selva, extinguishing the fires. The townspeople cheer when they see Lucio and me. They might not know exactly what we are, but they know the darkness that blanketed their small town has vanished into thin air. Above us the sun beats down, as bright and hot as ever. The wet ground practically sizzles beneath our feet.

"How do you feel?" Lucio asks.

I look at him like he's just asked me whether the sky is blue, a question with an answer so obvious, it's hardly worth asking. Every muscle in my body hurts. It feels like enormous bruises are blossoming on my internal organs from the demon's phantom grip. I'm covered in dirt and sweat, and my throat is raw from breathing in that hot, fiery air. Tears have dried on my face, and my clothes are stained with soot and ash. There's an unconscious man lying on the floor of the shack behind us who will never fully understand what happened to him. Another man has been reunited with his family. I search the crowd until I see him: his hand is resting on his wife's swollen belly, and a little girl is burying her head against his legs while a little boy wraps his arms around his father's waist.

I turn to Lucio. "I feel"—I pause—"*good*," I answer finally. Not just good: I feel like *myself* again. "How's that possible?"

"Real luiseach work," Lucio answers with a grin, like that explains everything. Which, I guess, it does. He pulls me toward the motorcycle.

"Wait!" I shout, turning to run back to the shack. There is a crowd of people in there now, attending to the man on the ground. I have to crawl between their legs to find what I almost left behind.

I slip the rusty knife back into my pocket where it belongs and run back outside.

"Can I ask you something?" I say before I swing my leg over trusty Clementine.

"'Course," Lucio answers, fastening his helmet's strap around his neck and handing me mine.

"Aidan's research is all about humans moving on without us—and if most of them could, they would, right?" Lucio nods. "But Michael Weir's spirit escaped Aidan's lab and turned dark because he thought he had unfinished business here on Earth. And he's not the only spirit in the world who feels like that—that his life got snuffed out too soon. What about the others who don't want to move on?"

Lucio cocks his head to the side. "Aidan has theories for that too. He thinks that over time spirits might be able to linger without going dark."

"But how much time?" My skin is still pink from exposure to the fire demon's heat. "What if we're extinct before that happens?"

"We'll just have to eliminate all the dark spirits before we go."

Yet another use for the word *eliminate*. Lucio makes it sound so simple.

Certain Powers

Nolan is so obviously heartsick that, under different circumstances, I might actually feel sorry for the boy. But instead, I keep my focus on using his weakness to my advantage. To his credit, I don't think he's the type to spill his secrets easily. Lucky for me, he is so tied up in knots over the girl that he can't help himself.

"I'm supposed to be protecting her," he moans miserably. "But I don't even know where she is!"

I nod sympathetically. I know exactly *where she is. I just can't get there.*

"But Victoria's letter"—how I hate saying that woman's name, even now—"said that it was your job to guard information. You can do that even when she's thousands of miles away. I can help you."

"I know," Nolan nods. "You have *been helping me, sharing what you found in the professor's papers. It's just a matter of time before we find something that will be useful to her."*

The poor boy waits eagerly every day as I show up with a fresh notebook or file folder filled with the professor's notes. He pores over them each day, as though all the information he's supposed to be guarding is just another page away, as though the very next line might be the one that explains everything. He's waiting to call Sunshine until he's found the answers he's looking for: why they can't touch, why her mentor thinks luiseach are going extinct, why she's been taken so far from him.

He has no idea that all of my research is fake. That I'm the one writing barely sensible scribbles in the tattered notebooks he believes sat in the university's basement for so long.

"But," he continues, "there's been nothing to make heads or tails of Sunshine's message."

"Maybe we should listen to it again."

Nolan reaches for his phone and presses play. I've heard this message at least a half dozen times by now, and every time my body reacts to that girl's voice: goose bumps prickle on my skin; a knot of adrenaline surges across my belly.

Halfway through the message I reach out and press pause. "What does she mean by handling multiple spirits?"

"The day before she left with him, she had a sort of . . . breakdown in the hospital parking lot. There was an accident, and there were multiple casualties, and there were just too many spirits coming at her at once."

"What do you mean, a breakdown?"

Nolan shrugs. "I wasn't there. But she told me it was terrifying. Her heart was pounding, her temperature dropped, and she could barely move."

"Wow. Sounds scary." In fact, it sounds like a weakness. I force my lips into a straight line.

Nolan nods. "It was." He presses play again. Sunshine's voice fills the room once more, finally saying the words I was most hoping to hear: I wish you were here. Because if she wants Nolan there, he can go, even with

Aidan's protections in place. And I can go with him, as long as he wants me at his side.

"I should have called her back." Nolan speaks over her voice asking him to do just that.

"You wanted to wait until we found some information that could help her." He's told me as much before.

"That's not the only reason."

"It's because you can't touch her." Nolan nods like his head weighs a million pounds. I bite my lip as though I'm trying to decide whether or not to confess something. Finally I say, "There's something I saw in my research. I wasn't sure whether I should tell you—"

"Tell me," Nolan interrupts, and his voice is so firm that it almost makes me jump.

"Well," I begin, "I saw something in the professor's notes about certain powers a luiseach's mentor can have." I pronounce the word correctly now, just as Nolan taught me. "A mentor can"—I pause as though I'm searching for the right word, as though I haven't planned out every aspect of this conversation—"can control certain aspects of his mentee's life."

"Like what?" Nolan asks darkly.

I shake my head frantically. "Maybe I shouldn't have said anything. It's just . . . I couldn't think of any other explanation for why you two can't touch each other! Not when other protectors and luiseach can."

"So you think her mentor"—to Nolan's credit, he's never actually told me Aidan's name—"put some kind of spell on her so she feels sick anytime she touches another person?" Nolan shakes his head, answering his own question. "No. I've seen her touch her mom, touch Victoria. There must be something different about when we touch."

I look down at the table, tracing the wood with my fingers like I'm too shy to look into his eyes when I say, "Maybe it's because when the two of you touch, it's a romantic sort of touch. You know, not platonic."

I figured this out weeks ago—Aidan's machinations are the only explanation for what's going on between Nolan and Sunshine. I was pleased that Aidan thought to do such a thing, to limit her attachments to the human world. At least some part of him couldn't deny what might have to be done.

When I look up, Nolan is blushing feverishly. "But why would he do that?"

"To control her," I answer simply. Oh Aidan, you made it so easy for me to turn this boy against you. *"Like she's nothing more to him than a puppet on a string."*

Nolan stands so quickly that his chair clatters to the ground behind him. "I have to tell her."

"Maybe we should wait," *I say hesitantly.* "I mean, we don't know for sure—"

Nolan shakes his head, righteous indignation clear on his face. "She has to know what Aidan did. I'm supposed to be protecting her. If he could do something like this, who knows what else he's capable of?"

CHAPTER THIRTY-ONE
Almost

It's sunset by the time we arrive back at the campus. Clementine screeches to a stop outside of the mansion.

"Thanks," I say, handing Lucio my helmet. What's left of my hair is still damp.

"You're welcome." He smiles.

"Can I ask you something?"

"'Course."

"How did you learn to do that? I mean, earlier—how did you learn to combine your powers with another luiseach if there were no luiseach left here to train with you by the time you were old enough?"

"It wasn't easy," Lucio admits. "It was pretty disappointing, actually, after all that time watching luiseach on the playground, waiting for it to be my turn. But one by one they all left over the years, and I knew I'd be facing my lessons alone." He cocks his head to the side. "But Aidan is a good teacher. He took time away from his lab to make sure I'd learn everything the luiseach on the other side of the rift learned. And Victoria was here sometimes, you know. She'd pretend to know a lot less than she did, taking lessons alongside me." He smiles at the memory.

Victoria told me her work took her away from home when Anna was young. I should have guessed her "business trips" brought here down here.

"Sounds like she was a better luiseach than she was an art teacher."

Lucio laughs. "Yeah, can't quite imagine her doling out paint-brushes and grading collages."

"It wasn't her strong suit," I agree.

"She was good at her real job," Lucio says, his voice turning solemn. He looks away, like he's thinking about what Victoria gave up—her powers—to help set her daughter's spirit free.

"Why did he have to make Anna my test?" I whisper, drop-ping my head into my hands. I don't understand what Anna has to do with any of this. And I certainly don't understand why the time isn't right for her spirit to move on.

Lucio speaks before I can ask. "Looks like Aidan is back in his lab." He gestures to Aidan's SUV parked in front of us.

"I guess we should go tell him what happened." Suddenly I remember something else I never got to tell him, about the man in the black hat I saw at the airport, the man I saw again in the fishing village. I wonder: Did Lucio see him too?

Before I can ask, Lucio says, "I'm glad Aidan is still working tonight."

"Why?"

"I didn't want him to see it when I finally kissed his daughter."

Thoughts of the man in black vanish as Lucio wraps his arms around me, his face hovering just above mine. His fingers rub my chin, and I can feel the blisters where the fire burned him earlier. Warmth radiates from his lips, and I can't seem to stop my own lips from pursing in expectation.

I close my eyes, but it isn't Lucio's face I imagine in front of mine. It's Nolan's. The last time I saw Nolan he wanted to kiss me good-bye. It would have been our first kiss. It would have been my first kiss. But I wouldn't let him touch me. I *couldn't.*

Being with Nolan never felt like being with Lucio has felt. It certainly didn't feel like *this*: cool hands, soft breath, waiting mouth. When Nolan touched me, it never felt quite right.

Lucio's lips feel soft against mine as he kisses me, but it only lasts a moment as I pull away. Being touched by someone else right now feels wrong too.

"I'm sorry," I breathe.

Lucio shakes his head. "I'm sorry," he says. "I shouldn't have just *assumed*—"

I cut him off. "It's not your fault. It's just—" Just what? Just that there's this boy back home whom I've never kissed and barely touched and can't stop thinking about every time *you* touch me?

"You don't have to explain," Lucio offers. "Really." He turns and heads into the house.

I don't think I could explain even if I wanted to.

In the bathroom I look in the mirror above the sink and survey the day's damage. I peel off my T-shirt, ripped and shredded in patches where the fabric just sort of melted away from the demon's heat. The metal rivets on my shorts are still dangerously hot, but I manage to slide them off without undoing the button and zipper, feeling the weight of the weapon as the shorts drop to the ground. My face is covered in soot, and my skin is nearly as pink as that man's had been when the demon possessed him. I was burned all over when I ran into him. But it will heal: demons can't really damage us.

Though it could, apparently, damage my hair. I guess technically hair isn't part of *me*—it's not actually alive.

Before it caught fire, my hair was tied up into a ponytail on top of my head, which I guess explains why it burned the way it did. The flames started at my neckline, so first they ate off the long pieces hanging down from the pony tail, the pieces that were pulled up my scalp and into the elastic band that held everything in place before it too turned to ash.

Now I study my reflection so I can see exactly what is left: the hair closest to my neckline has been singed almost completely off, as though someone took a razor to it. The hair closer to the top of my head didn't burn completely, but the tips of my ponytail burned off. The layer of hair I have left isn't even long enough to pass my shoulders.

On the bright side, the frizzball is a whole heck of a lot smaller.

I must be feeling better if I'm back to looking on the bright side of things. I'm not sure I could have found the bright side of things with a magnifying glass yesterday.

Slowly I unwrap the strip of cloth from Lucio's T-shirt. The cut on my palm is long but not deep. I run it under cold water in the sink, biting my lip when it stings.

I can't believe I almost kissed Lucio. Or almost let him kiss me. *Don't lie to yourself, Sunshine. You almost kissed him.*

Maybe he was the one who started it, but I had plenty of time to stop it before we got as close as we did. He literally announced his intentions ahead of time. I could have run away from him right then and there, but I didn't. I waited until our lips were only a heartbeat apart before I pulled away.

Lucio is not the boy I want to kiss. I mean, it's not that I don't want to kiss him. Not exactly. It's just . . . I want to kiss Nolan more.

Nolan. I miss the sound of his voice and his calm assurance that every problem has a solution that can be found if we just look hard enough. I should have asked him to look for the solution to this problem—to *us.*

Why does it feel like I just cheated on my boyfriend? Nolan isn't my boyfriend. Can you call someone your boyfriend when you've barely touched him and never kissed him?

But today isn't the first time I've felt this way. It's felt like cheating every time Lucio touched me, every time I leaned against him to soak up his warmth, every time I compared him to Nolan.

So now I don't just feel like I have a sort-of boyfriend I can't kiss; it also feels like I've been having an affair with someone I *could* kiss but won't.

I get into the shower, washing off the soot and the sweat from the day. By the time I emerge from the bathroom, the sun's long since set. I go to my room and shut the door behind me, climbing under the covers even though I'm still soaking wet. The tips of my newly short hair brush coolly against the nape of my neck, and I remember Lucio's fingertips brushing against the very same spot.

I lift my phone from the nightstand. I should call Nolan and apologize. But what exactly would I be apologizing for? Besides, it's abundantly clear that he does *not* want to talk to me. He hasn't called me once since I got here, not even after I left him a message practically begging him to.

Victoria's letter said Nolan was my protector, that our lives would be tied together for as long as we lived. But no one ever asked him whether he wanted that job. I can't help what I am—I was *born* a luiseach. But maybe Nolan doesn't have to be a part of all of this.

If I let him go, maybe he could live a *normal* life. He could find a regular girl—no, not entirely regular. Nolan would still want someone quirky, maybe even someone who believed in ghosts and spirits just like he does. But this girl would be able to walk down the street without tripping over her shoes, and she'd be able to make it through the day without any spiritual interruptions. She'd have a regular name like Jessica or Jennifer or Elizabeth, and she'd be able to touch him, to hug him, to kiss him.

He'd be so much happier with a girl like that. And if I care about him as much as I think I do, I should want him to be happy. Even if that means being happy without me.

I toss my phone onto a pile of dirty clothes on the floor across the room. I won't trudge out into the forest behind the house, searching for a signal so I can call him again, won't leave him another message updating him on the latest luiseach shenanigans, asking him to call me back. Maybe, if enough time goes by, he'll forget he ever heard the word *luiseach*.

Maybe he'll forget he ever knew a girl named Sunshine.

In my dreams tonight I'm not a helpless infant, crying mournfully. There is no face hovering above my own, no arms holding me too tight.

I'm back in Ridgemont, with a bird's-eye view of a crowded coffee shop on Main Street. I scan the crowd, and my heart skips a beat when I see Nolan. He's wearing his grandfather's leather jacket. His hair is falling across his forehead. I try to call out to him, but no sound comes out of my mouth. I try to reach for him, but my arms aren't there. I'm not a baby in this dream, but I'm still utterly powerless. In this dream I'm not anything at all, really. I'm just a set of eyes watching what's happening, like it's playing out in front of me on a movie screen.

A girl sits down across from Nolan, her back to me. She has long hair—not short and jagged like mine is now—that cascades down her back in perfect, nonfrizzy curls. She holds herself so easily that I can tell she's never tripped over anything in her life, never stubbed her toe just taking her pants off, never forgotten to put glue down before dropping a jar of glitter over her collage.

She never turns from Nolan's face. Clearly she isn't distracted by spirits whizzing past. Unlike me, she's not constantly haunted. She can focus on him completely.

She reaches out and rests her hand on top of his. Her grip is soft and sure, and she doesn't so much as cringe when their skin makes contact.

I manage to wake myself up before I see what happens next. Before she does more of the things I can't. Before she reaches over and touches his knee. Before she rests her forehead against his. Before they kiss.

My heart is pounding and I'm covered in sweat, just like after one of my baby nightmares. And just like I do when I wake from one of those dreams, I reassure myself that it wasn't real. I practically conjured that girl myself before I fell asleep tonight, thinking about the normal girl Nolan might date if I were out of the picture.

Though I have to admit, I'm a little surprised my subconscious gave her hair as curly as my own.

CHAPTER THIRTY-TWO

On the Precipice

In the morning it's back to my not-so-real luiseach work. My complete-and-total-opposite-of-real luiseach work. By the time I make my way across the courtyard Lucio is already inside, waiting for me at the top of the stairs, close enough to the door that I can almost feel the spirits, but far enough that I'm capable of having an actual conversation without my teeth chattering or, you know, passing out.

"'Morning," I mumble. Lucio is standing so it's impossible to walk down the hallway without touching him. I plant my hands on either side of his torso to step past him. He's wearing a hooded sweatshirt today, similar to the ones Nolan wears, except Lucio's is bright green, while Nolan's are usually gray and navy and brown.

Was he wearing one in my dream last night? No, he had his jacket. Light brown, almost the same color as his eyes. I hope Mom got it back to him after he left it behind on our porch the day I left town.

"Why are you wearing a sweatshirt?" I ask Lucio finally. "It's already at least eighty degrees outside."

"Outside, but not in there." He nods in the direction of Aidan's lab. We walk down the hall side by side. "We have to tell Aidan how well it went yesterday."

I reach up and finger my newly short hair. Even after a shower, complete with apple-scented shampoo and conditioner, it still smells like fire and ash. "I'm not sure how well it went."

Lucio doesn't look at me when he talks. "You completely destroyed that demon. Aidan thinks your sensitivity is a weakness, but I'm not so sure anymore."

"Why not?"

"It was because you felt so much that you kept fighting the demon, even after it looked like we'd already won. If you hadn't felt the demon reaching for that man's heart, we'd have lost him."

Before I can answer—or argue—Lucio opens the door to Aidan's lab. I'm immediately struck dumb by the drop in temperature. Wearing a sweatshirt was the right idea. I'm dressed as inappropriately as ever, in plaid shorts and a blue T-shirt with white flowers embroidered into the neckline.

"Is it just me, or is it colder than usual?" I ask, teeth chattering. I can see my breath.

From inside the room Aidan nods. "A few more spirits joined us last night."

A lump rises in my throat. A few more spirits joining us means that a few more people died.

Lucio steps inside first, and I follow. My heartbeat speeds up, but I'm getting used to the way it feels: I imagine the blood rushing through my veins like it's trying to win a race or something.

The spirits hit me all at once. I see flashes of five, ten, twenty different lives, all overlapped like pieces of film layered on top of each other in a darkroom. A little boy playing baseball on top of a man with a walker on top of a woman with white hair and dark brown eyes holding her grandchild.

Image on top of image, life on top of life, spirit on top of spirit.

And somehow, louder than all of that, comes Lucio's voice: "Try to concentrate on just one at a time."

I've tried and failed at that before. This would be so much easier if Helena and Aidan's experiment had actually worked, if I'd had the powers they intended, if I was strong enough to see just one spirit in the whirlwind of spirits swirling around me.

Blinded by all the lives playing out in my mind's eye, I feel Lucio take my hand and squeeze. "One at a time," he repeats. "One at a time." He says it over and over again like a chant. Finally he adds, "Play to your strengths. *Use* your empathy."

I take a deep breath and seek out the woman with the white hair, training my gaze on her hair, the way it's swept away from her face into a tight bun. Her name is Estella. She died in her sleep a few months after her ninety-eighth birthday. She had two children and two grandchildren. Her eldest daughter died when Estella was in her seventies, and she has been waiting to see her again ever since. She loved her life, but she did not fear death because she believed her daughter was waiting.

I gasp as another life flashes before my eyes. A man who died in a horrible accident with a chain saw, the half of his face he still has left stares at me, trying to get my attention.

No. Think about Estella. *Only* Estella. I reach out my arms and draw her toward me.

Estella. I touch her, and her spirit washes over me like water, and then through me. Suddenly I am at peace.

And just as suddenly, all is turmoil again.

"You're not supposed to do that," Aidan snaps. But I can't concentrate on anything—not Lucio's voice saying *one at a time* or Aidan's voice, so clearly displeased. The spirits are all over me again, begging me to help them like I just helped Estella.

The cold is overwhelming, and the spirit whirlwind is only getting stronger, pulling one direction and then another. I manage to make my way out into the hallway. Lucio and Aidan follow, Aidan slamming the lab's door shut behind him.

Almost immediately the peaceful sensation comes back.

"You helped that woman move on," Aidan says sourly.

"I know!" I can't help it. I'm grinning.

"That's not our goal here!" Aidan looks furious.

"But I've never done that before! Never been able to concentrate on just one spirit when there were a dozen more asking for my attention."

"What were you two talking about, use your empathy?" Aidan asks finally.

Lucio answers, "We thought that perhaps you'd—we'd—been thinking about it backward. Sunshine can use her sensitivity to her advantage."

"What advantage can there possibly be in being unable to focus?"

"But maybe this time it was what *allowed* her to focus," Lucio counters. I nod vigorously.

Aidan raises a single eyebrow, just like I do when I'm feeling skeptical. I bet this is the first time Lucio has ever come up against Aidan when it comes to his research. Aidan cracks his knuckles out of frustration. "We already know that helping multiple spirits move on isn't Sunshine's strong suit. That's not what we're working on anymore!"

"Maybe not," Lucio agrees, still not backing down. "But you have to let us celebrate the fact that she did it. I mean, at the very least, it shows how much stronger she's gotten since she arrived here, right?"

Aidan looks like one of the doctors Mom's always complaining about, the ones who are too distracted by the facts and figures written on the chart in their hands to notice the progress the patient in front of them is making. They're the doctors who give up hope too soon, she always said. The ones who don't take the human spirit into account.

For the first time I realize that Mom—my scientific, rational, skeptical mom—has been talking about the human spirit for years! I just never noticed it before. Maybe believing in me—in all of this—wasn't as hard for her as I thought it would be. Maybe some part of her believed in it all along, even if she didn't know what to call it or that her own daughter had anything to do with it.

"You two don't understand," Aidan sighs finally, waving us away and sticking his hands in his pockets. "We'll talk later."

"Her name was Estella," I explain as we emerge into the sunlight. Lucio takes off his sweatshirt immediately, tying it around his waist. He's wearing a bright blue sleeveless T-shirt and the same cargo shorts he pretty much always wears. He's the first person I've ever met who dresses as colorfully as I do. Luiseach thing, I guess.

"What happens to you after you help a spirit move on?" I ask. "Are you able to remember anything about their lives?"

Lucio shrugs. "They all kind of blend together. I definitely don't remember details like when they were born or—"

"December sixth." I interrupt.

"What?"

"December sixth was Estella's birthday." Lucio looks at me incredulously, and I shrug. "I can't help it," I say finally. "Much as Aidan might want me to."

Lucio shakes his head, then runs his fingers over his scalp, his parents' names dancing on his finger.

"About last night . . ." he begins.

"You're not going to use that old line, are you?" I say, but my joke falls flat.

"I just wanted you to know that I don't mind waiting."

"Waiting?"

"If you're not ready or something. If you don't want to start something with all this going on," he waves his hand at the campus around us.

I stop walking, so Lucio does too, planting his feet in the dirt beside mine. "I don't want to wait," I answer before I can stop myself.

"You don't?"

I shake my head. Lucio turns to face me, steps even closer to me.

"That's not what I meant!" I shout, stepping backward so quickly that I trip and fall to the ground. Lucio helps me up, his hand warm and soft against mine.

"What did you mean?" he prompts softly.

"I meant . . ." I pause, not entirely sure how to answer that question. *I meant that I want to talk about Estella with someone else. To hold that same someone else's hand. To hug that same someone else and kiss that same someone else and let that someone else's forehead rest against mine.*

The someone I actually do want to do all of that with isn't the boy standing just inches away from me, whose hand holds my own so gently.

Finally I know why I didn't kiss him last night and why I won't kiss him now. I know why it feels like cheating every time Lucio and I stand close to one another. I'm not just cheating on Nolan but on *myself*, on my own feelings. There's a reason why I hate the idea of Nolan moving on with someone else and why I don't want to try to move on either. Because no matter how much I like Lucio . . .

I'm in *love* with Nolan.

A Road Trip

"I think I know where she is!" I shout triumphantly when I walk into the coffee shop the next day, as though the revelation only just occurred to me, as though I haven't known where she's been all along.

"What are you talking about?" Nolan asks, keeping his voice low, like he's scared the other patrons will know what we're talking about and go off in search of Sunshine too.

"According to Professor Jones's notes, there's a luiseach training facility south of the border."

"In Mexico?"

I nod. "That's where she said she was, right?"

"But that's an entire country," Nolan protests. "She could be anywhere."

"True, but you said he was taking her to begin her training, right?"

Nolan shrugs. "I'm not exactly sure what his plan was."

I bite my lip, trying to conceal my displeasure. I'd been hoping for a more enthusiastic response. "Okay, but this is at least our best lead, right? Professor Jones's notes say he's actually been to this place."

Honestly I haven't a clue what Professor Jones's notes might say, but

I do know he went down to our campus more than once. When Abner was alive, he and Aidan were the best of friends. More than ten years ago Aidan was the one who helped the professor's spirit move on when he passed away, even though he was far from the nearest luiseach at the time. He used his strength to pull Abner's spirit to him, across the thousands of miles separating them.

Aidan and I had long since been estranged by the time Abner died, but I felt it nonetheless.

"Come on," *I whine, hoping that I sound like no more than a needy young girl.* "You said you want her to know about what her mentor did to her, keeping you two apart?"

Nolan nods. "I'm going to e-mail her, but I'm not sure she'll read it." *He sighs, his tawny hair falling across his eyes.* "She's probably angry I never called her back."

Under other circumstances I might point out that luiseach are unlikely to hold grudges, especially against their protectors. But better he believes the girl is furious with him. Better he thinks he needs to make a grand gesture to get her back. Like driving thousands of miles across the country and into the jungle.

"Even if she reads your e-mail, you have to explain all this to her in person. It's too complicated and too important."

"I know, but I can't just drop everything and head into the middle of nowhere. Do you even know exactly where this place is?"

I shrug. "We'll find it. It's supposedly huge. Come on," *I moan.* "Road trip?"

"Why do you care so much?" *Nolan says, but he's smiling.*

"You're my friend. I want to help you. Isn't that what friends do?" *And I need you in order to step foot on that campus, I think but do not say. Without Nolan there may as well be a thousand-foot wall surrounding the property, keeping my people and me out and the others in. Instead, I say,*

"You're her protector. And the one thing we know for sure about protectors is that it's their job to get luiseach the information they need. Which means you need to get this information to her ASAP."

Nolan nods. "I know," he says firmly. He brushes his hair out of his eyes, and I see that they're focused in a way they've never been before. Protectors instinctively want to stay close to their luiseach, and now that Nolan sees a way to get to his luiseach, his instincts are kicking in.

Finally he says, "Guess it's time to hit the road."

CHAPTER THIRTY-THREE
Back on the Grid

I dig my phone out from under a pile of dirty, sweaty, dusty clothes. The battery is dead. (Of course.) I find the charger deep inside my duffle and plug it into one of the sockets on the wall. After a few minutes the screen comes to life, but it's still not charged enough to use, so I sit on my bed and wait.

I start pacing the room. I bite my nails and change my clothes, like I'm worried about looking nice when I call Nolan. *Super-dork.* I pick my favorite T-shirt, the one I stole from Mom with the Mustang on the front. I go into the bathroom and play with my ragged hair. Maybe when I get back to Ridgemont, Mom and I can go to a salon and see if a stylist can make sense out of it. Maybe it will look like a dramatic and edgy fashion statement.

Next I start pacing the hall. But after a few laps, it feels so small and narrow that I start opening doors and pacing the other rooms on the floor one at a time.

I open the door to the nursery last. It's dark but cool, and instead of pacing, I move slowly across the room, running my fingers along the edges of the dust-covered crib and changing table. I open a cabinet and smell the talcum powder and baby wipes, long since dried out.

I lift a tiny white onesie from a drawer and bring it to my face. It takes me a second to recognize the scent: lavender and spices—the perfume from the master bedroom. I rifle through the drawer until I find a sachet filled with herbs, tied shut with a tiny pink satin bow.

I fold the outfit as well as I can in the darkness and put it back where I found it. I leave the room, shutting the door tightly behind me. I check on my phone: 20 percent charged. That's plenty—I'm in no condition to wait for it to be fully charged. I run down the stairs and out the door, holding my phone out in front of me like a lantern as I trudge through the garden and up the hill behind the house.

Finally bars appear at the top right-hand corner of the phone's screen. I start to dial Nolan's number—I actually know it by heart, even though it's stored in my contacts—but I can't seem to make myself press *Send*.

He didn't pick up the last time I called. He didn't respond to the message I left. Maybe he never listened to it at all.

I sit cross-legged on the ground and lean against a tree trunk. Mud sticks to my bare legs. This entire place feels dirty—not just the dusty house and the dilapidated buildings, but the *air* itself feels thick, almost sticky.

I take a deep breath and clear my phone's screen. I check for text messages. One from Mom, just saying *hi* and *I love you*, and several from Ashley, checking in to see how I'm doing and telling me that Cory Cooper won't stop calling her, that he wants to get back together . . . what should she do? I smile. I'm literally the last person Ashley should be turning to for relationship advice.

No texts from Nolan. No voicemails either. I bite my lip. What are the odds that he e-mailed me instead?

When I see his name at the top of my inbox, I'm so happy that tears actually spring to my eyes.

Sunshine, I don't really know how to tell you this, but I've been doing some research, and I think Aidan is up to something.

Up to what? I keep reading, and my tears of joy quickly shift into tears of anger.

My mentor/father—*blah,* who cares about the stupid slash anymore!—has the power to keep me from Nolan, from any and every person I might have wanted to touch and kiss and love. Memories of every awkward almost-kiss and slow dance and crowded party from middle school onward flood my brain.

My hand shaking, I lower the phone even though I haven't read all of Nolan's e-mail.

Ashley always teased me. We thought I was the only sixteen-year-old in the world with virgin lips. Just another thing to make me different from most of the kids at school, another thing to make me a weirdo.

And apparently it was all Aidan's fault.

I stand and start running, clutching my phone to my chest like a Teddy bear. My hands are shaking so hard that I'm scared I might drop it. I hug it tighter. Even from far away, even after the way I rejected him, Nolan is still protecting me: conducting research, getting me new information. I never *could* have let him go, never had a chance to set him free to find a normal girl. He was never *going* anywhere.

Now I'm crying because I miss him so much.

Why would Aidan do this to me? I was beginning to like him—sort of—and at least starting to trust him. I even felt sorry for him! That empty nursery and the master bedroom frozen in time, the way he carried me from the lab and made me warm, plus the way he looked when he spoke about Helena—the woman he loved, the woman he gave up to save me.

But now . . . maybe he never really wanted to *save* me. He only wanted to *control* me. I trip over a root in the garden and stumble, but I manage to catch myself before I fall to the ground, tightening the muscles in my core. Out of breath, I stand still, trying to gather my thoughts. Maybe all Aidan ever cared about was being *right* and proving everyone else *wrong*.

I stand in the center of the courtyard between the mansion and the lab building and shout Aidan's name until I'm hoarse. I recall a snippet of Estella's life that I saw earlier: a fight between her youngest daughter and her husband. Estella took her daughter's side, screaming and shouting until her husband saw reason. I know I'm not alone. When we first moved to Ridgemont, I thought that living in a haunted house meant that I'd never really be alone again. But now I understand that I will never be alone, not as long as I am able to help spirits move on. As long as I help them move on, some part of them will stay with me.

When Aidan finally emerges into the sun, I hold my phone out in front of me so he can read what Nolan wrote.

He looks every bit as uncomfortable as he did on the plane that day when I first asked him about Nolan. Now I know it had nothing to do with being a normal father, nervous about the idea of his teenage daughter dating. Now I know there's nothing *normal* about it. It was just another secret he kept. A trick he played on me.

"How could you?"

"I limited your ability to touch anyone romantically."

"I know that," I shake the phone for emphasis. "But why?"

"I knew we would be apart for sixteen years. I couldn't keep you from human relationships—with your mother, your friends. But I thought I might be able to keep you from falling in love."

Is that why I never felt sick when Lucio and I touched? Because all along, I had . . . *stronger* feelings for someone else?

"What's wrong with falling in love?" I'm still panting from running across the campus. Or maybe because I can't stop crying. I stuff my phone into the back pocket of my shorts, right next to the rusty knife.

For an instant Aidan looks sadder than I've ever seen him. Sadder than I've ever seen anyone. Sadder than Victoria looked when she told me about Anna and her husband. Sadder than Mom looked the day she let me leave.

"You know what's wrong with it," Aidan says gently.

I shake my head. *What is this guy talking about?*

"I would have put the same measures in place between you and Katherine if I could have, but because you were a baby when she adopted you, I knew you needed to be touched, carried, held."

"Kat," I correct through gritted teeth. Aidan keeps speaking as though I never said a word, but when he mentions her again he uses the correct name so I know he heard me.

"And, of course, I needed you to bond with Kat to ensure that she would want to raise you."

I take a step back. I can't stand the way he talks about my relationship with Mom—so . . . *clinically,* like it only existed to get me safely to my sixteenth birthday, when he could take over.

I've never missed my mother so much in my entire life. And that's counting the months when she was possessed by a demon.

I lift what's left of my hair off of my neck. It seems miraculous that back at home it's still winter. Ridgemont is probably drenched in fog and covered in clouds so thick that not even a single ray of sunlight can break through. People are rushing to and from their cars, blowing on their hands to keep warm, wool hats pulled tightly over their heads. Maybe there's snow on the ground.

A cool breeze fills the air, drying my sweat. The spirits in Aidan's lab can't escape, but they're making their nearby presence known. The breeze whips what's left of my hair off my shoulders. I shiver.

From the look on Aidan's face, it's obvious he notices the change in the air too. But I'm not about to let him change the subject.

"My mother did more than raise me. She *loved* me, because that's what good parents do." The words I don't say hang in the air between us. Kat is a *good* parent. Unlike Helena. Unlike *you*.

"I know," Aidan answers wearily. "I must admit, I was hoping you wouldn't be quite as close as you are."

Why? I can't even get the word out. Is everything all science and research to him?

The answer hits me so suddenly that I stop crying and panting and sweating. I might stop breathing altogether for a few heartbeats. I just stand there in the breeze, stunned.

This has nothing to do with Aidan's certainty that he must be right. It has everything to do with the fact that Aidan knows he might be *wrong*. Aidan didn't want me to get too attached to my humanity—to my *life*—because he knew that I might have to give it up.

"Is this the real reason you didn't want Nolan to come here?" All those times I asked Aidan why Nolan couldn't be here—when I insisted that this work would be easier with my protector at my side—and Aidan told me this was work I had to do without my protector.

Whether or not Nolan was my protector had nothing to do with it. Aidan just didn't want me spending time with the boy I cared for.

"You and Nolan would have bonded more deeply, working together here. It would only have made it harder for you."

I shake my head. "Do you really believe there's a way to make it easy?"

Aidan doesn't answer.

A lump rises in my throat, as big as a boulder. "So you'll kill me too, if you have to?" The words come out as little more than a whisper, but from the look on Aidan's face, I know he hears me.

I take a few steps backward, blinking in the sunlight. This is like something out of a bad horror movie: the mad scientist lured the innocent girl into the desert, lulled her into a false sense of security, when secretly he had dastardly plans of his own.

The breeze whips my hair into my eyes, brushing away my tears.

"All this time, even when you told me you brought me here to protect me, you've also been prepared to kill me?" I wave my hands at the campus around us—the mansion behind me where Lucio is sitting alone, the trees swaying in the breeze, the lab in front of us, filled with spirits.

This is why Aidan was so upset when I helped Estella move on. It was proof that he was wrong about me. I'm not some kind of magic key, the missing piece he just needed to slide into place so spirits could move on by themselves.

"Your powers *are* different," Aidan says finally. "Our experiments did change your abilities."

"Just not the way you needed them to," I supply. Aidan doesn't argue. And now a new unasked and unanswered question hangs in the air between us:

Have you already made up your mind to do it?

CHAPTER THIRTY-FOUR

Imprisoned

I thought this campus was a fortress to protect me. But maybe all along it was meant to imprison me.

There's a knock at my door. "Go away, Aidan!" I shout.

"It's not Aidan," Lucio's voice answers. He opens the door.

"I didn't say you could come in."

Lucio shrugs. "I know. But I thought you needed a friend. And I thought you might not admit it if I gave you the chance to answer." He plops down on the unmade bed beside me, propping my pillows up behind him, stretching his strong legs out in front of him, folding his arms across his chest.

I can't even remember if I've ever seen Nolan's bare arms. How do I have such strong feelings for a person whose forearms I've never seen? Lucio is right. I need a friend. I'm just not so sure that he is my friend. Not anymore.

"Were you in on it too?" I ask.

"In on what?"

I stand up and start pacing again, as restless as a tiger in a cage. *In on Aidan's tricks to keep me from being with Nolan. In on keeping me here, on this campus, befriending me and distracting me, knowing all along that Aidan might do exactly what he claimed he was protecting me from.*

"You keep walking like that, you're going to drill a hole in the floor," Lucio says.

I don't smile, and I certainly don't laugh. Doesn't Lucio understand that being still is impossible right now? I don't think I've ever had so much energy. I can't stop my fingers from drumming against my thighs. My feet feel like they want to run away.

"I hate Aidan," I whisper. Hate tastes sour and bitter and cold, like the time I accidentally drank vinegar.

Lucio gets off the bed and crosses the room, catching hold of me so I can't pace anymore.

"You don't hate him," he insists.

I shake my head, tears slipping down my cheeks. Who knew anger could turn into sadness so quickly?

"I do."

Aidan is just as bad as Helena. *Worse!* Helena may have wanted to eliminate me, but Aidan saved me only to control me, to hold me captive, to take me away from the people I love, to keep me at arm's length just in case he needed to . . . I hate to even think it.

At least Helena was honest about what she was going to do to me.

At least Helena didn't try to get me to care about her, knowing all along that she still might kill me.

I shake my head frantically. *It doesn't matter.* Neither of them is really my parent. My only *real* parent is Kat. That fact has never felt more true than it does right now.

"Aidan loves you." Lucio reaches up to hold my head so I stop shaking it. "In his way."

"Well, then, that's not a way I want to be loved."

Lucio drops his hands. "It's not so bad," he says. I bite my lip. Aidan is the only person Lucio has left to love him.

"Haven't you ever doubted him?" I ask finally. "Did you ever consider joining the others?"

"You mean joining the luiseach who murdered my parents?"

I take a few steps back, lifting my hand to cover my mouth as though I want to put the words I just said back inside. "I'm sorry," I whisper.

Lucio sits on the bed and pats the empty space beside him. I cross the room and sit.

"I have thought about leaving," he admits heavily. "After I passed my test, I thought *I'm strong enough now.*"

"Strong enough for what?" I ask, even though I think I know the answer.

"Strong enough to track down the luiseach who killed my parents and punish them for what they did." He closes his eyes. "You can't imagine how angry I was. Angry at Aidan for putting my parents in danger. Angry at my parents for staying with Aidan instead of having the good sense to join the other side of the rift before it was too late." He opens his eyes and holds his gaze steady with mine. "Angry at you for being born and tearing all of us apart." Lucio swallows hard. "So the day after I passed my test, I packed my bags and left this house before dawn. When I got outside, there was Aidan. Fully dressed in the middle of the night, leaning against Clementine like he didn't have anywhere else to be."

"What did he say?"

"I didn't give him a chance to say much of anything at all. I started shouting, said I didn't care that revenge went against everything we are—the light, the kindness, the forgiveness. We help all spirits move on—those who lived good lives and bad, without prejudice, you know?"

No one ever told me that, but then no one ever had to. I've never come across a spirit I didn't want to help move on.

"I screamed that I was my parents' son, and it was my job to exact justice. By the time I finally stopped shouting, my throat hurt and I was covered in sweat."

"I know the feeling." I think of my outburst in the courtyard. "What did Aidan say when you finally gave him a chance to get a word in?"

"He said that the luiseach on the other side believed what they believed as deeply as we believed what we did. They thought what they'd done was for the greater good too. So how could he hate them? He said he had never hated Helena, no matter how much she wanted to eliminate his child." He pauses. "But he knew he couldn't keep me from hating them, if that's what I wanted. Then he got up and walked back into the house."

"He didn't try to stop you?"

Lucio shakes his head. "Nope. I thought for sure he'd block my way or lock me up or something. But he just stepped aside."

"And that was it?"

Lucio smiles wryly. "Not quite. Before he went back inside the house, he reminded me that if I left Llevar la Luz, I wouldn't live here anymore. Which meant that once I stepped foot off the property, I wouldn't be able to come back without an express invitation from someone who did."

"He told you he wouldn't invite you back?"

"He didn't have to." He runs his hands over his scalp, a gesture I've come to recognize as a sign that he's thinking about what to say next. "Llevar la Luz is the only home I've ever known. And Aidan is the only parent I've got left. And that morning, after Aidan left me alone, I sat on my motorcycle—a gift from Aidan and named by him—and watched the sunrise. I realized that as homes and adopted parents go, I didn't have it *that* bad. I had a man who wanted me to turn my back on hate, to stay here and continue the research that he believed could save the world."

"Do you believe it too?"

"I'm not sure," Lucio answers honestly. "But Aidan does. And that's enough."

I bite my lip. "I'm not so sure he believes it anymore. Not after what happened today."

Lucio nods. "Maybe not," he concedes. "But I still believe in him."

He reaches out and puts his hand on my shoulder and squeezes, but for once his touch isn't reassuring. How can it be, when he pretty much admitted that Aidan might be planning to eliminate me too?

"I'm sorry," I whisper, leaning away from him. "I think I want to be alone."

Lucio nods. "I'll be around if you need me," he offers.

"I know," I answer. I try to smile, but my jaw muscles aren't cooperating. "Thanks."

As soon as the door clicks shut behind him, I take my phone from my back pocket. Nolan's e-mail is still up on the screen, waiting for me to finish reading it. I scroll all the way down to the last paragraph.

I'm coming to get you, Sunshine. It'll take me a while to make the drive down there—Google Maps says 34 hours, plus some time for traffic and pit stops—but just sit tight and wait for me. We'll figure this out together. There has to be a way to undo what Aidan did.

How does he know where I am? *I* don't even know exactly where I am. But then again Nolan is pretty much a genius. If he could find out what Aidan did, then finding out where I am was probably a piece of cake.

And luckily I did invite him to come here. Not just in the message I left him but pretty much every day since I arrived here, I've been silently begging him to join me.

He must not be mad at me. You don't go on a quest to rescue someone you're angry with.

Suddenly I feel like a princess in a fairy tale, waiting for her prince to storm the castle and rescue her. But unlike Sleeping Beauty or Rapunzel or Cinderella, I'm not content to sit around waiting. I have to *do* something.

I practically bounce to my feet, the tile cracking beneath me. I start packing, turning the messy pile of clothes on the floor into a messy pile of clothes in my duffle bag. I plug in my phone so it can actually finish charging. I go across the hall and grab my toothbrush and toothpaste from the bathroom. I lift the stuffed owl from the floor and hold it, staring into its blank, glassy eyes. Once I get back to Ridgemont, I'll be able to focus all of my energy on pulling Anna toward me and helping her move on.

"I'll name you Dr. Hoo, the sequel," I whisper as I stuff the toy into my already overstuffed bag.

It's not stealing. It was meant to be mine all along.

Once my duffle is completely packed, I sit on the edge of the bed, listening for the sound of a car entering the courtyard below. Nolan drives his grandfather's old enormous beat-up navy blue Chrysler. It practically moans every time he accelerates and shudders when it shifts into park. I'll definitely be able to hear him coming.

I'll run out the door before Aidan can stop me. A great escape. And unlike Lucio, I don't care if I never get invited back.

Nolan could be more than halfway here by now. *Sit tight.* I doubt anyone in the whole world has ever sat as tight as I'm sitting right now. My legs are crossed and my arms are folded, and it feels like every single muscle in my body is clenched in anticipation, ready to spring into action the instant Nolan arrives, to run out the door so quickly that Aidan won't be able to stop me. I uncurl myself long enough to look down at my phone and read the last two sentences of Nolan's e-mail one more time.

We'll figure this out together. There has to be a way to undo what Aidan did.

Does that mean he loves me too?

Fury

"I don't think you should come with me."

We're standing outside the coffee shop. My eyes narrow reflexively. I force myself to behave as though Nolan's words don't make my blood boil. "Why not?" I play with the hem of my sweatshirt. I can't wait until this facade is over and I can go back to dressing in my own clothes again. These mass-produced clothes are functional, but they have no history, not like the vintage clothes I usually favor. The threads in this shirt, these jeans, these shoes might have been stitched just a few days before I bought them. They have no history.

"Because she's never met you, and because I don't know what kind of shape she's going to be in when I find her. And because. . . ."

He trails off, but his meaning is clear: because I don't want to show up with another girl when I'm trying to rescue the girl I really want to be with.

Teenagers are infuriating.

"Nolan," I begin, pretending the strain in my voice is because it's cold out here rather than the true reason: I'm shaking with fury, "I really think

I should come with you. You don't know what it's going to be like when you get there. You don't know how Aidan is going to react to seeing you."

Now it's Nolan's eyes that narrow. "I never told you his name."

"What?"

"I never told you Sunshine's mentor's name."

Inwardly I curse. How could I make such an amateur mistake?

"Helena," Nolan prompts, "How did you know his name?"

I try to look nonchalant. "It must have been in one of the professor's files."

Nolan shakes his head. "Even if Aidan was mentioned in the professor's files, there couldn't have been anything linking him to Sunshine. You couldn't know he was Sunshine's mentor."

I don't answer.

"Helena," Nolan says finally. "Who are you?"

No point in pretending anymore. The boy is a protector, after all. I wouldn't have been able to go on fooling him forever: protectors excel at putting the pieces of a puzzle together.

I stand up straight instead of slouching. I hook my curls behind my ears instead of letting them fall across my face. No more pretending to be less than half my age.

"I think you know who I am, Nolan." I use my real voice, so much deeper and more powerful than the one I put on for his benefit. The boy takes a step back. "Or anyway, I think you have a guess as to what I am."

Nolan shakes his head in disbelief. "But why are you here with me instead of down there with them?"

"Let's just say that Aidan and I had a falling out about sixteen years ago."

I reach out and grab Nolan's arm before he can step even an inch farther from me. "Get in the car." I nod in the direction of my pale blue rented subcompact. "You're driving me to Mexico."

He tries to shake off my grip, but I hold tight. I laugh at the surprise on his face. "I'm a lot stronger than I look."

"So am I," *he answers.* "And I'm not taking you anywhere."

"Don't you want to save your beloved luiseach?" *I spit.* "What I told you about Aidan was true," *I add, before he can object.* "He really did keep Sunshine from touching you."

"How about what you said about protectors and luiseach? Is it true that they can fall in love and be together?"

"It's rare," *I admit.* "But don't pretend you didn't know that. You know that the only way to create a luiseach child is with two luiseach parents. If luiseach were constantly falling in love with their protectors, we'd have gone extinct long ago."

"But you are going extinct," *Nolan says.* "That's what Aidan thinks."

"And he's right," *I answer huskily, dragging the boy away toward the parking lot.* "At least, he's right as long as the girl lives. But once she's gone . . ." *I trail off, setting my jaw. Of course I know our numbers were dwindling before the girl's birth—we were limited by the fact that it takes two luiseach to make one—but at least we were still able to reproduce somewhat!*

And some luiseach are better than none.

Without closing my eyes, I search for the strongest nearby spirit: what's left of a high school athletics star. Its strength pushes Nolan along behind me. "I see it's going to take a little bit of persuasion to get you to do what I need you to do."

It doesn't matter why he wants me at his side when he steps foot onto Llevar la Luz. I'll be able to go with him even if the only reason he wants me there is to stop the pain.

It's time to show him just how strong I am.

CHAPTER THIRTY-FIVE

Focus

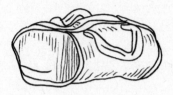

With all this nervous energy coursing through my body, the last thing I expect is to fall asleep while I'm waiting for Nolan. But I do. And I dream.

I see Nolan and that girl again. The *normal* girl, with her frizz-free curls and her nonhauntedness. I see them from the back—she's leading him across a parking lot, but wait . . . her fingers are digging into his arm so deeply that she's clawing holes in his jacket.

That's not *normal*. There's nothing *normal* about that.

Now she's pulling him down a pinecone-littered street that looks more like a path out of a fairy tale than an actual street in an actual neighborhood. She turns onto a long driveway, dragging him behind her all the time. I'm so far away—floating above them like a disembodied pair of eyes again—that it takes a second for her face to come into focus, like looking through the viewfinder of my old Nikon and adjusting the lens.

If my disembodied pair of eyes had a mouth, this is when it would gasp. If I had legs, this is when they would run to Nolan. If I had hands, they would wrap their way around her fingers and pry her away from him.

I've seen her face before.

It's the face from my nightmares, the dreams that began the first night I slept in this house. This is the woman who stood over me as a helpless infant. The woman who tried to kill me.

When I wake up, I can smell her: lavender and spices.

I thought I'd never want to talk to Aidan again, but instead I'm banging on his door at eleven at night in the pitch-dark hallway. The wood splinters beneath my fist. When Aidan finally opens the door, I see that he's still fully dressed, but his white shirt is wrinkled, and it looks like he hasn't slept for days, maybe weeks. His eyes are bloodshot, and the dark circles beneath them are so dark, they look like bruises. How have I never noticed this before? Does he usually hide it somehow? I don't wait for him to step out into the hallway before I ask, "Did Helena try to kill me?"

Aidan blinks. "What?"

"You said that you insisted that you be the one to eliminate me, remember? But before that—did she try to do it herself?"

"Why are you asking?"

"It's important!" I try not to shout. I hear Lucio moving around in his bedroom nearby. "Please!" I beg, even louder now, more desperation in my voice.

Slowly, like his head weighs about a thousand pounds, Aidan nods.

"When you started to cry, Helena insisted that Victoria bring you downstairs. She held you close and you stopped crying—you must have smelled her milk. But instead of feeding you, she held you tighter. And tighter still. As though she thought she could squeeze you right out of existence."

"What?" Aidan and I both spin around and see Lucio standing in his own doorway, wearing nothing but his shorts. "I thought I made that part up. I had nightmares about it for months."

I should have put the pieces together sooner. Why didn't I realize that every night I was experiencing exactly what Lucio thought he saw when he was there?

Aidan nods. "I know. Argi and I thought it would be better to hide the truth from you. You were so young." He steps around me and puts a hand on Lucio's shoulder. "I'm sorry I lied to you."

"What happened after that?" I whisper. "How did you stop her?"

Aidan turns back to me. "I had to rip you from her arms." His grip is tight on Lucio's shoulder. "I pretended that I *wanted* to do it. That I believed it was the only way I could make amends for the evil I'd let into the world."

"You thought I was evil?" I pant, no longer sure of what's truth and what's fiction.

"Of course not. But I had to convince your mother—"

I know I shouldn't waste time with interruptions, but I can't help myself. "Why do you insist on calling her my mother? My real mother has been there for me every day for the last sixteen years. That's what it means to be a parent. That's what matters. Helena is not my mother, just like you are not my father!"

Aidan takes a step back as though I slapped him. I ball my hands into fists and bite my lip to keep from apologizing. I shouldn't feel bad for saying that, not after everything he's done. I shouldn't care that his Adam's apple is working up and down, up and down, almost as if my incredibly composed, never wrinkled, and almost never rattled mentor/father is trying not to cry.

"She would have killed you if I hadn't convinced her to let me do it." Aidan's voice is barely louder than a whisper.

"I know." I shake my head vigorously, trying to hide the tears springing up in the corners of my eyes. "I saw it."

"What do you mean?"

I explain that the nightmares started as soon as I moved into this house, as soon as I walked through these halls and breathed in these scents and slept under this roof. Finally I say, "I don't think they were ever dreams. They were *memories*. Things that happened here, in this house. Which means that what I saw tonight wasn't just a dream either." Nolan is still in Ridgemont. Helena is holding him prisoner.

"What did you see tonight?"

"Helena has Nolan," I answer hoarsely. My heart is pounding nearly as fast as it does when a spirit touches me. "We have to go back to Ridgemont."

"You should have told me you were having visions."

"I didn't know they were visions until tonight. I thought they were just bad dreams!" The desperation in my voice shocks me. "It doesn't matter anymore. All that matters now is saving Nolan."

"Of course it matters! I'm trying to understand what your powers are, and now all of a sudden you discover you have a new power, and you think it's beside the point?"

"It *is* beside the point! We have to save my friend."

"We're trying to save the *world* here, Sunshine, not just one person," Aidan counters wearily. "Don't you understand that by now?"

Doesn't he understand that I don't want to save a world that Nolan might not be a part of? "Are you going to help me get to Nolan or not?"

"Absolutely not," Aidan snaps. "I'm not about to hand you over to Helena."

"Lucio?" I face the boy who said he was my friend. A lump rises in my throat.

"I'm sorry, Sunshine," he answers. "I'm with Aidan on this one."

"You're with Aidan on *every* one!" I turn on my heel and run upstairs. I sit on the edge of my bed until I hear the sound of Aidan's and Lucio's bedroom doors clicking shut. Then I grab my bag and tiptoe down to the front door, begging it not to squeak as I pull it open and slip outside.

CHAPTER THIRTY-SIX

Trapped

It's drizzling outside, but it's so hot out that the rain feels like a warm shower. The sky above is covered in clouds, barely giving off any light at all, but I manage to feel my way through the darkness to climb behind the wheel of Aidan's SUV first. Funny, just a few months ago I was scared to drive from my high school to the hospital, and now I'm prepared to drive from Llevar la Luz to Ridgemont. Or at least to the Mazatlan airport.

"What are you doing?" I look up. Aidan's white shirt glows in the moonlight, turning see-through as the rain soaks it. His voice sounds tinny and far away through the metal and glass between us.

"I have to get out of here."

"You *can't* get out of here. It isn't safe for you off the property."

I laugh, but it comes out sounding like a cackle. "It's not safe on the property either."

"You won't get far."

"Why not?" I adjust my grip on the steering wheel, squeezing it so tightly, I think I could break it.

"Well, for one thing, you don't have the car keys."

I lean my head against the wheel. I can't so much as turn the headlights on. "Fine." I get out of the car, slamming the door behind me. I slip my backpack over my shoulders and drop my duffle bag on the ground—I can leave it behind. All I really need is my phone and my passport. I walk to Clementine and hop on. The keys are in the ignition.

But before I can turn on the engine, Lucio grabs me and lifts me off the motorcycle with one arm and shoves poor Clementine onto her side with the other so quickly it's like he has night vision. Still holding me, he kicks in the metallic pipes on the side of the bike with all his might.

"What's wrong with you?" I shout, struggling against his grip. The rain makes his skin slippery.

"I'm not letting you kill yourself."

"I'm not trying to kill myself! I'm trying to save my friend."

"What exactly do you think is going to happen when you come face to face with Helena?" Lucio pants as he kicks the metal at his feet. Finally he lets me go and doubles over, gazing at what's left of his beloved motorcycle.

"You can't leave, Sunshine," he says, his breath ragged.

"I can't stay," I counter.

Once more, despite the heat, a cool breeze blows down from the direction of Aidan's lab, so forceful that the rain starts to fall sideways.

"What's got them so worked up?" Lucio's voice is thick with worry.

Despite the darkness, I can see Aidan nod in my direction.

"What are you two talking about?" The wind is whistling now. I have to shout to be heard.

"I think your sensitivity works both ways," Aidan shouts back. "The same way you feel their emotions, they can feel yours."

"But I haven't actually helped any of those spirits move on."

"Sunshine, at least half the spirits in that lab have come into some sort of contact with you."

"If that's true, then how come it's never happened before?"

The answer is so obvious that Aidan doesn't have to say it: I've never been this upset before.

He turns to Lucio. "We have to get them to calm down before—"

Behind us the mansion seems to groan. I turn around and see that the vines climbing the walls are shifting in the breeze. They look alive.

"Promise me you won't leave," Aidan orders.

"I'm not promising you anything." One of the vines rattles loose, waving in the wind like a loose power line surging with deadly electricity.

"We're surrounded by the jungle," Aidan points out rationally. "You wouldn't get far without help."

Finally I nod. He's right about that much.

But that just means it's time for me to call in reinforcements.

Behind the mansion the breeze whips the leaves from the trees; they fly through the air like snowflakes in a blizzard, sticking to my skin. For once there aren't any mosquitoes; the wind seems to have blown them all away. It's so cold, I have to blow on my hands to keep warm. I shiver, hoping there isn't anything waiting for me in the darkness: snakes and jaguars and other wild, hungry creatures.

Lions and tigers and bears, oh my.

Dorothy was just trying to get home too. I pace the woods, using my cell phone as a flashlight, waiting for service to kick in. Mom said she would come and rescue me, but by the time she got here—by the time she booked a flight and switched planes and drove from the airport to Llevar la Luz and then drove us back and onto another plane . . . by then it might be too late. And I have no way of getting out of this godforsaken place myself. It's not like there's a highway close by where I can hitchhike my way back to the airport, and it's not like I would actually get into a stranger's car anyway—I'm desperate, not stupid. So I call the only friend I have within driving distance. The screen is slippery with rain, but I manage to dial.

"Sunshine?" Ashley asks groggily.

If she needs an express invitation to get here, then I'm going to give her one. "Hey, Ash," I begin, shouting to be heard over the wind. "Remember the time you said you wanted to spend spring break in Mexico?"

CHAPTER THIRTY-SEVEN

Calm

According to the directions I e-mailed Ashley, it will take her eleven hours to drive here. Thank goodness for GPS: using my phone, it could locate me even in the middle of nowhere, even in a place that has no address and exists on no map.

I told Ashley to look for a driveway hidden by enormous leaves, a secret entrance to a secret place. And Nolan said it would take thirty-four hours to drive between Ridgemont and this place. Which means I won't be back home for nearly two days.

But it's the fastest way I can think to get there.

The wind whistles around me, burning my ears as I trudge through the mud back to the courtyard. I point the light at the crumbled pile of metal that was once Clementine, crushed and twisted on the ground, barely recognizable. Just the memory of what Lucio did makes me angrier, and the wind picks up, spinning the cycle in circles on the ground. The metal groans.

I tried calling Nolan a dozen times, but every time his phone went to voicemail, so I finally gave up. If he's being held against his will, he's probably not allowed to check his phone, right? I couldn't help sending him a text message just in case: *I'm coming,* I wrote. *You sit tight.*

I didn't write what I'm really thinking: *Please be okay. Please be okay. Please be okay.*

The wind blows dust into my eyes, and I have to plant my feet firmly just to take a single step. "Calm down!" I shout. Talk about the pot calling the kettle black. I don't think I've ever been less calm. I take a deep breath and try to concentrate.

It was just before midnight when I called Ashley, so she should be here sometime this afternoon. But how am I going to sneak out without Lucio and Aidan trying to stop me again? What if they imprison Ashley too?

I'm getting ahead of myself. First, I have to make it through the next ten hours without letting on that I have a getaway car en route. I start pacing, even though it feels like the wind is pushing and pulling me in every direction. Despite the spirit-filled chill in the air, I'm sweating.

Step, step, step. *They'll never let me leave.* Change direction. Step, step, step. *But I have to leave.*

I shout it out loud: "I *have* to leave!"

The breeze shifts, and an explosive sound fills the air. A window in one of the buildings across the courtyard shatters, sending shards into the air like hailstones. I scream, crouching down in a circle and covering my head with my hands.

Across the courtyard I hear another window break.

Then another.

And another.

Llevar la Luz is falling apart. If Aidan is right about the connection between the spirits and me, *I'm* the reason why.

Suddenly I know how I'm going to pass the next ten hours without making Aidan and Lucio suspicious. I have to get the spirits to calm down. If I can stop this wind, Aidan and Lucio will believe that *I've* calmed down too.

I don't even bother using my cell phone as a flashlight anymore. The breeze is enough to guide me: I walk headlong into it. Each step takes enormous effort, like walking into a hurricane or swimming upstream. It's so cold that the rain is turning to sleet. If this goes on much longer, it might even turn to snow.

It feels like it takes forever just to walk across the courtyard. I'm not sure I ever really realized just how enormous a place this is. It was meant to house hundreds of luiseach, not just three.

Or not just two, as one of us is getting out of here.

It's even windier inside. The door slams shut behind me so hard that I'm not sure I could open it again if I wanted to. No place to go but forward then. The wind blows harder with each step I take, lifting what's left of my hair off my shoulders so hard that if feels like someone is standing behind me, pulling my hair from my scalp.

Inside the lab Aidan and Lucio are shouting. It sounds like the first few minutes in *The Wizard of Oz* when it's still in black and white and Auntie Em is calling for Dorothy, and they're all terrified because a twister is coming.

Research papers and Aidan's notebooks swirl around the room in the chaos. I'm struck by a large piece of paper on my leg. I look down and see that it's the map Aidan had tacked to the wall, the one with four red circles and dates by each circle. Quickly I fold it and stick it in my back pocket. The map is coming home with me. Maybe Nolan will be able to make sense of it.

"Michael Weir's spirit wasn't this worked up when it escaped!" Lucio cries. A flashlight spins around in the breeze, casting strange shadows on the walls. It gives off enough light that I can see that Lucio's eyes are closed. He's trying to reach out to one spirit at a time like he always told me to do. "You have to let me move them on before it's too late," he begs.

"No!" Aidan yells to be heard over the whistle of the wind, but his voice is as even as ever. "We'd have to start all over again."

"Better to start over again than risk all of them turning dark!"

My teeth are chattering so hard, it's a wonder they don't crack right down the middle.

"No!" Aidan repeats. "They won't turn dark in this much warmth."

"What warmth?" Lucio counters. "It's freezing in here. And it didn't seem to stop Michael Weir's spirit." His muscles flex with the effort it takes to stay upright in this windstorm. "None of the old rules apply anymore."

What magic did Aidan have to work to lock these spirits inside? Victoria had to give up her powers to create the energy it took to send Anna and her demon to our house in Ridgemont. How much energy did *this* take? Perhaps he made a deal with another luiseach, just like he did with Victoria. Split another person in two *for the greater good*.

How much energy would it take to set them all free? I remember a lesson from physics class: the law of conservation of energy. Energy is never created or used up; it's just moved from one source to another. I wonder whether I have enough energy in me to set all of these spirits free.

I rub my hands up and down my arms, feeling the ridges and bumps of the goose bumps beneath my fingers. The wind sends the papers that had been neatly stacked on Aidan's cold metal table flying around the lab. The flashlight smacks into the wall so hard that its batteries fall out, throwing the room into darkness.

Neither Aidan nor Lucio notices me stepping inside the room. It starts as soon as I step over the threshold: image after image, flash after flash, one life and then another. Every memory looks and feels *angry*. I stumble, crashing against the table with a *whomp*.

"Sunshine!" Lucio catches me before I hit the ground. We lean against each other to stay upright. I reach out blindly and lace my fingers through his. "You have to get out of here. It isn't safe for you."

I manage to shake my head. Understanding crosses Lucio's face. I close my eyes and *concentrate,* just like I've been taught.

I hold my breath and seek out one spirit, just one. The man with the walker. His name is Joseph. But this time the memory of his life that flashes before me isn't one of him calmly walking up and down the hallways of his retirement community. This time it's a fight he had with his caretaker, when he was refusing to take the medicine she offered him. When he was so sick of suffering that he just wanted to let go.

Just like he wants to let go now.

"Get her out of here!" Aidan shouts.

"No," Lucio counters. "Maybe she can calm them down."

My thoughts exactly, I think but do not say.

"I want to help," I manage. And not just because Ashley will be here in less than eleven hours. The spirits in this room are suffering. It's bad enough they're trapped in here. Now they're trapped and reliving some of their worst memories. Their anger shoots through my body. I slide my hands from Lucio's and ball them into fists, digging my fingernails into my palms.

In a flash I feel another set of hands on me. It takes the combined strength of both men to keep me upright. They lean against me. I feel warmth coming from the center of their bodies, from their heartbeats, nearly as fast as my own.

I can do this.

I'm so sorry you're trapped in there. I would set you free if I could—but no, I wouldn't. The last spirit to escape this lab became a fire demon. A breeze whips across my bare neck, sending shivers down my spine.

No, I wouldn't set you free. But I would help you move on, like I did Estella. I imagine it: one right after the other, like some kind of one-person luiseach assembly line in a spirit factory.

I wish you could move on by yourself, like Aidan wants. I wish you could feel the peace that comes with releasing your grip on this Earth.

I know your son loved baseball and that you could always taste the pills the nurse crushed into your applesauce.

The wind shifts, the deafening whistle just one octave lower. The flashes of Joseph's life change before my eyes: instead of seeing all the times he couldn't do what he wanted, I begin to see the times he succeeded: the race he won in high school, the promotion he worked so hard for.

I must be succeeding. I lower my fists.

Leaning against Lucio and Aidan, I seek out another spirit.

The woman with white hair and dark brown eyes holding her grandchild.

I know your granddaughter's name is Maria and that your grandson loved dogs.

And then another. A man who never got to say good-bye to his husband.

I know how much you loved each other.

And another.

I know you're sorry you got behind the wheel when you were too tired to drive.

And another.

I know how much you loved your wife.

And another.

And another.

I'm shivering, but I'm also sweating from the effort of concentrating so hard. My teeth are clenched so tightly that I can feel them grinding against one another.

I tell every single one of them *I know how you felt in life. How you feel now, in death. I can feel it too.*

"You're suffering," I say out loud. "I'm suffering too. And I will suffer until each of you has gotten to move on like you should."

One by one, the images that flash before me go from the worst moments of these people's lives to the small, petty inconveniences, to just the normal, everyday sorts of things. Finally the memories shift from frustration and powerlessness to success and accomplishment.

Because *I'm* accomplishing something.

What's more, I *can't* think of Nolan. There just isn't room in my brain for worry. Not with all these lives taking up so much space.

Finally the wind quiets, dying down until it's nothing more than a hum, barely blowing my hair back at all. Aidan takes his hands from me, stepping back like he can't believe what he just witnessed. Exhausted, I slump against Lucio, who hugs me gently.

I have no idea how long we've been in here.

But it must have been hours. Nearly eleven, in fact.

Over the hum of calm spirits I hear a car horn blasting up from the courtyard.

I twist myself from Lucio's embrace and break into a run. It's time for me to go home.

CHAPTER THIRTY-EIGHT
Ashley to the Rescue

The storm has passed; there isn't a cloud in the sky. I squint as my eyes adjust from darkness to light. The campus is still wet from last night's rain, and the humidity is as strong as ever. I can't wait until I'm breathing in the air conditioning blasting from the vents of Ashley's dashboard.

It looks like Ashley's shiny blue hybrid is glowing in the brightness. Soon we'll be cold and wet and beneath miles of cloud cover back home. I can practically taste the fog on my tongue.

Before I can stop her, Ashley jumps out of the car and throws her arms around me.

"Where is this guy?" she shouts.

I shake my head and toss my bags into her backseat. "Let's just get out of here." I expected Aidan and Lucio to run after me, but they're still somewhere inside. Somehow their absence makes this all feel even creepier. What are they waiting for? Aren't they going to try to stop me?

I grab Ashley's arm. She raises her gaze to take in her surroundings: the courtyard, the mansion, the shattered glass at our feet, the jungle closing in.

"What is this place?" she breathes. This is definitely not the vacation-type scenario Ashley had in mind when I first said I needed her to drive to Mexico.

"It used to be a sort of college campus," I answer. "Aidan—my birth father—was like, the dean or something."

Before Ashley can ask anything more, the sound of someone whooping fills the air. Not just someone. *Aidan.* I turn in the direction of his lab—somewhere inside that big building, my serious, composed mentor/father is literally cheering. Within seconds Lucio has joined him, shouting in Spanish.

The sound is getting closer. They're running down the stairs. Finally running after me.

"We have to go, Ash. *Now.*"

Ashley folds her arms across her chest and taps her foot against the muddy ground. "What the heck is going on here?"

"It's too complicated to explain in ten seconds." I tug at her arm. "We'll have plenty of time on the drive to Ridgemont."

"To Ridgemont? I thought I was driving you back to Texas."

"I have to get home. There's not a second to spare," I add, even though it makes me sound less like a real person in a hurry than the heroine of a romance novel. "Come on," I beg, and she follows me back to her car.

"Sunshine!" It's Lucio's voice. "Sunshine, wait!"

I don't answer and I don't turn around.

Ashley opens the drivers' side door and puts the key in the ignition. The engine comes to life, but Lucio is still shouting my name. I can hear his footsteps bearing down after us. Followed by another set of footsteps. *Aidan's.*

"Sunshine, please." Aidan appears beside the car so quickly that I actually jump in my seat. He tries to open the door, but I've already locked it. "You can't leave now. We had a breakthrough."

"I don't have time for your breakthroughs," I shout breathlessly. I bet that outside the car the wind is picking up again, the spirits getting riled up along with me.

"It's not safe out there! And now that things have changed—"

"Nothing has changed!" I yell back. "I have to get back to Nolan."

"Everything has changed!"

I refuse to look at him. I won't look at anything but the dashboard in front of me. I don't want to see the trees whipping in the breeze, the vines hanging over the mansion swaying from side to side, threatening to crush the whole thing to the ground. I turn to Ashley.

"Floor it," I say, and she does.

Ashley waits until we've left the campus behind, until we're on an actual paved roadway and there is even the occasional other car on the road before she opens her mouth to ask, "Sunshine, will you please tell me what the heck was going on back there?"

"It's complicated."

"We have a fairly long car ride ahead of us. I think we have time for complicated." I don't answer and Ashley sighs. "You don't have to tell me everything," she offers gently. "But you do have to explain *some* of this. Like, for starters, what the freak happened to your hair?"

I burst out laughing. In no time I'm laughing so hard that I can't even sit up straight, and Ashley is giggling right along with me. I shake my head, struggling to catch my breath. I don't notice at first when my laughter turns to tears. But soon I'm crying so hard that I can't even see the road in front of us. I can't even see a few inches in front of me. All I can see are the tears in my eyes, blurring everything so that the world is even more confusing.

Ashley pulls over. She unclicks her seatbelt and reaches across the front seat, taking me into her arms. For a few seconds I let her rock me back and forth like she's my big sister instead of my best friend, but then I pull away, shaking my head.

"No," I say through my sobs. "We don't have time to stop. We have to keep going, as fast as we can."

Ashley must hear the desperation in my voice, because she nods and restarts the car.

"There are tissues in the backseat," she offers without taking her eyes off the road.

I twist around and grab them. "Thanks," I say, sniffling.

"Sunshine, talk to me."

I take a deep, ragged breath. Then another, then another, until finally I'm breathing almost normally. "Like I said on the phone last night . . ." I concoct a version of reality that will make sense to my friend. She's as skeptical about ghosts as Mom used to be, so I'm not about to tell her what's really going on. Instead, I say that my birth father isn't who I thought he was, and I needed to get out of there. It's not that far from the truth.

Things get a little trickier when I explain why I absolutely must get to Nolan as quickly as possible. Luckily Ashley has no trouble believing I'm in love with him. "I've been rooting for you two to get together for months now!" she squeals. She doesn't even balk when I explain that we're rushing home so

I can tell Nolan how I feel before he falls into the arms of this other girl he's been seeing since I left town. It sounds like something out of a romance novel, but Ashley buys it, hook, line, and sinker. Thank goodness my best friend is boy crazy.

Ashley would never guess Nolan is in real danger and I need to get him out of harm's way before it's too late. Not that I have any idea *how* I'm going to get him away from Helena.

Or how I'm going to get *myself* away from her once Nolan is safe.

CHAPTER THIRTY-NINE
Homecoming

Ashley and I take turns driving. I force myself to sleep when it's her turn; I have to be strong to face Helena. As we drive the landscape shifts: out of the jungle and into the desert, and then up through Texas. It reminds me of driving from Austin to Ridgemont with Mom back in August, though it's hard to believe just how much has changed since then. The weather goes from balmy to frigid somewhere along the way. At a rest stop in Idaho I put a sweater on over my T-shirt, change from shorts to long jeans, and slip the knife and map from one back pocket into another. I'm dozing when we cross the state line into Washington.

I dream of Nolan. No—it's not a dream. I know that now. It's a *vision*. He's sitting. He's struggling to get up, but an invisible force is holding him down. He's bleeding from a gash above his left temple. I read somewhere that a cut to just the right part of the temple can kill a man. Drops of blood drip onto the chair's upholstery. A chair that looks so familiar . . .

"The GPS says we're only seven minutes away from your house." Ashley's voice wakes me. Groggily I open my eyes. We're driving through downtown Ridgemont—well, as much as Ridgemont has a downtown—turning onto Main Street. It's nearly midnight, and all the storefronts are dark. I gaze longingly at the pizza place where Mom and I had take-out on our very first night in this town. That seems like a million years ago. For most girls *homecoming* is a word associated with dresses and football and glittery plastic crowns.

Not for me.

Ashley turns a corner, and I find myself staring at the coffee shop where I dreamed of Nolan with Helena.

Wait. Just wait. This isn't a homecoming. I'm not going *home*. Not to my actual house. I've got to get to wherever Helena is holding Nolan hostage. I close my eyes and try to remember every detail of my vision. I know I recognized it, but it feels out of reach somehow, like a word on the tip of my tongue that I can't remember.

"Stop!" I shout.

Ashley slams on the brakes so hard that if I hadn't been wearing my seatbelt, I would have slammed into the windshield. I turn around and look for cars honking like crazy behind us, but it's late at night in our quiet little town, and the streets are empty.

"I didn't mean *stop,* stop." Slowly Ashley presses on the gas.

"Be more specific next time. What kind of *stop* did you mean?"

"I meant . . ." I pause. "We're not heading for my house. That's not where Nolan is."

"You sure you want to go straight to Nolan looking like this? Don't you want to, I don't know," Ashley continues like she's ticking items off a list: "Shower, put on some makeup, maybe some clothes that you haven't been wearing for this many hours in a row?"

Somewhere Nolan is struggling. Nolan is fighting. Nolan is *bleeding*. I shake my head.

"Okay then, where to?"

I purse my lips, but it's too hard to concentrate with the coffee shop staring me in the face. "Pull over for a sec," I say. I close my eyes as she shifts the car into park. In my visions I saw Helena dragging Nolan down a pinecone-littered street. I saw him sitting in a pretty plush chair. Light pink, with little flowers embroidered into it.

And then, as though I'm adjusting the lens on my camera, everything snaps into focus.

"Can that really be where she took him?" I ask out loud.

"Can where really be where who took who?"

I take a deep breath and direct Ashley to number three Pinecone Drive.

"*This* is where Nolan is holed up with some girl?" Ashley asks. The headlights from her car are bright enough that even in the thick Ridgemont darkness, she can make out the Victorian-styled wedding cake of a house where Victoria Wilde lived. Where her daughter, Anna, died. "Not exactly my idea of a romantic rendezvous."

"Not mine either," I agree, but my voice is shaking. On the other side of the house's front door a woman who wants me dead is holding the boy I love prisoner. Sweat pools at the nape of my neck, the moisture curling what's left of my hair.

I unlock my door, but I haven't even stepped outside when I feel a presence.

"Anna! What are you doing here?"

"Who are you talking to?" Ashley rolls down her window and searches the empty space around her little hybrid.

I don't answer; instead, I get out of the car. I'm cold, but for the first time in months it's not only because a spirit is near. I'm cold because it *is* cold. I take a deep breath, savoring the familiar Ridgemont chill. There are patches of snow on the ground, and I can see my breath. The clouds hang thick, so low that it feels like I could reach my arms up and touch them.

"Please let me help you move on," I beg. "You can't stay here." And it will give me strength. Strength I desperately need right about now.

Ashley sticks her head out her window. "Seriously, who are you talking to?"

Again, I don't answer. I lean back against the car. It's been almost three months since I exorcised the water demon, setting her spirit free.

"You know what happens to a spirit who lingers too long," I say, even though Ashley thinks I'm speaking to the air. If anyone knows what's at stake when a dark spirit manifests, it's Anna. But her certainty fills the air around me: she doesn't believe she's at risk. Her life flashes before my eyes: learning to ride a two-wheeler, baking cookies beside her father, hugging her mother when she was home from one of her long business trips, clutching the stuffed owl that matches the one in my duffle bag.

Anna had a happy life before the demon showed up. Her joy fills the air around me, charging it like electricity.

She's trying to make me feel better. To make me feel *stronger,* even if she won't let me help her move on.

"More proof that my father was wrong about my empathy making me weak," I mutter. It's the first time I've referred to him as *my father* like that, out loud. It surprises me how easily the words just slipped out. Why would I say those words for the first time now?

I shake my head, and the images of Anna's life disintegrate. I turn around to face Ashley. "You should go." My voice isn't trembling anymore.

"Go?" she echoes incredulously. "I'm not going anywhere. I'm not leaving you alone like this."

"Like what?"

"Sunshine, you're standing out there talking to yourself in the dark. I know you want to see Nolan, but maybe you should get some rest or something first. Let me take you home."

"I told you, I don't have that kind of time."

"If the boy loves you, she's not going to be able to take him away in a matter of hours."

"You don't understand."

"No," Ashley agrees. "I don't understand. I'm worried about you. This isn't like you. *None* of this! Believe me, no one was more excited to see you so worked up over a boy, but I have a hunch that whatever this is, it has just as much to do with whatever happened back there with your birth father as it does with Nolan."

Once again Ashley has no idea just how close to the mark she is. I wish I could explain it all. Someday, somehow, I *will.* If I have enough somedays ahead of me.

I turn back to look at number three Pinecone Drive. It looks just like it did in December, right down to the patchy snow on its lawn. Narrow, with a set of disproportionately wide stairs that lead to an enormous front porch. The second floor with its big wrap-around terrace, and the third floor has that same pointy turret like the house is a teeny, tiny little castle. I think part of me was expecting it to look different. Like there had to be something on the outside to give away all the sinister stuff going on inside.

I lean down and reach through the open window to hug my friend good-bye. "I love you," I say. "Thank you for everything."

"I've literally never heard you sound so serious." When I pull away, I see the fear in my friend's eyes. But she must see in mine that there is nothing she can say that will make me get back in the car.

"I'm going to get Kat." She turns back to her phone, my address still programmed into her GPS, and shifts into drive. "I really don't understand what's happening here, but I can tell you need your mother."

"Ashley, don't—" I begin, but she pulls away before I can finish my protest.

I'm left alone on Pinecone Drive, across the street from my old visual art teacher's house. No—not alone. I can feel that Anna is still close. Her spirit sends pleasant shivers up and down my spine, almost like she's putting her arms around me.

I put one foot in front of the other and make my way to her old front door.

CHAPTER FORTY
Inside

Should I knock? Ring the doorbell? Instinctively I start to slide my hand into my back pocket, but before I can so much as touch the knife, someone opens the door from the other side.

Victoria.

I throw myself into my old teacher's arms.

If Victoria is here, then everything is going to be okay. Maybe she's already saved Nolan. Maybe she's already sent Helena running scared in the other direction, and we can all just go home and take a break from all this luiseach drama.

Or maybe . . . maybe Helena is holding her prisoner too. I loosen my grip so I can look Victoria in the eye, but she keeps hugging me tight. Has Helena been trying to force Victoria onto her side of the rift? No. That wouldn't do Helena any good—Victoria doesn't even have her powers anymore. Can Victoria even sense Anna's presence?

That's when I realize: the instant Victoria opened the door,

270

Anna vanished. Why did she disappear on me? Even with my teacher's arms around me, I feel suddenly, terribly alone.

Victoria's long, almost-black hair is soft against my face. She's wearing the same flowing, witchy clothes she's always worn, clothes I thought made her look creepy before, but now I realize they're just part of what makes Victoria look like Victoria, just like my colorful vintage choices are part of me. It'd be strange to see my old teacher in jeans and a T-shirt instead of a long gray skirt and matching peasant top, with a crocheted shawl around her shoulders.

From somewhere inside the house a husky voice inside calls, "Let our guest inside, Victoria."

I follow my old teacher into her living room. It's just the same as it was four months ago, bright and preternaturally warm.

Except for the fact that now Nolan's blood has stained one of Victoria's plush floral chairs. He struggles to get up when he sees me, but he can't. Goose bumps rise on my forearms, a cool breeze in the otherwise warm room. A spirit is near.

Nolan's head tilts to one side. Invisible hands press like ropes into the sleeves of the jacket I love so much (Mom must have gotten it back to him after all), and I can see him wince in pain as they squeeze ever tighter. His blue jeans look even more worn than usual, and his tawny hair is pushed back behind his ears instead of falling across his forehead. He hasn't changed his clothes or showered for at least two days, not since Helena brought him here. And judging by the circles under his eyes, he hasn't slept either.

A woman stands facing him, her back to me. She seems to tower over him, despite the fact that she's at least six inches shorter than he is, just like I am. Her hair is pulled back into a tight bun, but I can tell that it's thick and long and curly, just like mine used to be.

I hold my breath as she turns.

I've dreamed of her for so many nights, but now here she is, come to life right in front of me. The brown eyes that started out warm and then narrowed as she squeezed my helpless infant body.

"Apologies for the blood," she says, gesturing at Nolan's forehead. "We had a bit of a scuffle before I could secure him. The boy seemed to think he had a chance at escape." She smiles. Nolan struggles ever harder. Helena flicks her wrist, and Nolan stills as though an enormous weight is sitting on top of him. His face twists in pain.

I focus my energy on the spirit in the room to see him. His name was Ryan Michaelson, and he was a promising college football player with a real chance at going pro. Now his neck is twisted from a fatal football injury, bones bulging out of one side. He's angry because his life was cut short.

"You're *using* a spirit who doesn't want to move on?" I ask, shocked by the cruelty of it. This is one lesson I wouldn't want to learn.

"Only for a short while longer," she answers, a fake sort of sweetness in her voice. "His strength is coming in handy at the moment. As soon as my task is complete, I will force it on." For an instant her face relaxes: the circles under her eyes vanish, the tightness around her lips releases. With a start, I realize we have the same mouth.

But just as suddenly her features shift. She looks starving, like she hasn't eaten for months, as parched as someone who hasn't had anything but tiny little sips of water to keep herself alive for weeks at a time. She's been manipulating this spirit for days to torture Nolan.

There's something else in her face. *Surprise.*

Maybe she can't quite believe the girl she's been hunting for so many years just walked right into her clutches.

Or maybe she's just surprised to see me all grown up. Maybe for all these years she's been thinking of me as the baby she let go.

"Why don't you offer our guest a seat?" Helena says to Victoria. Her voice sounds like no voice I've ever heard before, hoarse yet powerful. She sounds a thousand years older than she looks.

That's the second time Helena referred to me as *our* guest, like she and Victoria have been living in this house together. But Victoria would never have willingly allowed Helena into her house, would never have just stood by while someone tortured Nolan.

Would she?

"Sit down, Sunshine." Victoria nudges me toward the couch where I sat when she answered my questions just a few months ago.

I look at my protector, gasping for breath beneath the weight of the former football player, and then back at my old teacher, who looks perfectly normal. Well, as normal as she ever looked. She still has deep hollows beneath her eyes and the palest skin I've ever seen. But she doesn't look any *different* from the way she looked the last time I saw her. She certainly doesn't look like a prisoner. After all, prisoners don't get to answer the front door.

Aidan said he and Lucio were the only two luiseach left who didn't want me eliminated. Could he have possibly meant *Victoria* abandoned him too?

"How could you?" A lump rises in my throat, and I swallow it down, determined not to cry in front of Helena. "I thought you were on our side!"

Before Victoria can answer, Helena speaks. "She was. Until your father decided to use her daughter rather than save her when he designed your test. That's just like him, you see, putting his little experiments above the lives of others."

I can hardly argue with that. I'm furious at him for exactly the same thing.

"Please," Helena says. "Sit down."

I sit. There's a plush ottoman in front of me, and Helena is standing on the other side, angled so I can't quite make eye contact with Nolan. Keeping my eyes open, I concentrate on the angry spirit. I shiver as I reach out to him. Maybe if I can just get him to loosen his grip . . .

"Uh-uh-uh," Helena wags her finger at me. Nolan groans as the spirit redoubles his efforts, every bit as strong as the body it left behind.

Helena squares her shoulders. Even though she's small—like me—she seems like a wall between Ryan Michaelson and me. Between Nolan and me.

"Why are you hurting him?" I ask. "It's me you want."

"I needed him to take me to Llevar la Luz," Helena answers, confirming that she's known where I've been all along, every bit as calm and scientific as Aidan, even in dire circumstances. They must have made quite a team, barely breaking a sweat even as they took on demons. "I thought Nolan just needed a little persuading, but he's been unusually resistant. Lucky for me, I don't need to go to Llevar la Luz anymore."

She gives the tiniest little nod, and Nolan groans again, this time in relief. I crane my neck so I can see his face. It looks like he isn't in quite so much pain anymore. But Ryan Michaelson is still working for Helena, holding Nolan down. He can't stand. And he certainly can't run.

"If you don't mind my asking," Helena continues politely, "how exactly did you know we were here?"

"I saw it." No point in lying.

Helena looks just as surprised as she did when I walked into the room, but she quickly regains her composure, saying softly, "And you love him too much to let him suffer when you knew you could stop it."

Months ago, in this very room, Victoria referred to Nolan as my boyfriend, and I was quick to correct her. This time I don't correct Helena when she says I love him.

Though I have to admit, this wasn't quite the way I envisioned Nolan finding out. I wanted to tell him myself, not have him hear it from the woman who wants to kill me.

I stand and plant my feet firmly against the carpet, expecting her to lunge for me, ready to fight. But Helena just steps aside, clearing the path between Nolan and me.

"The boy is free to go," she says. Ryan Michaelson's spirit vanishes: the chill dissipates, and Nolan is unfettered.

I practically leap across the ottoman. I put my arms around him—nausea be darned!—and use one of Victoria's pretty throw pillows to apply pressure to the gash above his right temple. "I'm so sorry," I whisper. "This is all my fault."

With effort, Nolan shakes his head. He reaches up and takes one of my hands in his. After months spent in the Mexican jungle, my skin looks so dark next to his, but somehow our hands still seem to fit together perfectly.

The warmth of being near Nolan turns into heat as I struggle to control the sensations rushing through my body. Sweat forms at the base of my neck, and without my long hair to catch it, the moisture drips down my back, in between my shoulder blades. Touching Nolan feels simultaneously so right and so wrong, but at least now I know that all those *wrong* feelings are just a trick manufactured by Aidan. They're not *real*.

"Can you stand up?" I ask, putting my arm around his shoulder to help him. I may be shorter than he is, but I can feel my muscles working. All that strength I built up in the jungle has come home with me.

"I think so," Nolan whispers.

"Let's get you out of here," I say, helping him to his feet. I just have to get him to safety. And then . . . I don't know what happens *then*.

Nolan shakes his head. "I'm not leaving without you." It's clear from the look on his face that he knows what Helena intends to do with me.

Before I can protest, Helena's voice makes me jump. I hadn't forgotten that Nolan and I weren't alone in the room, but it just didn't *feel* like anyone else was part of our conversation.

"Well, then," her hoarse voice begins, "I'm afraid we have a problem. Because I can't let you leave *with* her."

CHAPTER FORTY-ONE
Kissed

Nolan seems strong enough to stand on his own, so I turn to face my birth mother. "I won't give up without a fight."

"No," Helena agrees. "I don't imagine you will. You inherited your father's willfulness."

"Maybe I got it from you." I raise an eyebrow. After a few months living with Aidan, I know I got *that* from him. "You seem every bit as stubborn as Aidan."

Helena sinks onto the couch across from us with a sigh. She looks relaxed, but she warns, "Don't try anything." She nods slightly, and I feel a spark in the electric current of nearby spirits. Helena could pull them all close in a heartbeat. And this time they would restrain me, not Nolan.

I nod that I understand.

She brings her hand to her forehead and closes her eyes just the way Mom does when she's battling a headache. "You can say good-bye," she offers, gesturing at Nolan. Suddenly I feel grateful to the woman who wants to kill me, the woman who's been hurting the boy I love. She's going to let Nolan go.

But before I can say a word, he protests. "You're not actually going to say good-bye to me, right? We're going to get you out of here. Away from *her*," he spits, nodding in Helena's direction.

"No, we're not," I say firmly.

"You're just giving up?" He pushes the sleeves of his jacket up over his elbows, and I see dark bruises on his forearms, reminders of the spirit who held him down.

"I didn't say that. But *we're* not getting me out of here. If I'm getting out of here alive, I'm doing it myself. I'm not letting you risk your life to save me again."

"You risked your life to save me," Nolan counters, every bit as logical as my father, like the math of me saving him without letting him save me back just doesn't add up.

That's the second time I've thought of Aidan as my *father*. As my *parent*. A parent who underestimated me. His protections aren't enough to keep me from Nolan. I ignore every bad feeling, silently saying *No* every time my body tries to pull me away.

"I have to tell you something," I begin, but Nolan cuts me off.

"I love you," he says plainly, just as calmly as if he were telling me it was raining outside.

"I love you too." It's just as undeniable as the fact that the sky is blue (or gray, here in Ridgemont), water is wet, or owls can fly.

Slowly I stand on my tiptoes and press my lips to his. Back in January there were about a million reasons why I didn't let him kiss me, and one of those reasons was that I didn't want our first kiss to be a good-bye kiss. But right now kissing him good-bye seems better than not kissing him at all.

As his lips press against mine, I feel something shift inside me. It starts with butterflies dancing across my belly like someone just started playing their favorite song. And then, just as suddenly, everything settles down. There's no lurching of adrenaline. No queasiness. No nausea. There's only the warmth of being close to Nolan. Our kiss is like something out of a fairy tale, powerful enough to break a sorcerer's spell. For now, at least.

I don't ever want to stop kissing Nolan. I don't want to stop saying good-bye, because then he'll be gone. But I have to get Nolan out of here.

So I pull away and start dragging my friend to the door. Maybe I can call him my boyfriend now, even if it's just in my head. I glance at Helena; her head is still in her hands, but her body reacts to every step we take, ready to spring. Nolan and I are holding hands as we slide past Victoria, who's hovering by the entrance to the living room.

"Just run outside with me. We're almost at the door." Nolan tightens his grip on my hand as if to say *I'm dragging you out there with me whether you want to go or not.*

The electric hum sparks again, making me jump. Helena isn't going to let me go anywhere.

I still feel the shadow of Nolan's lips against mine. I don't try to twist my hand from his grip. I let him think that I'll run with him. He doesn't know how strong I've become over the past couple of months. But before I can force Nolan to leave, the door swings open from the other side.

Aidan and Lucio burst into the room, blocking the way out.

Helena is on her feet, with wide open eyes at lightning speed. Lucio doesn't stop at the door.

"Sunshine! You're alive!" Lucio throws his strong arms around me and buries his head in my neck. I feel his breath against my skin, fast and desperate, like he sprinted all the way here from Mexico. Nolan's eyes widen with surprise. I'm sure mine do too.

CHAPTER FORTY-TWO

Too Late

"I thought we'd be too late!" Lucio exclaims, swallowing hard. I step back from Lucio, taking Nolan's hand. Lucio's eyes dart between Nolan and me, trying to understand what he's seeing. Maybe I should have told Lucio about Nolan.

"You *are* too late." It sounds like the kind of thing you'd hear from the villain in a movie, but in a movie Helena would be brandishing some kind of a weapon: a gun, a grenade, maybe even a sword or a crossbow. In real life her bare hands are clenched at her side, ready to call spirits to her bidding.

She sounds almost sad as she directs her attention toward Aidan and continues. "My compatriots and I have done all we could to bridge the gap, but our numbers are dwindling— luiseach live long lives, but we don't live forever. Without enough luiseach to counterbalance the spirits in the world, darkness is inevitable. We must eliminate the girl while there's still time."

"There's still time." Aidan's teeth are clenched.

Helena shakes her head. "What about the fire demon that tormented Lado Selva?" Aidan looks surprised. "Oh yes, I know all about Michael Weir, the spirit who escaped your lab and turned dark even in the warmest of places."

"An anomaly," Aidan counters.

"No, dearest." She makes the pet name sound like a curse. "It's becoming all too commonplace."

Understanding hits me like a bolt of lightning. Helena isn't the enemy. She never was. The *darkness* is. Images flash across my mind. The man watching us at the airport, the man in the fishing village who hid in the shadows. Somehow he has everything to do with the darkness. He's the face of the darkness! A face I can see, even if the rest of them can't. I should've told Aidan about him ages ago! I'm about to explain everything when Helena speaks, her voice cold as ice.

"The girl came to me willingly. The world can't wait for your science to catch up with it."

"But I've made so much progress!" Aidan insists. "Let me show you."

Suddenly the temperature drops as Anna's spirit fills the room. Nolan looks at me questioningly. I stand on my tiptoes to whisper a single word in his ear. "Anna."

"Do you feel that girl?" Aidan shouts. "Our daughter saved her spirit on New Year's Eve, and in the months that have passed, she has not turned dark. She is half-luiseach, half-human—Victoria's daughter," he adds, gesturing to my old visual arts teacher. "And her spirit is strong."

I blink, remembering what Lucio told me that day in the desert. Aidan had theories that spirits might be able to linger without going dark. Is *Anna* what he was talking about?

Helena turns furiously to Victoria. "You were lying all along," she shouts. "I should have trusted my instincts."

"I had to protect the girl," Victoria explains.

"What is she talking about?" I shout, more confused than ever.

Much to my surprise, it's Helena who answers. "Your lovely teacher was a double agent. She was working for Aidan all along. My dear husband planted her here, to watch me. To keep me distracted. I'd have been better off waiting for you to emerge at the borders of Llevar la Luz."

Another spark, but this time it's different. *This* is more like a spark that never ends, a bolt of lightning that brightens the sky forever.

Now Anna's spirit isn't the only one here. Lucio watches as I move closer to Nolan. His body is something of a buffer, and at first, none of the spirits can touch me, but even the strongest protector is no match for this many spirits. Helena lifts her arms as Lucio and Aidan get to work, but for every spirit they help move on, two more come to take its place.

"She must be drawing spirits from across the country to this house," I manage to whisper to Nolan, who looks stricken.

"I'm so sorry, Sunshine," he replies. "I told her that multiple spirits made you weak. I didn't know . . ."

"It's not your fault." I squeeze his hand in mine.

Spirits criss-cross the room with the force of a tornado. Spirits who want to move on and spirits who wish to stay behind.

The sensation is overwhelming.

Helena stretches her arms out wide like she is inviting all the spirits in the world to join us. Her face is white as paper, but she isn't even out of breath.

The temperature drops even further. I've never been so cold in my entire life. There isn't room for a single coherent thought in my brain. I can't focus on one spirit at a time. There is only life after life and death after death—car accidents, cancer, old age, heart attacks, gunshot wounds—crashing over me like waves. My teeth chatter so hard that I can't even muster the words *I promise* out loud.

Helena's voice rises above the din, her gaze fixed on Aidan. "You abandoned our mission to protect the life of one girl." Her voice sounds like she hasn't had a drop to drink for days. "You put the entire balance at risk for the sake of your precious *progress*."

Aidan shakes his head. "No," he insists. "I've never lost sight of our mission. All along it's been at the heart of everything I've tried to do."

"Even hiding this girl?" Helena's fingers wrap around my arms as she pulls me away from Nolan. Nolan tries to keep his hold on my hand, but Helena sends a spirit crashing his way, shoving him aside.

"*Especially* hiding her!" Aidan counters. His voice is louder and more full of emotion than I've ever heard it before. "She is able to do things no luiseach ever has. And now we've had a breakthrough, Helena." He lowers his voice when he says her name. "We've had a breakthrough," Aidan repeats, holding up his hands as Helena drags me across the room. "Because of our daughter—"

"Our daughter is to blame!"

"No!" Aidan counters. "She is the *key*. Yesterday, just before she left our campus, more than a dozen spirits moved on by themselves. Without my help. Without Lucio's. Only with hers."

My heart's pounding so fast that I can barely catch my breath.

"Helena," Aidan says solemnly, "they moved on by themselves." I have to concentrate to hear him.

"Impossible!" Helena's fingers twist through my hair, and I feel the warmth of her flesh against my back. Despite myself, I lean into her, desperate for her warmth.

"Possible," Aidan counters.

"Let's see a demonstration, then," Helena says. "Work your magic, Sunshine."

"I didn't do anything," I manage to say. "I just said . . ." I pause, remembering the words I thought before I left Llevar la Luz: *I'm so sorry that you're trapped in there. Do you know what happens to spirits who spend too much time on Earth? Even the kindest of them turns into something unrecognizable. You're not meant to stay here so long.*

I wish you could feel the peace that comes with letting go of your ties here on Earth.

I know how you felt in life. How you feel *now, in death. I can feel it too.*

I'm limp in Helena's arms.

"You expect me to believe this girl is capable of all that?" Helena shouts. "That this girl, who can't even open her eyes in the presence of a few dozen spirits"—I didn't realize my eyes were closed—"could change the world?"

"Yes," Aidan answers calmly, his voice a million miles away.

"Well, I don't. These are just more of your lies to protect the girl who will ultimately be the cause of our demise!" Helena says, and she tightens her grip on me, bringing her hands up around my neck. The spirits have weakened me enough that I can't fight back, but she can't count on them to finish the job.

I am a luiseach after all. Spirits can't kill me, so Helena begins to squeeze.

CHAPTER FORTY-THREE

The Awakening

I wake up on the front porch, my teeth still chattering. What just happened? How did I end up out here? Am I dead—is this just my spirit escaping all that chaos?

I look down at my body. It's still there. I rub my hands together, still cold. I exhale, and vapor floats out of my mouth. I feel my heartbeat, faster than it should be, but at least it doesn't feel like my heart is about to explode anymore.

I'm still inside my body. I'm still alive.

"Sunshine?" I look up. Lucio is crouched beside me. Nolan stands over him. "Are you okay?"

There's no way to answer that question, so I counter with one of my own: "What happened?"

Lucio looks up at Nolan like he's asking a question. Nolan nods. "Helena couldn't go through with it," Lucio says finally.

"Couldn't go through with it?" I echo.

"She couldn't kill you," Nolan answers. As always, he provides the information I need to complete the picture. Helena couldn't kill her own daughter—the girl who shares her hair and her mouth, the girl who is exactly her height.

"Let's get out of here," Nolan says, reaching down and pulling me up to stand. I immediately feel queasy. Guess our kiss couldn't break the spell completely.

"We wouldn't get much farther than the edge of Victoria's front yard." Lucio nods toward the street in front of us.

Nolan can't feel it, but Lucio and I can. Helena arranged all the spirits that were criss-crossing Victoria's living room into a ring around the house. They're lined up around Victoria's house like a fence.

"We never covered this particular trick in my lessons," I say to Lucio.

"I don't think Aidan actually knows how to do this."

"I guess he wasn't the only one who spent the past sixteen years doing research."

"Guess not," Lucio agrees.

"Will someone please tell me what the heck is going on here?" Nolan can't see or feel the spirits. He might even be able to walk right through them if he wanted to. I explain that we're surrounded. "Helena is holding us prisoner," I finish.

In unison we look back at the house. The front door is open wide. We can hear Aidan and Helena shouting at each other.

"Now we know why he made Anna my test." I don't know why I'm speaking so softly; it's not like they'd be able to hear me over the sound of their own voices. "He needed her spirit to be part of this." Lucio and Nolan both nod.

"I've never heard him yell like that," Lucio says softly. "Not even at you," he adds with a smile. Nolan doesn't seem pleased with Lucio's inside joke.

"The darkness is growing stronger," Helena shouts. "There isn't a moment to waste."

"Then why didn't you eliminate her when you had the chance? You must still believe—"

"Belief has nothing to do with it."

Aidan doesn't respond. Helena's voice is calm, even when she says, "There's no one left on your side but a powerless woman and an orphan boy." Lucio flinches. I place a hand on his forearm.

"There may be fewer of us, but that doesn't make us wrong," Aidan counters.

"They could go on like this all night," I whisper breathlessly.

"All night?" Lucio laughs, but there's no joy in it. "They could go on like this *forever.*"

I glance at Nolan, pressing my hands to my lips. Blood still drips from the wound on his right temple, and even though I can't see them, I know his arms are bruised beneath his jacket. This isn't the first time he's been hurt because of me. The shouting inside the house grows louder.

I might be able to put an end to all of this. Repair the rift, protect Nolan, protect Kat, protect the entire human race. I shiver, shoving my hands in my pockets to keep warm, wrapping my fingers around what's inside.

"Nolan, I have something for you." I slide a wrinkled piece of paper from my back pocket.

"That's Aidan's map!" Lucio exclaims, recognizing it at once.

"I thought Nolan might be able to make some sense out of it."

Nolan immediately starts scanning it with his eyes. "Four places, four dates?" he murmurs thoughtfully.

"Those are the four dates and places across the globe where

one luiseach has died suddenly." Lucio hesitates before adding, "One luiseach every four years since Sunshine was born."

I gasp. Nolan's face looks grave, but he keeps his eyes focused on the map in his hands. Just as I thought, Nolan will make sense of the map. And now that he and Lucio are both distracted, it's time for me to act.

I take a step backward, away from my friends.

Did the spirits in Aidan's lab really move on without help after I left? Or was Helena right when she accused Aidan of lying? I shake my head. After what happened inside Victoria's house, I know that it doesn't matter whether or not Aidan was lying.

I'm not strong enough to help all the spirits in the world.

Aidan was wrong. I'm not the luiseach to end all luiseach.

And if he's *wrong,* then isn't the next logical conclusion that Helena is *right?* That just by existing, I'm preventing the birth of more luiseach? And one thing is certain: the world *needs* more luiseach. Since my birth our numbers have diminished even further. No births, and now—thanks to the map—I know that there have also been deaths.

It only stands to reason that if I weren't here, luiseach would have a better chance of survival. Nolan and Lucio are too busy poring over the map to notice I'm walking away from them.

Suddenly the sound of screeching brakes pulls me from my thoughts. Ashley's car squeals to a stop across the street. She hasn't even turned off the engine when Mom comes bolting out of the passenger side.

CHAPTER FORTY-FOUR
Falling

Mom freezes halfway across the street. For a second I think that the spirit force field has stopped her somehow, but then I see the look on her face. She's staring at me, and she doesn't like what she sees. She can tell that her daughter nearly had the life squeezed out of her.

Just by looking at me, Mom can see that everything is wrong.

"What's going on?" she shouts furiously. She sent me away with Aidan so I could get stronger, and here I am, looking (I assume, as I can't see myself) every bit as bad as I did that day in the hospital parking lot. Worse, probably.

"Where is he?" Mom shouts. "I'm going to give him—" I shake my head before she can say *a piece of my mind*. There was a time when all I wanted was to give Aidan a piece of my mind, back when he was just my nameless, faceless mentor. That was before I realized how horribly spooky that expression is. And before Aidan was an actual person with a name and a personality and an inexorable link to me.

"Sunshine!" Mom gasps, still frozen in place. "I don't understand any of this, but I—"

"I love you too," I call out before she can finish. My second time saying those words today. They're so small—just one syllable each—but they sound enormous to me.

Mom is the first person I ever loved, but she's not the last. I love Nolan, and I love Ashley. I love Victoria and Anna, and given time, I think I might have loved Aidan and Lucio and even Helena too. At least now I know that some part of her loved me. The part that couldn't kill me.

I step onto the lawn, then turn to glance back at the Victorian house behind me. Lucio stands on the front porch, shivering not just because spirits are near but because of the Ridgemont chill. Maybe he's never seen snow, just like the tall man from Lado Selva.

Nolan tears the map in half and flips one side to the other, rearranging the order of countries from left to right. He starts tracing invisible lines with his fingers from one red circle to another, his brain working to connect the mysterious luiseach deaths as Lucio watches over, answering any of Nolan's questions that he can.

Through the front door I see Aidan's profile. His face is contorted painfully, and his perfect hair has fallen across his forehead, but he's too distracted to push it back in place. He looks like he's fighting for his life. Actually, I guess he's fighting for *mine*. Everything he's done for the past sixteen years—all that research, allowing himself to become completely isolated—has been to save my life. With every failure he was reminded that I might have to die.

I turn around. Mom seems to have regained the ability to move because she's finally stepping across the invisible—and, to her, imperceptible—spirit fence and onto Victoria's front lawn. Just a few more steps and she'll be next to me, putting her arms around me and whispering that everything's going to be all right.

But it's not. Not unless I do this.

I reach into my back pocket and grab the knife. It's become a torch and a thunderstorm for me before. I just hope it will become what I need now.

On the porch behind me Nolan begins to slump over, still weak from Helena's torture. He leans heavily against a pillar, panting. Blood drips from the wound on the left side of his face. I'm aware of each individual *drip, drip, drip* as his blood lands onto the map now laying on the ground below him.

A thought flashes across Nolan's face, and he leans down and draws a fifth circle on the map, using his blood that has pooled up below him. It looks like he's tracing the circle right where we are on the map, in Ridgemont.

Lucio reaches out a hand to steady Nolan, slumped over the map. Lucio, who stayed by Aidan's side. Whose parents died for *the greater good.*

I finally understand: They didn't die just to keep *me* safe. They believed they were keeping the *world* safe, because they believed Aidan was right and Helena was wrong.

Saving the world is *the greater good.* Maybe it's the greatest good there is.

Nolan's tawny hair falls across his amber eyes, the way it always does when he's figuring something out. With Ridgemont as the fifth circle, Nolan traces lines between the five circles on the map, using his blood-link ink. It looks like he's drawing a star.

Suddenly he looks up, and I know he's figured out what I'm about to do.

"No!" he shouts. He tries to run down the stairs, but in his current condition he isn't fast enough.

I throw the knife onto the ground. The earth splits open at my feet, leaving an unbridgeable chasm between Nolan and me. Now he won't be able to stop me.

The knife materializes against my sneakers. Its work isn't done yet. I turn back to Mom. The ground shook as it opened up, and she's fallen onto her hands and knees.

"Sunshine, what are you doing?"

"You said you'd support me no matter what."

Her face twists with shock. Mom *always* understands what I'm talking about. "I can't support *this,*" she counters, tears streaming down her face. I pick up the knife and throw it into the ground a second time.

Once more the ground opens up, this time on the other side of me. Now Mom can't reach me either. I'm standing on an island all alone.

Standing next to her pretty blue car across the street, Ashley screams. Maybe she's trying to make sense out of this—maybe she thinks it's an earthquake or some kind of natural disaster, not a paranormal weapon at work. Everyone else knows better.

Aidan and Helena run onto the front porch, followed by Victoria, drawn by the sound of the earth breaking in two. Mom's eyes go wide at the sight of my old art teacher—I never actually told her Victoria was still alive.

"Sunshine!" Aidan shouts. "What are you doing?" He looks nearly as horrified as Mom, his voice every bit as desperate.

Despite the space that divides me from everyone else, I'm suddenly, *blissfully* aware of all the love that surrounds me. It practically emanates from each of my friends and family, almost like how it feels when a spirit touches me. But instead of making me cold, this love envelopes me with warmth. Even Helena's face—the face of the woman who wanted me *eliminated* for so many years—looks different. Except for our eyes, she looks more like my mirror image than ever.

Aidan was right about one thing: I *feel* everything. I never could hide my emotions. Mom always said I'd make a terrible gambler. Love is written all across my face. Love is all I feel.

What I do next comes as easily as water flowing downstream. I focus on the electricity in the air, on all the spirits surrounding us. Hundreds more join us within moments. This time their lives and their deaths don't overwhelm me. This time my feelings are strong enough to overwhelm *them*. They feel what I'm feeling: love. Feeding off my emotions, the spirits spark a windstorm ten times stronger than what happened at Llevar la Luz, when all I could feel was anger.

The love I feel at this moment is so much more powerful than my rage was then.

The spirits and I work together. They swirl around me, lifting me. They raise me up above Mom, Nolan, Lucio, Aidan, Helena, Ashley, and Victoria, wonder written plainly on their faces. They shout as I go higher and higher, but the wind is so loud, I can't make out the words they're saying.

I won't linger. There is no unfinished business waiting down there for me. Once the spirits have lifted me high enough, I begin to help them move on, sending them all my love.

I feel serene, just like the spirits releasing their bonds to Earth. Before, I struggled with helping multiple spirits move on because I repressed my emotions. But right now helping hundreds of spirits move on at once is as easy and natural as taking my next breath.

I've become a luiseach unlike any other.

The wind ceases, and there is a moment when everything is still. Time moves in slow motion as I begin to fall. Gravity starts pulling me down, down, down, and time slows. What happens to luiseach when we die? Nolan never came across *that* in his research. Do we move on, as humans do? Do we go dark if we linger too long?

I look down toward my friends and family, shouting my name: Lucio, with the tiniest hint of an accent; Ashley, high pitched and terrified (I hope someone will explain this to her when it's over); Victoria, mournful and melodic; Helena, hoarse and surprised; Aidan, solemn and deep.

And Mom. She crawls toward the edge of the chasm, reaching out to me, but the space between us is too wide. Her voice doesn't sound like anything I've ever heard before. She sounds like she's outside of herself somehow, but not the way she was when the demon possessed her. This sound is unmistakably *human*. It's the sound of anguish.

Then Nolan, clear as a bell.

He holds up the map so I can see it. I look at the lines he traced between the circles. The last circle around Ridgemont is the final point on a perfect five-pointed star.

"Someone was expecting another luiseach death in Ridgemont!" he shouts loud enough for me to hear. "Someone *organized* this!"

Lucio said the darkness was organized.

Out of the corner of my eye I see a gray-black blur in the distance. A man surrounded in shadow. I've seen him before. Seen his black coat and wide-brimmed hat. Seen his face. The face of the darkness.

He's been watching all of this.

He's been waiting for it.

He wants me to die here today.

My death will complete whatever powerful spell the darkness has been conjuring up. A spell that stretches the world over. *I was wrong about all of this.*

Suddenly, instead of peace, I'm filled with terror. Instead of falling in slow motion, I'm accelerating toward the ground rapidly. The fear of death consumes me. My ears ring as the pressure of making such a terrible mistake builds inside my head. I thought I was freeing the world of my burden on it, on everyone, but my death will only make things worse. The voices of the people I love fade, and suddenly I'm alone as I fall toward a mistake of my own making.

The chasm below me opens even wider, deeper into the earth. I look down. Swirling at the center of the chasm below me is a whirlpool of darkness. No, not just darkness. Dark *spirits.* Hundreds, thousands of demons are waiting for me down there.

Terrified, I close my eyes. In my mind's eye I see an enormous white owl flying toward me. No, not flying: a little girl is throwing a stuffed animal up and down, laughing as its cotton wings flap back and forth in the breeze.

Her youthful voice calls my name, getting louder, following me down. But why? Anna can't stop me from falling. She's a spirit, nothing more than a presence beside me. She can't take shape, can't hang onto me, can't pull my weight upward against gravity to save me.

I gasp as Anna's ice-cold hands twine their fingers through mine.

And pull.

LOOK FOR BOOK THREE IN THE SERIES

The Haunting of Sunshine Girl

COMING 2017